SUSAN WITTIG ALBERT

A WILDER ROSE

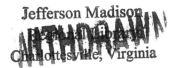
Jefferson Madison
Charlottesville, Virginia

A Novel

Persevero Press
www.PerseveroPress.com

A Wilder Rose

This is a work of fiction. Names, characters, places, and incidents are the product of the author's imagination or, in the case of historical persons, are used fictitiously.

Publisher's Cataloging-in-Publication data
Albert, Susan Wittig.
  A wilder rose / by Susan Wittig Albert.
  p. cm.
ISBN-10: 0-9892035-1-4
ISBN-13: 978-0-9892035-1-7

Includes bibliography.

1. Wilder, Laura Ingalls, 1867-1957 --Fiction. 2. Lane, Rose Wilder, 1886-1968 --Fiction. 3. Authorship --Collaboration --Fiction. 4. Mothers and daughters --Fiction. I. Title.

PS3551.L2637 W55 2013
813.6 --dc23

pcn to come

For Bill Holtz, whose interest in Rose made this book possible
and Bill Albert, whose support made it happen

We are never aware of the present; each instant of living becomes perceptible only when it is past, so that in a sense we do not live at all, but only remember living. And we are blind to conditions forming our lives, until those conditions are becoming part of the past.

Rose Wilder Lane
Old Home Town

$\mathcal{C}$ONTENTS

A NOTE TO THE READER

A Wilder Rose is the true story of Rose Wilder Lane and her mother, Laura Ingalls Wilder, whose creative collaboration produced *Little House in the Big Woods* and seven more books in the Little House® series. It is the tale of two exceptional women: a mother who had a fascinating pioneer story to tell but whose writing skills were not up to the challenge of shaping and polishing it for publication; and a daughter, a gifted and much-published author who had both the skill to turn her mother's stories into memorable books and the publishing connections that would get them into print.

Fortunately for us, their teamwork (complicated, vexed, and reluctant on both sides) has been documented in Rose's unpublished diaries and journals and in Laura's unpublished letters. Rose's Line-A-Day diaries, particularly, allow us to witness her struggle with the daily angers, frustrations, and fears that distanced her from her mother and the duty, compassion, and caring that pulled her closer. They especially help us understand the difficult contexts of time, place, and politics within which these women lived and out of which their writings were born.

But while the story itself is true, *A Wilder Rose* is a novel. With the diaries, journals, and letters as my guide, I have taken my own imaginative journey through the real events of those years. I have treated the real people as fictional characters and the real events as fictional events. I have chosen some storylines to expand and dramatize and omitted others; I have put words into people's mouths and listened in on their internal dialogue; I have invented incidents and imagined settings. In all this, I am exactly as true to the real events, settings, and people of *A Wilder Rose* as Rose and Laura were true to the real events, settings, and people of the Ingalls family's pioneer wanderings across the American plains. The books they wrote are fictional representations of Laura's life as a child growing into young womanhood; *A Wilder Rose* is a fictional representation of Rose's life in the 1930s and her struggle—not always successful—to make sense of it all.

In the eleven years spanned by this novel (1928–1939), Rose Wilder Lane lived and worked under the long, dark shadow of the Great Depression, the Dirty Thirties, and the often desperate, always unrelenting need for money. In fact, the Little House® books might never have been written if the stock market hadn't crashed in 1929, wiping out her savings and leaving her stranded at her parents' farm. There, she was available to work with the family stories her mother provided—and could use those same remembered stories as elements of her two most acclaimed novels, *Let the Hurricane Roar* (1932) and *Free Land* (1938).

Rose wrote no more fiction after she finished working on *These Happy Golden Years* in 1942, but she didn't lose her voice. Instead, she found her passion and turned to writing on behalf of American individualism. Her book, *The Discovery of Freedom: Man's Struggle Against Authority* (1943), was barely acknowledged when it was published, two years into the Second World War. Today, it is recognized as one of the most passionate documents of twentieth-century American libertarian thought.

Susan Wittig Albert

PART ONE

1. THE LITTLE HOUSE ON KING STREET DANBURY, CONNECTICUT: <u>APRIL 1939</u>

With an audible sigh, Rose Lane rolled the letter out of her Underwood typewriter and signed it—*Much love as always, Rose.*

She dropped the letter onto the stack of orange-covered tablets her mother had sent her a year and a half before. Now she was committed. Like it or not, she had to finish the rewrite and get the typescript of her mother's book in the mail by the middle of next month. It meant putting off her own paying work—the nonfiction article she was writing for *Woman's Day.* But she'd had the manuscript so long that the book had missed Harper's 1938 list. Mama Bess had forwarded a chiding letter from her editor, Ida Louise Raymond, making it clear that *By the Shores of Silver Lake* had to be finished quickly in order to appear in this year's fall catalogue.

But she should be able to meet the deadline. Her mother had already agreed to the changes that had to be made. "Do what you think best," she had written, sounding resigned. "It's your fine touch that makes all the difference." If there weren't too many interruptions, Rose would finish the pen revisions in a few weeks. This time, though, she would pay somebody—maybe Norma Lee, who could use the money—to retype the manuscript, which would at least get *that* job off her desk.

The window was open over the kitchen table, covered in yellow-and-blue oilcloth, and the yellow dotted swiss curtains blew gently into the room. With the breeze came the scent of lilacs and the sound of the radio: the Andrews Sisters' hit song, "Bei Mir Bist du Schoen," banned the month before by Hitler's Nazi regime because the composer and the lyricist were Jewish. The swingy tune was punctuated by the irregular beats of Russell Ogg's hammer as he worked on an upstairs study for Rose. When it was finished, she wouldn't have to write at the kitchen table. And bookshelves, ah, yes, there would be bookshelves! At last, she could begin emptying the boxes of books, her personal library, that Mama Bess had shipped from Rocky Ridge, the Mansfield, Missouri, farm. When that job was done, she would finally feel settled, as settled as she ever felt anywhere, more settled than she had felt since she and Helen Boylston—Troub—had moved into their Albanian house.

Rose leaned back in her chair, enjoying the rich fragrance of chicken pie (the chicken obtained from a local farmer until she had her own flock) and apple cobbler (the apples from her own backyard trees). Supper would be a celebration of sorts, the first anniversary of her purchase of the little farmhouse. Situated on several acres some four miles outside of Danbury, on the extension of King Street, it was a small two-story white clapboard house with a porch on the front and a woodshed on the back. It had come with lush lilacs and gnarly apple trees; two tenacious tomcats who preferred to stay when the previous owners of the house had left; and a manageable nine-hundred-dollar mortgage, which had put Rose's initial investment at just thirty-five hundred dollars. The pretty woodland around the house sloped gently down to Sterns Pond, the three-acre lake where, one Saturday morning last month, Russell and his wife Norma Lee had caught enough largemouth bass to feed the three of them and the Levines, Don and Ruth, who had come over from Norwalk for a fish fry and an evening's conversation.

Outside, Rose heard a car door slam—the Oggs' old Ford coupe—and quick steps on the back stairs. "Hello," a light voice called. "It's me."

The back door opened and Norma Lee came in with a sack of groceries. In her early twenties, she was an attractive young woman, dark haired and dark eyed, with a high, wide forehead and prominent cheeks, narrowing to a pointed chin. Rose, who at fifty-three had not quite come to terms with being short, pudgy, and very gray, envied her young friend's trim figure. Her jacket, slim skirt, and blouse had likely come from a used clothing shop in the city, since the Oggs were making do on something like twenty dollars a week. Still, she looked stylish and nicely put together, whatever she wore.

But Norma Lee wasn't just a pretty girl. She was bright, perceptive, and full of dynamic energy. She had earned undergraduate degrees in English and journalism, was taking classes in English at Radcliffe, and had already mapped out her future as a reporter and feature writer. Rose, both mentor and surrogate mother, had helped her place an article in *The Forum* about the flat that she and Russell rented in a New York tenement. DeWitt Wallace had excerpted it for the upcoming August issue of the *Reader's Digest* (Rose had given her a boost there, too).

Norma Lee put the brown paper bag on the counter, sniffing. "Chicken pie! Oh, Mrs. Lane, my favorite! Russell's too." She began taking things out of the bag. "Thought I'd pick up a few items for the weekend. Extra butter, eggs, sugar." She held up a brightly labeled can and danced a little jig, demonstrating delight. "Baker's Coconut."

"You're sweet," Rose said. "We'll bake that cake tomorrow."

Norma Lee and Russell had become the latest addition to what Rose thought of as her family: Rexh Meta and John and Al Turner, her three "somewhat-adopted" boys, all of them far away. Since Norma Lee and Russell had come for an extended visit, getting settled in the new house had been easier, even fun. Russell was dark haired, tall, gangly, and painfully thin—he certainly needed to get a few good meals under his belt. His career interest was photography, but he was handy around the place, always willing to add a wall here, take one out there, dig a garden, plant a tree—and he was unfailingly cheerful about it. Last week, she had drawn the plans for a small chicken coop that Russell had agreed to build. When the weather was reliably warm, she planned to get a batch of baby chicks and start a laying flock—white Leghorns, she thought, like the chickens her mother used to raise at Rocky Ridge.

Russell was handy, yes. But it was Norma Lee's company that Rose enjoyed most. The girl loved to help hang wallpaper, paint woodwork, and sew curtains. But most of all, she clearly loved the times when she and Rose put their heads together over a piece of Norma Lee's writing, the teacher offering advice and criticism, the student attentive, focused, taking it all in—and there was always a great deal to take in. Rose wielded her red pencil freely, and Norma Lee made no secret of her belief that Mrs. Lane (she said the words with a warm affection that belied their formality) wrote every bit as well and maybe even better than the writers in the literary canon she was studying.

To which Rose, laughing, responded that Norma Lee was young and impressionable and would meet a great many very good writers in the course of her career. She enjoyed being appreciated. But more than that, she liked having young people around— especially young people with energy, ideas, a clear-eyed relish for life, a fresh-hearted belief in the hoped-for improbable. Their optimism boosted her out of the blues that sometimes threatened to swamp her. And Norma Lee had become a friend—Rose's first real friend since Troub. Irrepressible Troub, short for Troubles, for her habit of taking tumbles, big and small, and landing on her feet with a grin and a toss of her head. Rose and Troub had shared a house and a life in Tirana, in Albania, in those hopeful, hedonistic years before the world spun merrily off the cliff.

Tirana. Today, this morning, the word rang like a bell with the bitter peal of loss. Last evening, Robert Trout had reported on the *CBS World News Roundup* that Mussolini had invaded Albania. King Zog—Ahmet Bey Zogu, who had once proposed to Rose (or perhaps this was a fanciful story she had invented to entertain Mama Bess and her Mansfield friends)—was likely to be deposed. And who could tell what would happen to Rexh? Rexh Meta, the ragtag Moslem orphan with the dirty red Turkish fez who had rescued her from a dangerous, perhaps even deadly situation when she was traveling in the Albanian mountains. Rose had sent the boy to a vocational school in Tirana and then, when he'd demonstrated his gift for learning, funded his Cambridge education. Rexh was married now, and he and his wife and little daughter—Borë-Rose ("a rose in snow," she was called, to Rose's delight)—were living in the thick of it. Rose had cabled him last week, offering safe haven if he and his family wanted to emigrate. But Rexh was committed to his country. She knew he would never leave.

Rose herself would have liked to return to the Balkans, to revisit the mountains and the ancient tribal ways she'd written about in *The Peaks of Shala* in 1923. But to go back was impossible. Even before the threat of a Europe-wide war, the Albania she loved existed only in the realm of places and people remembered and written about—seen and experienced vividly then, in dimensions and bright colors, now fading to a soft sepia, the figures and faces blurred, the voices indistinct. Her dreams, that dream and others, seemed to have shrunk within a ruthless, implacable circle of reality, starved by the dwindling of imagination, darkened by the flickering out of an inner intensity. In a way, it was a relief not to have dreams—to have, instead, what she had now. A few friends, this little house and its domestic pleasures of paint and wallpaper and garden. It was enough. She was learning to content herself with the possible and leave the improbable to those who still dreamed.

"Sweet?" Norma Lee asked with an easy laugh. "I am not sweet. I am sneaky. I am manipulative. If you have butter and eggs and coconut, you can bake Russell that cake he lives for." She took off her jacket and hung it on the peg by the door. Holding her loose dark hair away from the flame, she bent over the gas stove to light her cigarette, then put the teakettle on the burner. "Hey—I'm ready for a cuppa. You want one?"

"You'll singe your hair doing that, Norma Lee. Use a match." Rose pushed the typewriter to the middle of the table and picked up her own cigarettes. "Tea would be grand."

In a few moments they were settled at the table with their cups and cigarettes, the lilac breeze brushing over them, Russell's hammer and the radio silent for the moment, a phoebe singing, bright and clear, in the maple outside the window.

Norma Lee glanced at the typewriter and then at the orange notebooks. "What are you working on? Some new fiction, I hope." She paused and added, with a certain casual significance, "It's been awhile, hasn't it?"

That was Norma Lee, always ready with questions and impertinent little nudges, always impatient to read what Rose was writing, to understand how the piece worked, where it was going, what it would look like when it got there. Of all the writers Rose had fostered over the years, and there had been dozens, this one had the most intense curiosity, the most discipline and focus, the most interesting *ideas*. This one was going to make it.

"I was writing a letter to Mama Bess," Rose said matter-of-factly. She hadn't written a piece of fiction for almost two years. Not since *Free Land,* which had been recommended by the *New York Times* for a Pulitzer. Of course, there had always been arid stretches over the course of her nearly thirty-year writing career—what writer didn't dry up now and then? And she had ideas for nonfiction, for articles, plenty of them, mostly having to do with politics or the economy. But she had never gone this long without an idea for a *story*, and the drought was beginning to frighten her. She tapped her cigarette ash into a glass ashtray that bore the logo of the *Saturday Evening Post.* "The editor at Harper says she needs my mother's book by the end of next month. Otherwise, it won't get into the fall catalogue."

"That's *Silver Lake*, I suppose." Norma Lee made a wry face. "You can't put it off? If you had a few free days to work on your own material—"

Rose cut in. "I've put it off long enough. I promised my mother I'd finish it."

Norma Lee kicked off her patent-leather pumps and flexed her toes in her cheap rayon stockings. "I hope Mrs. Wilder knows how lucky she is to have you for a daughter. I've seen the loads of work you put in on her stuff. Really, Mrs. Lane. No other writer would do it—or *could* do it. And your name isn't even on those books, which in my opinion is a serious crime!"

Rose smiled tolerantly. She and Norma Lee had met in 1936, at the end of the summer that she had finally managed to escape from the farm. She was living at the Tiger Hotel in Columbia and working on her mother's fourth book, *On the Banks of Plum Creek.* That September had been hot and lonely, and Norma Lee—a bright and observant honors student at the University of Missouri and an intern at the *Columbia Daily Tribune*—had blown into it like a cheerful autumn breeze. She had been assigned to interview an author. Rose, whose novel about pioneer life, *Let the Hurricane Roar,* had been serialized in the *Saturday Evening Post* and then published as a book, was the closest thing to a famous author the city had ever seen. A story about her would be a scoop. Norma Lee pounced.

Rose and the girl were a good match, and they quickly became friends. One evening, in an unguarded moment, Rose had shown her the work she was doing on her mother's draft of *On the Banks of Plum Creek,* which had led Norma Lee to read the three books that were already in print: *Little House in the Big Woods, Farmer Boy,* and *Little House on the Prairie.* She had admired them, which had led to long conversations about the writing and editing process, about Norma Lee's journalism classes and her ambitions. Satisfying conversations for Rose, whose natural eloquence was ignited into exuberance by an enthusiastic listener, as a spark lights a Roman candle.

The next summer, 1937, Rose had moved to the Grosvenor Hotel in New York, where she settled down to work on another *Saturday Evening Post* serial, *Free Land.* Norma Lee had followed (didn't all would-be writers end up in New York?) and she'd been around when Rose received Mama Bess's draft of *By the Shores of Silver Lake.* Deeply inquisitive about the workings of authorship and the making of books—and especially Rose's work on her mother's books—she made it her business to see what was going on. Impertinent or not, she made no secret of the way she felt about it.

And Rose had to admit that Norma Lee was right about the amount of work she put into her mother's books. Mama Bess was an oral storyteller. She could recall dozens of stories about her family's pioneer wanderings, but when she wrote them down, they sounded like . . . well, they sounded like stories told by your favorite grandmother in front of the fire on a winter's night, without—as George Bye, Rose's agent, had once said—the benefit of any dramatization or fictional technique. The anecdotes were rich in nostalgic detail (especially when Mama Bess was prompted with specific questions) but stitched together with no attention to pattern or theme or structure. The characters were realistic because most of them were drawn from her personal experience of real-life people, her father and mother and sisters and their friends. But the basic elements of narrative—plot and scene and point of view and theme—were hard for her to manage.

Still, over the six or seven years they'd been working together, Rose and her mother had fallen into a more-or-less satisfactory pattern of collaboration. Mama Bess made notes for the book on scraps of paper and the backs of old letters and bills. Then she wrote a pencil draft in the five-cent tablets she bought, a half-dozen at a time, at a local grocery. Sometimes she made more than one pencil draft, then sent the final one to Rose.

Rose read it carefully and pointed out the major changes that needed to be made—since she'd left the farm, she'd put these into her letters. Mama Bess almost always objected. To change *Silver Lake* the way Rose wanted, one letter lamented, would mean starting over from scratch. But eventually, she agreed. "Change the beginning of the story if you want," she had finally said. "Do anything you please with the damn stuff if you will fix it up."

Rose then rewrote the material—shaping scenes and chapters, creating narrative transitions that pieced the anecdotes into a coherent story, crafting dialogue, adding details. Then a revision of the typescript in pen, for style, and a final typing, usually with more edits. She mailed the finished book to her mother, who forwarded it to George Bye, the literary agent they shared, with a cover letter that Rose drafted for her, never (of course) mentioning her daughter's intervention. George Bye sent it on to Ida Louise Raymond at Harper. The proofs made their circuitous way back to Rose, who corrected and returned them to her mother to be returned to Harper. It was the long way around Robinson's barn, as Mama Bess always said, with a little laugh that was part conspiracy, part guilt. But the indirect transmission was necessary to maintain the fiction that Laura Ingalls Wilder was the sole author of the books and that her daughter's only contribution was some minor editorial and publishing advice—very far from the truth.

By this time, Norma Lee had a general idea of the collaborative process and had listened eagerly on the infrequent occasions when Rose dropped the pretense. But the girl had been sworn to secrecy from the beginning.

"If anybody ever asks, tell them I am only marginally involved," Rose had instructed firmly. "Just say I do some of the technical work on the manuscripts. They won't know what that is, and they won't want to give away their ignorance by asking."

Rose, who knew the book business inside and out, had covered her tracks with care. And nobody ever asked, not the Harper editor, not their literary agent, neither of whom had met her mother. Ida Louise Raymond and George Bye probably suspected what was going on, but they didn't want to know, for obvious reasons. As far as they were concerned, the little white-haired farm lady—pioneer child heroine and untaught literary genius, who wrote her books in pencil on five-cent school tablets, sitting alone at her desk on a remote Ozark farm—cut a delightfully appealing figure in bookselling and book review circles. Readers and librarians and teachers and schoolchildren loved the idea of an author who, as a little girl, had lived an adventurous life on the American prairie. Laura Ingalls Wilder was good for business.

And anyway, who the dickens cared? as Rose often put it to herself. These were books for children. *On the Banks of Plum Creek* was not *David Copperfield.* Her mother's books had been well received from the beginning, yes, and to be completely honest about it, Rose was astonished at their continuing popularity. She had told her mother once that there was no opportunity to make a name with juvenile fiction. But that had been in the years before the big publishing houses began to create children's departments and the departments had created children's books and an audience of child readers. She had been right, at the time—unless, of course, you were writing under a house pseudonym like Victor Appleton, churning out dozens of formulaic Tom Swifts and Don Sturdys. Now, it was different. The economy was easing and good books for children were big business.

But children's books still didn't loom large on the literary horizon. Perhaps someday, but now, no. And *that* was more to the point, in Rose's mind. "I don't want my name on my mother's books," she said now. "They're juveniles, Norma Lee. Successful writers don't work for both the juvenile and adult markets. All my other book-length work, including the ghostwriting, has been for an adult market."

Rose had already told Norma Lee about the books she had ghostwritten for Lowell Thomas during the early days of the Depression, after the magazines stopped buying and there was no money to pay the bills. Books with titles like *Born to Raise Hell: The Life Story of Tex O'Reilly, Soldier of Fortune* and *Old Gimlet Eye: The Adventures of Smedley D. Butler, as told to Lowell Thomas.* All of them had been "as told to Lowell Thomas," although they had actually been "as told to Rose Lane," who rewrote them from a scramble of notes and often illegibly penciled pages and sent them back to Mr. Thomas, who published them under his and his clients' names.

And there was *White Shadows in the South Seas,* which she had ghosted for Frederick O'Brien in 1919. The book had gone on to become a best seller and an Academy Award-winning movie and had earned O'Brien a small fortune—while she, unfortunately, had been cheated out of her share of the royalties. She had sued but settled out of court for a fraction of what she was owed.

As far as Rose was concerned, what she had told Norma Lee about her ghostwriting experiences had been a cautionary tale—the things that writers (she hadn't been the only one) resorted to when markets got tight. The times were better now. The magazines were buying again and the newspapers were hiring. If Roosevelt didn't wreck things by imposing more of his New Deal nonsense or by dragging the country into a European war, it would keep on improving. There was plenty of work for writers with ideas.

Norma Lee stubbed out her cigarette. "I guess I can understand why you don't want your name on the books. But they're selling well and earning royalties. Don't you resent that, even a little bit? Shouldn't you have your share?"

Resent it? How much did she resent it? Rose pushed the first question away, not to be answered, not even for Norma Lee, and replied to the second.

"I don't want a share of the royalties. I want the money, all of it, to go to my mother. It's not that much, actually. Last year, it only amounted to around two thousand dollars." That was very good money for Mama Bess, who for most of her life had scraped by on a few dollars a week, but less than a tenth of the amount *Free Land* had brought. "Now that she has her own income, I don't have to support her. And earning makes her feel good—makes her feel that she doesn't have to depend on me."

"But she *does* depend on you," Norma Lee objected. She pointed to the letter on the stack of orange tablets. "She depends on you to write the books that she takes the credit for. Doesn't she feel obligated to give you something in return? And doesn't she feel . . . well, guilty about the deception?" Norma Lee wrinkled her nose. "She should, if you ask me. There's an ethical issue here, isn't there?"

"Nobody's asking you," Rose snapped, short and hard. Like a good journalist, Norma Lee knew how far she could push it and then always pushed it just a little bit farther. But the ethical issue was Mama Bess's business. It was among the subjects—the *many* subjects—that they never discussed, although Rose had suspected from the beginning that her mother felt deeply uneasy about the deception. That was her mother's way: the more troubled she was about something, the less likely she was to say anything about it to anyone. Which meant that there was no way to know for certain, for it was almost impossible to break through that politely silent façade to what was underneath.

After a pause, Rose softened her tone. "Morality doesn't enter into it as far as I'm concerned, Norma Lee. Writing is a job for me, a way to make a living. It has always been that way, from the first day I became a reporter for the *Kansas City Post*. I am always surprised and even a little incredulous when I read that one author or another actually *loves* to write and would do it dawn to dark, even though he or she didn't earn a nickel." She chuckled drily. "But that's not my style. Sometimes I write because I get mad—that's why I wrote *Free Land*. But I usually write because I need the money. When I don't, I do things I really *like* to do. Gardening, needlework, writing letters, talking with friends."

"But you're not working on your mother's books for the money or because you're mad about something or another—"

Rose shook her head. "Norma Lee, you are missing the point. Working on those books is my way of supporting my mother and father financially. What's more, if I earned royalties from the sales of those books, I'd have to pay income tax on it, at a higher rate than my mother does. This way, we both get to keep a little more of what we earn." She smiled crookedly. "And I'm sure you know how I feel about the Infernal Revenue Service. It's just another way for the government to stick its fingers into our pockets."

"Yes, I know," Norma Lee replied seriously. "You've told us about that." She tilted her head to one side. "But you've never told me how you got *involved* in your mother's books. You've told me about your work as a telegraph operator right out of high school, and the reporting for the *Kansas City Post* and the *Journal* and your real estate career in California. And the feature writing you did for the *San Francisco Bulletin* during the Great War, and your autobiographical novel and the books you wrote about Jack London and Charlie Chaplin and Henry Ford." She frowned. "I'm leaving somebody out."

"Herbert Hoover," Rose said. The book had first come out in 1920 and was still selling—modestly, but selling. Hoover might be a scapegoat for the Depression, but he wasn't forgotten.

"Oh, yes, President Hoover. And I've heard about your travels for the Red Cross in Europe and the Middle East after the war and the two years you lived in Albania with Troub." She pulled her brows together. "Let's see—when was that?"

"Nineteen twenty-six, twenty-seven, twenty-eight." That had been only a decade ago, but it seemed like a century, a millennium, Albania itself now as distant as the moon, and Troub too, long estranged. "Then I went back to Rocky Ridge. My parents had both been sick, the winter was terrible that year, and Papa couldn't get any help at the farm. I had a good writing income and investments in the stock market. I thought I would build a tenant house and hire somebody to live there and work the farm, then build a retirement cottage for them. And then I could travel back and forth, from the farm to the city and back to the farm, when I was needed there." She shook her head heavily, feeling the weight of what she had done. "Foolishness. Idiocy. Dreams and schemes, those houses. A waste of money." She dropped her voice. "Worse, a waste of time." A waste of time, yes. But the time had wasted *her*. Those years, those awful, awful years, when there was no work, when—

"Really?" Norma Lee said sympathetically. "Was it really that bad?"

"Of course. There was the Crash and farm foreclosures and bank failures—" Rose pulled in her breath. And failures of hope and wonder and imagination and dreams. And love, yes, of love. When love failed, when love was swallowed by disappointment, by resentment . . .

"Tell me." Norma Lee leaned forward, her dark eyes intent, searching. "Tell me, please, Mrs. Lane."

Rose turned away to glance at the clock. "Time to take that chicken pie out of the oven." She pushed her chair back and got to her feet. "You go tell Russell to wash up and then you can set the table. We'll eat in about fifteen minutes."

Norma Lee put out her hand. "*Tell me*," she said again, more urgently. "I love the stories you've told us about all the things you've done in your life. And your writing—your work as a writer—is so important to me. I know I have a lot to learn from your experience. And I really want to know about *this*. How you got involved. Why you've done what you've done for your mother."

"I don't know why you'd want to hear it, Norma Lee." Rose went to open the oven. "It was an unhappy time. The magazine fiction market hit bottom. Those summers were damned hot, and no relief. They were the years of the Dust Bowl, and the air was thick with blowing grit. Nobody had two nickels to rub together. Roosevelt was setting himself up as a dictator." She pulled on a pair of oven mitts, took out the pie, and set it on the top of the stove. "If we were unhappy, if we were depressed, if everybody was a little crazy, it was no wonder. That's it. That's the story. Doesn't bear repeating."

Norma Lee shook her head stubbornly. "I still want to hear it. It'll go no further, I swear. Whatever it is, it's just between you and me. We could do it this weekend."

Rose paused. There were mysteries that easy tellings, like her mother's simple tales of the plains pioneers, could scarcely convey. Even the most artful story ultimately failed, for the deepest feelings—the urgency that drove desire, the desire that compelled choice—were hidden in the secret places between the words. Why bother, when the effort was bound to fail? Or (and here was a thought that caught her, like a vine snaking around her ankles) why take the risk, when it might succeed too well, tell too much?

But perhaps there was something she *could* tell, something that might at least satisfy the girl's curiosity. And if she could give voice to even the simplest narrative of all that had happened, there might be something in it that would help her understand how she had come to the place where she was now, where she had no more stories of her own to tell, and no more mysteries.

"I'll think about it," she said.

And in the end, because Norma Lee didn't give up easily, and because there *was* a story to tell, and because she herself wanted to understand, she did.

2. From Albania to Missouri: 1928

Come home, she cabled, and I went.

Troub—Helen Boylston—always complained that I was at my mother's beck and call. Troub was right, of course. Still, the situation was desperate. My father was sick. My mother was sick. They had to have help. Who else could they turn to but me?

But the matter was more complicated than that. It was time to leave Albania, and both Troub and I knew it. We had gone to Tirana in 1926. We had been living in a lovely two-story villa, cool and dignified in its blue-gray whitewash, with a narrow front court and an archway that led into a lush walled garden. The house had been previously occupied by American diplomats and people were still accustomed to drop in to talk. So we held afternoon teas for the foreign service community—Germans, French, British, Americans, Greek, but *not*, of course, the Italians.

Ah, those lovely days. The air in that house was fragrant with the aroma of Turkish tobacco and electric with international intrigue in four or five languages. We drank tea and wine and yes, sometimes French champagne, and nibbled on whimsical Albanian pastries contrived by Yvonne, our French cook, and danced to the latest records on Troub's Victrola: "Who's Who Are You?" and "Let Me Call You Sweetheart" and "Tea for Two." Troub and I—two American women, reasonably attractive, well traveled, well read, and lively—were much in demand. From the wide windows, our guests could admire the view of Mount Dajti, stretched out like some lazy prehistoric beast against the bluest sky, or on moonlit nights, they would spill out onto the balcony and into the garden, where old Ibraim, our Albanian gardener (who could not read the labels on seed packets but knew every Albanian proverb ever conjured) had planted a formal bed of chrysanthemums edged with an unlikely lace of green lettuce. Ibraim came to Tirana as a refugee. He told me that he had finally scraped together enough *quindarka* to buy four oranges, which, in a moment of entrepreneurial inspiration, he had displayed on a white handkerchief on the sidewalk, thereby launching his career as a fruit stand man, from whence vantage point he had promoted himself to salaried gardener.

Ibraim's garden was gorgeous. The house was a fabulous delight. Tirana, with its white minarets rising out of the hot white dust of medieval streets, was a cabinet of treasures. I loved each inch of it and all of it and hated to leave—part of me hated it, that is. Another part knew that it was time and seized on Mama Bess's command to come home as if it were a rope tossed over a cliff to a weary climber.

It had been a lovely life, those two years in Tirana, in many ways an ideal life: exotic surroundings, Troub for companionship and conversation and sweet sustenance, and servants to cook and take care of the household so I could have all day to write. I went to Albania with the idea of living cheaply and writing—writing something that was true and real and *satisfying,* something I was passionate about, not just the magazine stuff I had been writing for a living during the last decade. Something that would express *me*, if I could ever manage to understand who I was.

But I was too many things, and wanted too many things, and could never decide which ones might be (if I would pay them the proper attention) most important. There were too many distractions in Albania, too many sights to see, things to do, to think about, to write about. It was too easy to lose focus, to scatter my energies, to fragment—perhaps (and this was the hard part) because I lacked the sense of purpose that would bind all the loose pieces of myself together.

And in the end, I didn't find the time or the energy to write anything more than the magazine stuff that paid the bills. I was supporting two households, even then: the household in Tirana and Mama Bess and Papa on their Missouri farm, some two hundred acres of hardscrabble Ozark mountainside that produced nothing but apples, milk, and eggs, and not enough of any of them for a decent living.

So I did what I had been doing ever since I left the *San Francisco Bulletin* at the end of the war. I rattled off a dozen or so magazine pieces and a serial, *Cindy: An Ozark Romance*. Carl Brandt, my agent, sold the serial to the *Country Gentleman* for ten thousand dollars, which mostly went to pay household expenses and repay debts. I managed to send some of it to George Q. Palmer in New York, for my brokerage account, which was keeping pace with the bull market in that go-go year. I remember writing my mother, who saw what I was earning and wanted to invest some of her own saved pennies with Mr. Palmer, telling her that stocks were leaping around like corn in a popper and we couldn't lose. Now, post-1929, I think of that with some irony. Then, I more often thought of the lines from the *Panchatantra*: *Money will get anything, get it in a flash. Therefore let the prudent get cash, cash, cash.*

Ah, yes. *Cash cash cash*: my mantra. I told myself that I longed to write something of my own, something significant that came from my center, emerged from who I was. Something like "Innocence," my best story, which had won second prize in the O. Henry Awards for 1922. I would be happy to write another story like that, or one about Albania and the bazaar and the minarets in the clear light of dawn and the haunting call to prayer.

But I was, in the end, unrelentingly, relentlessly practical: my haunting call was always for *cash cash cash*. I settled for writing what the magazine editors wanted. I put what I could into the Palmer brokerage account and spent the rest.

And there were plenty of places to spend it—the Tirana house, for instance. For me, houses are a vice. No, more than that: they are a seductive, enthralling, soul-stirring *joy*. My life is littered with the bones of houses that have enchanted me, on which I have lavished time and money—a curse and I know it, but there it is. So Troub and I happily painted and plastered and tore down walls and built new ones in our rented house and dreamed and drew sketches of the even larger villa we would build on the green hills above Tirana.

We had thought when we went there, Troub and I, that we would stay forever. But the medieval Albania I had seen and loved during my first visit in the early 1920s was being transformed into a misbegotten by-blow of European culture. Learning that was like tasting the bitter truth at the end of a disastrous love affair. Then came the earthquakes, tremors that opened cracks in the city's mud walls and shook our house so badly that we slept in our clothes, with our shoes under our pillows. And the political earthquakes—that *damned* Mussolini, who even then coveted Albania's strategic location on the Adriatic and was poised to march in and possess the country the minute the Albanian government collapsed.

There were practical considerations, too. I needed to see my agent and talk to my magazine editors and my stockbroker. I absolutely *had* to get something done about my teeth, which couldn't be done in Albania where dentistry was a blood sport. Altogether, my days seemed to be darkened by needs I couldn't fulfill and a kind of subterranean discontent I couldn't quite bring to the surface.

So it was almost a relief (not quite, but almost) when Mama Bess cabled: *Come home.* Yes, it would have been nice if she had said "please," but international cables are priced by the word. My mother pinched every single penny she took out of her little leather purse, then (when she had to) as now (when she doesn't). "Please" would cost too much.

Troub knew it was time to leave but wasn't crazy about the idea of going back to the farm. "By the time you get to Missouri," she pointed out, "it will be spring and your mother won't need you anymore. Anyway, she just wants to know that she can still make you do what she says. She has you under her thumb." Troub was a slim, athletic woman, younger than I by some nine years, intelligent, perceptive. She looked good in trousers, which shocked the Europeans and amazed the Albanians. "Your mother may seem like a sweet little old lady, with her white hair and blue eyes. But she is the most overbearing woman I have ever known. She bosses your sweet, long-suffering father, the dog, the cat, the cows, you." She quirked an eyebrow. "It's no secret. Ask your mother's neighbors. They'll tell you who wears the pants in the Wilder family."

I laughed at that, ruefully, but of course it was true. My mother had the appearance of everyone's ideal grandmother: diminutive and pretty, her hair going white now and her eyes a dark, deep blue. When she went into town to shop or to a club meeting, she always wore her best dress, a pert little hat, spotless gloves, and a sweet smile.

But her father had always said that she was as strong as a little French horse and there was a firm set to her mouth that belied any softness in her face. The two of us had fought a battle of wills since I was old enough to realize how *good* it felt to be willful, if not willfully *bad*. She was afraid of what I would come to if she let me go, and I was afraid of what I would come to if she held on.

Finally, at seventeen, I taught myself Morse code. My friend Ethel Burney's father was the agent at the Frisco depot and had a telegraph key at home that Ethel and I learned how to operate. Then I took the train to Kansas City, where I got a job as a telegrapher with Western Union. I worked for the company there and in Mount Vernon, Indiana, until 1908, when, not yet twenty-two, I began a new life in San Francisco.

Yes, I left home to earn money (*cash cash cash*), some of which I dutifully sent back to Mama Bess. But mostly, I left to escape her instructions on how to behave, her small-town moralizing, her worries about what people would think if I did this or said that. And to escape the parochial quicksand of Mansfield, which, if I had stayed, would have swallowed me, heart and soul and every original and rebellious thought in my head.

In the next twenty-some years, I went home occasionally and kept in dutiful touch by letter. But mostly I was on the move, onward, outward. I married Gillette Lane and divorced him nine years later; in the interim, I lost a baby boy and buried with him a piece of my heart. I went to the East Coast, then to the West Coast, then to the East Coast again, then abroad. I was a wife, a real estate salesperson, a newspaper reporter, a feature writer, a freelance writer.

"There's all the world, all the world, outside, waiting for me!" I wrote that in 1919, at the end of *Diverging Roads,* my first novel, the disguised and fictionalized story of my young life. There's all the world, all the world, waiting—but I was still my parents' only child, with an only child's obligations, which fell heavier on me now that my parents couldn't manage the farm.

Papa—lame since he had suffered a stroke or maybe contracted polio when I was still a baby—was now past seventy. Mama was sixty and (though we didn't know it at the time) diabetic. I was duty-bound to see that they were taken care of. I once read that the sociologist Jane Addams called this burden the "family claim," two words that probably explain it well enough: a bond—no, a bondage, braided of strands of guilt, duty, and affection. This powerful bond held daughters (especially only daughters) to parents in those days, the days before the Great War, before the Twenties roared and girls bobbed their hair, hiked their skirts above their knees, painted a red cupid's bow on their lips, and kissed their mothers goodbye.

So when Troub advanced the opinion that I was afflicted with an immoderate sense of obligation ("You are your mother's little *slavey,*" she said), I defended myself. I invited her to think back to the world as it was at the turn of the century, when I left home, already inoculated with the idea that adult daughters are responsible for the care of their aging parents. If mine had been able to support themselves (like Troub's father, who was a prosperous dentist), it would have been a different story.

My mother liked to present the Wilder farm as a great success in her *Missouri Ruralist* articles. But she and Papa and I knew that it had never been more than marginally productive. Rocky Ridge was one of the larger farms in the county (in a word, they were land-poor), but it was too hilly and the stony soil was too thin and poor to support much more than her chickens, his cows, and the apple trees that were now long past bearing. Papa and Mama Bess grew most of their food, so they weren't in danger of starving. They earned a few dollars selling milk and butter and eggs in town, my mother made a little money as secretary-treasurer of the local Farm Loan Association, and there was the five-hundred-dollar "subsidy" (the word I chose for this annual payment) that I had been sending them since 1920. Mama Bess, whose mantra was *save save save*, had even managed to piece together a cash reserve out of those few crazy-quilt scraps of income.

But she told me that she still dreamed of walking down a long, dark road with wintry trees closing in on either side, knowing with a bone-chilling fear that it was the road to the county poorhouse. Now, they needed me. I had no choice. I had to go home.

Troub gave me a searching look. "I have the feeling that your mother, and even your old hometown, are a kind of safe haven for you, Rose, a refuge. You head for home when the big wide world gets too scary. But I hope you remember how you felt the last time you were there alone, with your parents—and even when we were there together. You hated it."

A safe haven? A refuge? I doubted that. But the other part was certainly true. I hated the isolation, the feeling of being exiled. I despised the parochial pettiness of the townspeople. And I loathed the unrelenting drudgery of the farm and household work, which my mother rationalized and romanticized in the columns she wrote for the *Missouri Ruralist.* I countered that in an article called "Veal Cutlets" that I wrote for *Harper's Magazine,* itemizing the chores that had to be done at Rocky Ridge. The firewood to fetch, the stoves to feed, the ashes to shovel. The floors to sweep and scrub, the lamps to clean and fill and light, the beds to make, the clothes to wash and iron. The potatoes to peel and biscuits to bake, three meals a day to cook and serve and wash up after. The milk to strain and skim, the cream to churn, the chickens to feed, the pigs to slop, the garden to plant and weed and harvest, and all of it mindlessly, continuously, endlessly.

I didn't intend to go back to that drudgery. This time, I had money, *cash cash cash.* And a plan.

Troub, seeing the handwriting on the wall, gave a resigned sigh. "How long are you thinking of staying?"

"Only as long as I have to, and not a minute longer," I said. "Will you come with me?" Troub and I were close, as close as two friends could be, and closer. We needed each other. I didn't like to think of going back to the farm without her.

"I'd come in a minute if it weren't for your mother," Troub said frankly. "I'm pretty easygoing, Rose, but the farmhouse is crowded with four of us, and there's no place to escape. She's always begging us to have a cup of tea with her, or go to a club meeting with her so she can show us off, or drive her to town. And all in the sweetest of ways, of course, which makes it impossible to refuse." She made a face. "And then there's the bickering."

I sighed. What Troub was saying was perfectly true. A few years before, I had bought my parents a car—a 1923 blue Buick they named "Isabel"—and my mother could drive just as well as my father. But she preferred to be driven and, in a smooth-as-cream voice, would ask us to take her into town. For her regular Wednesday trip to the grocery, she would put on her best hat and gloves and call out instructions for every stop and turn, as if the driver—my father or me or Troub—were her chauffeur.

As for their bickering—well, Troub was right again. My father was a lamb. I adored him, and Troub did, too. But my parents argued endlessly about the farm: whether they should hold on to a piece of it or sell it to a neighbor; whether my mother should give up her chickens or my father should sell his cows or both; whether they could afford to buy another heifer or perhaps a pig. Eventually, my father would escape to the workshop or the barn, but in the meantime, the voices from downstairs (Troub and I usually worked or read upstairs on the sleeping porch) would be vehement. And loud, because Papa hard of hearing.

"You have a point," I agreed. "But I have a plan."

Troub snickered.

"No, seriously," I said. "The first order of business is to hire somebody to help my father with the farm work. That means building a tenant house, something simple that can be put up in a few weeks. About the crowding and my mother—" I glanced at her. "That part of my plan will take a little longer, but it will be an answer to everything."

"Oh, really?" Troub wrinkled her freckled nose, interested but skeptical.

"Yes, really." I made myself sound more confident than I felt. I wasn't sure that my mother would go for my scheme. "I'm going to build them a modern cottage with electricity and central heating and hot water and an indoor bathroom, all on one floor, so Mama Bess doesn't have to climb the stairs. Just the other day, I saw a Cotswold cottage in a magazine, an English-style bungalow that would be just about perfect. There are plenty of pretty places to build it on the farm. All my mother has to do is pick the spot. They could be moved in by October, snug and ready for winter."

"A new house." Troub, who has plumbed the depths of my passion for houses, eyed me doubtfully. "Won't that be expensive?"

"The price for the house I saw was around twenty-two-hundred dollars, so even with the extras I have in mind, it's not likely to be more than four thousand dollars. And the Palmer account just keeps growing—I can afford it."

Troub cocked her head. "What about the old farmhouse?"

"That's where the real fun comes in." I was beginning to get excited, the way I always do when I am about to be seduced by a house. "I could fix it up for *us*, Troub— do some painting, wire it for electricity, install a furnace and get rid of those awful stoves. It would be our place to stay in, to travel from. When we're there, we could hire somebody to cook and clean for us, and I could write. And we could invite friends from New York—Genevieve, Catharine, Mary Margaret. I'm sure they'd jump at the chance to spend a few weeks at a writing retreat in the country."

Inviting friends had been one of the thorny issues the last time Troub and I had stayed at the farm together. Mama Bess complained that we sat up too late and made too much noise, and Papa was annoyed when he found the outhouse occupied. ("Every time a fellow wants to use the john, there's some hen on the roost," he'd grumbled.) The farmhouse looked large, but the rooms were small, and there were only the two extra bedrooms upstairs. If four was a crowd, five or six was even more so—and (I had to admit) a serious disruption in my parents' daily routines. But if Mama Bess and Papa had their own house on the other side of the ridge, our visitors wouldn't bother them.

"A writing retreat." Troub sat up straight, catching my enthusiasm. "Like that place Mabel Dodge Luhan has in Taos."

"Well, not exactly," I said, but she was going on, getting excited, too.

"We could have our friends, and parties, and *both* of us could write."

A couple of years before, Troub had showed me her war diary. She was trained as a nurse and had volunteered in France in the last years of the war, where she'd specialized as an anesthesiologist and been promoted to captain. I saw what a splendid piece of writing she had done and mailed it off posthaste to the editor of the *Atlantic Monthly,* who quite naturally snapped it up. We polished it a bit and it ran as a serial in the magazine and would shortly be published as a book, *Sister.* Troub could be a fine writer if she settled down to it. But she had inherited a little money, enough so that she could choose to write, or not to. (Later, after the Crash, after the whole world changed, that would change, too. Before the next decade was out, she would be writing books for girls about a nurse named Sue Barton.)

I've never had the luxury of *choosing* to write. For me, from the beginning, writing has been a financial necessity, and would be now, especially given my ambitious plan for the farm. But I could manage it. All I needed was a thousand words a day, a dozen short stories a year, another book-length serial for *Country Gentleman* or even for the *Saturday Evening Post,* which paid better. By 1930, if I buckled down to work, my parents would be provided for and I would have a solid, secure fifty thousand dollars invested in the market. I could divide my time between New York and the farm. I could live where I chose and write what I liked, without having to depend on magazine fiction for a living.

Fifty thousand dollars. Now, looking back, knowing everything that would happen, wouldn't happen, *couldn't* happen, fifty thousand dollars seems like a maniac's mad hallucination. But it wasn't, then. Then, we were all caught up in the rah-rah-rah of the euphoric days before the Crash. The stock market was on its way to the moon and the future had no horizons. There was plenty of everything and more to be dreamed of and reached for. More, more, more. Fifty thousand dollars was a goal to be grasped, not a joke to be laughed at.

"Yes, friends and parties," I replied. "We can both write. And spend time together, doing just as we like. What do you say?" I wanted her to come: Troub was smart and funny, a good-natured, agreeable companion, someone I loved to talk to, a shield to deflect my mother's constant attentions. And more, of course, in ways we didn't put into words. I was greedy. But I couldn't insist.

Troub considered, scratched her freckled nose, grinned. "Guess I don't have anything better to do. Sure, Rose. I'll come." She added, carelessly, "For a while, anyway. For as long as it suits both of us."

That was Troub, then. We lost one another years ago, and probably she's different now—the Depression has changed us all. But in those days, she was happy-go-lucky, easy-come, easy-go. She had no plans of her own and no designs on a particular future—and that was what I loved about her. She didn't claim, didn't cling, didn't clutch. There were no obligations, other than to respond to each other in the truest of ways.

"I'd enjoy being out in the country again," she added. "Do you think your father would mind if I bought a horse and kept it in his barn? I could ride in the afternoons."

"He wouldn't mind a bit," I said confidently. "Papa likes you."

It was true. Mama Bess regarded Troub with more than a little jealousy and was always wondering, half-aloud and nervously, what others thought when they saw us so much together, and what they said about me behind her back, and what they said about *her* when they were talking about me. But Papa, who never cared a bean for what anybody thought, found Troub clever and fun loving and admired her tomboy energies.

"And he's a horseman," I added. "I'm sure he would be glad to help you find the perfect horse." A Morgan, probably. Papa loved Morgan horses.

Troub nodded. "Tell you what, then. I'll go home to New Hampshire and visit my father for a few weeks, then I'll join you at the farm." She flung both arms around me and kissed me. "Come on, Rose, smile. Another adventure, together."

So we packed bags and boxes. I made arrangements to sublease the Tirana house and cabled Mama Bess that we would book passage as soon as we could. We took Mr. Bunting, the white Maltese terrier we had bought in Budapest the year before, and sailed on the Italian liner *Saturnia* for New York, a gay sailing, with good weather and light-hearted company. Somewhere off the coast of Spain, I settled down with my journal, making plans for the new year, for the next three years, writing that I was looking forward to the fresh, sunny, open-air life of the farm, a busy life, active, energetic, free of the smoldering discontents that had darkened the past few months. I looked out across the fog-veiled Azores and thought how good it would be to live on an island and filed it away, a possible dream.

Disembarking in New York on February 16, we paid an unexpected $4.50 in customs duties for Mr. Bunting, checked into the new and luxurious Berkshire Hotel, and dashed out onto Madison Avenue. Around us, the city was booming. It was splendid and lively and invigorating and above all *exciting*, reminding me how much I loved the streets and shops and noise and energetic bustle and hurry, loved seeing my agent and stock-broker and editors and, most of all, friends—Mary Margaret McBride and Catharine Brody and Genevieve Parkhurst and Berta Hader—Berta, from our years together in San Francisco before the war and after the war, living through the winter together in an unheated house on Jones Street in Greenwich Village. Like starving survivors rescued from a desert island, Troub and I indulged in giddy rounds of restaurants and shopping and the theater and parties and talk talk talking about ideas and books and politics and people.

There was a certain sadness, too, which is another kind of indulgence. I saw Guy Moyston, and we sat together in the bus terminal cafeteria until one o'clock in the morning, saying (but not quite *saying it*) a final goodbye. I had loved Gillette Lane for a time but not forever; and Austin Lewis briefly and unwisely in San Francisco; and Arthur Griggs skittishly in Paris now and then; and finally Guy, who spent one sweet-scented Ozark spring with me at Rocky Ridge. I remember how empty the old farmhouse seemed after he left, and my mother said, "Now can you imagine what it's like when you go, and there is nobody? *Nobody*."

I had thought Guy detached and ironic and loved him for that, but now he wanted marriage, a conventional marriage, a doting wife in a little house and regular meals and company on the weekends. And although I still had a kind of love for him, I could not marry him. I could not *marry*, for there was all the world, all the world, outside, out there, beyond, waiting for me.

And in the meantime, there was New York. Yes, I thought, yes. Yes! Invigorating, enlivening, revitalizing New York, where every writer should live for at least a part of every year, where *I* would live for a part of every year, once my parents were settled. My stay at the farm, however long it was, would have to include at least two or three months of every year in New York.

And then . . . and then I was back in Missouri.

3. Houses: 1928

Days on the farm do not fill diaries.

But spring in the Ozarks is unspeakably lovely. In a single madcap April week, all the countryside becomes a green riot, glorious with violets and buttercups and wild pansies and anemones. And then the elms and dogwood and maples and white oaks assert themselves, and after that, in an impetuous rush, the white flume of wild plums and the pinks of peach blossom spill across the hillsides, while the fresh spring grass surges in an emerald tide across the meadows—all of it reminding me of that very first spring we lived at Rocky Ridge.

Our family had fled to Missouri from South Dakota after a series of disasters: the disease that lamed my father, the drought and hailstorms that destroyed the crops, the death of a baby boy, the loss of our house. I burned the house. Yes, yes, I did. My mother was sick in bed and, trying to be helpful, I stuffed too much slough hay in the stove and set the place ablaze. I was not yet three, but I quite well remember the searing despair I felt as I watched it burn and knew that *I* had done it. After that, there were stays with my mother's family in De Smet and my father's in Spring Valley, Minnesota, and two years in Florida and two more in South Dakota before my parents had saved enough for the Ozark farm they wanted to buy.

We traveled, Mama and Papa and I, in a black-painted hack with an oilcloth top and curtains, a wooden hencoop fastened at the back and Papa's mares hitched to the front, with their colts, Prince and Little Pet, following along. In the hack was a bedspring for Papa and Mama to sleep on, and Mama's writing desk and as many other of our scant possessions as could be tucked into or tacked onto the load. We traveled with our friends, Mr. and Mrs. Cooley, and their two sons, Paul and George. Earlier that spring, Mr. Cooley had scouted for land in southwestern Missouri, so the journey had a destination.

We reached it in the last days of a hot, dusty August, camping near the town of Mansfield, in Wright County, in the Land of the Big Red Apple. At least, that's the way it was promoted by the Frisco Railroad. A few weeks later, Papa and Mama Bess bought Rocky Ridge—forty acres and a log cabin—with a three-hundred-dollar mortgage (at a usurious 12 percent, compounded every three months) and a hundred-dollar bill, saved by my mother from her hundred days' labor as a dollar-a-day seamstress back in De Smet and terrifyingly lost for several breathless days in a cranny of her writing desk. And then, thankfully, found again, and we could all breathe.

The green Ozark woodland they purchased was beautiful: heartbreakingly, unpromisingly beautiful. My father, a flatland wheat farmer, would later say that the place had looked so rough and hostile—nothing but gullies and ridges and rocks and timber—that he was reluctant to buy it. But my mother had taken a violent fancy to the property, crying that it was the only land she wanted and that if she could not have *that* one, she did not want any. My mother didn't cry often—the Ingalls girls had been tutored in the stiff-upper-lip school, and she always said she didn't like a row. But when tears were necessary to get the job done, she knew how to use them. My easygoing father rarely opposed her when she was set on having her way. He didn't now, whatever his own judgment might have been. Rocky Ridge, they called it. The name was perfectly descriptive. This was a land of ridges and rocks, rocks and ridges.

Our first house at Rocky Ridge was the tiny log cabin that the previous owner had built on the lip of the ravine. Its most interesting feature, to me, was the newspaper pasted as wallpaper on one of the walls, and I stood stock-still, entranced, reading. "Carter's Little Liver Pills: What is life without a liver?" This philosophical question haunted me for years.

By the time we broke camp and moved into the cabin, we were down to our last bit of salt pork and cornmeal, with winter coming on. To earn money for food, my father cut wood and sold it for fifty cents a wagonload. With my mother on one end of the crosscut saw and my father on the other, they began to clear the land. The next spring, they set out the tiny apple trees—twigs, really—that had come with the property. My father was no orchardist, but his father had raised apple trees on the Wilder farm in upstate New York, and he was willing to give it a try. He was proud of his apples, when the trees came into bearing seven years later: Ben Davis, they were, and Missouri Pippin. He always said that the thing that made his orchard a success was that he took care of each individual tree, giving it whatever it needed, which meant a great deal of work.

Mostly, from those years, I remember the work, and it wasn't just the apples. My father turned the cabin into a barn and built a two-room frame house with a sleeping loft for me, a steep, ladder-like stair climbing up to it. My mother raised a garden and chickens and prepared every meal and washed the dirty clothes, and I was expected to help as far as my child-self was able, carrying water and stove wood and hoeing and weeding.

All this was hard work, backbreaking, dawn-to-dark work that took both my parents away from me, but especially my mother. It made her snappish and quick with her temper, so that many things I did or did not do correctly or left undone disappointed her. I *knew* her disappointment. I felt it like a lance.

Indeed, it has often seemed to me that in those days—except for a brief golden hour after supper and before bed—I had no mother, for she had no time to give me attention or affection and I was left to ask for it or beg for it or even to misbehave for it, which earned instead her sharp anger and my sullen guilt. Then, I thought this lack of mothering was my own particular privation and resented it, and pitied myself. Now, I know that many children do not receive the mother-love they need and that they keep on needing and wanting it for a long, long time, perhaps all their lives. Do I? Do I do what I do for her now because of the lack, the emptiness I felt then? I don't know. Perhaps. Perhaps.

But I adored her. I loved to watch her brush out her hair and braid it, loved the glints and gleams in her thick, roan-brown hair, which fell loose in a shimmer down to her heels. At home, she wore it in one braid down her back; for town, she coiled it like a shining crown on her head and fastened it with her tortoiseshell pins. Beneath a fringe of curled bangs, her blue eyes gave away her mood. When she was out of patience with me, they darkened; when I pleased her, they sparkled. When she was happy, she whistled like a meadowlark, trilling and chirping and spilling song as she worked. She was young, then, not yet thirty, and her skin was soft and smooth and smelled of soap and lavender. To this day, I can't catch a whiff of lavender without seeing her as she was in those early days, my mother, young and lavender-scented and lovely.

I especially loved the winter evenings in that tiny cabin, its log walls banked with snow and crystal icicles hanging from the eaves. In the fireplace, a fire of hickory logs blazed bright. On the hearth, my father, always silent, rubbed oil into a leather harness or smoothed a new wooden ax handle with a piece of broken glass. At the table, in the circle of golden light cast by the kerosene lamp, my mother knitted woolen socks for my father and read aloud to us, her voice softly murmuring, while I sat on the floor with a pile of corncobs, building a little house of my own. In that hour, I had both a mother and a father, a measureless treasure.

The next spring, my father traded a load of wood for a donkey that I named Spookendyke. I was supposed to ride him to school, although it can't accurately be said that I *rode* him, for the ungrateful beast had the perverse habit of slumping his shoulders so that I slid off over his ears. In the classroom, barefoot and shabby and painfully aware of being very poor, I was seated with the other barefoot, shabby mountain girls, well away from the town girls in their wonderful store-bought dresses. Oh, how I coveted Becky Hooper's red serge dress, trimmed with narrow bands of red satin, and Ethel Burney's white stockings, and my heart ached for Josey Franklin's shiny patent leather shoes. I said nothing to my mother about these longings, for even a pair of the plainest shoes was beyond my parents' reach. At home, I insisted that I would rather go barefoot to school than wear shoes. At school, I pretended that none of it mattered.

But it did. In the frontier Dakota settlement of De Smet, the men and women, alike in their buckle-down grit, had worn their poverty as an earned badge of honor, and while the Ingalls family was even poorer than most, they had achieved, by virtue of their courage and stick-to-it, a certain social distinction. My mother rarely talked about it, but I knew she had felt the brutal edge of her childhood poverty as keenly as I felt mine.

Mansfield was an established town with a closed social hierarchy built on seniority and wealth and evidenced (to me, at least) by satin-trimmed dresses and patent leather shoes. In Mansfield, poverty was a badge of shame, and my homemade dresses and bare feet were its insignia. While my father was courageous and my mother could even be gay in the face of our poverty, I was tormented, and my childhood was a nightmare.

In the years that were to come, my mother would gain entry into the town's clubs, and even start one of her own, the Athenian Club, in Hartville, the county seat. But as a child, I was on the outside, as anyone could tell just by looking at me. Except for the Cooley boys, Paul and George, I had few friends, and no wonder: I was odd and bookish and spoke my own language, Fispooko, to Spookendyke and the chickens and the family cow. Books were my life and my joy, when there was time away from the work I was expected to do and *wanted* to do to please my mother—books and the wild green hills and clear mountain springs where I dreamed under the hazel and sassafras hedges, edged with lavender horse-mint and orange butterfly weed.

The effects of that childhood poverty stayed with me long after I came to an easier place in the world. For one thing, it taught me to hide my insecurity behind a pretended nonchalance, an attitude of *I-don't-care*, which is perhaps my reason for spending money I don't have. It also—and this is more important, I think—made me a teller of tales, someone for whom the sheer pleasure of invention may overtake whatever facts might be involved, especially when I have an appreciative audience. I learned how to *pose*, how to adjust my story to my listeners or readers, a valuable asset for a writer of fiction. That doesn't mean that I don't always know where the truth lies, or that I am deceived by my own stories (although sometimes perhaps I am), or that I am not painfully honest with myself in my journals (as I *certainly* am). It only means that I learned, very young, to conceal the truth behind a fictional façade, which we all do to some extent—except that I have made a profession of it.

The apple twigs my father had planted were still years away from producing and cash was scarce. So when I was eleven, we rented out the little house at Rocky Ridge and moved to town, to a small yellow frame house that we rented for five dollars a month, just two doors east of Mrs. Cooley and the boys. Mr. Cooley had died and Papa took over his hauling business and his job as an agent for the Waters-Pierce Oil Company, selling kerosene, stove gas, turpentine, and linseed oil. The job required him to drive his team and wagon as far south as Ava and as far north as the county seat of Hartville, often in the worst of weathers. Mama Bess set up a boarding table in the front room of our house and cooked for railroad men and traveling salesmen.

All this effort brought a little more money and life was easier, but I was still miserable in school. I was precocious enough to be utterly impatient with the ignorance of our country teachers, and I preferred teaching myself to being taught by *them*. I remember once being instructed to paraphrase some lines of Tennyson's. I retorted that the lines meant more than the individual words and that you couldn't paraphrase poetry without reducing it. Tommy Knight could, though. When he finished his plodding summary, the teacher turned to me. "Let this be a lesson to you, Miss Wilder," he said darkly. "You fail because you do not try. Perseverance is a chief virtue. If at first you don't succeed, try—"

At this unendurable banality, I slammed my books on the desk, cried, "I won't stay and listen to such stupid stuff!" And stormed home. And didn't go back for the rest of the term. Instead, I lay in the barn and read borrowed books—*History of the Conquest of Mexico* by William Prescott, the Leatherstocking Tales, *Sense and Sensibility, Dombey and Son, Decline and Fall of the Roman Empire,* and anything else I could put my hands on. My sporadic attendance seemed to do me no harm, and I know that I profited handsomely from my reading.

Mansfield's school, like most rural schools of the day, went as far as McGuffey's *Sixth Reader.* When the town girls reached that great jumping-off point, many of them began preparing for their life's work, helping their mothers at home and tatting edgings for the tea towels they embroidered for their hope chests until they married the town boys and began having town children. Thus was a woman's life defined: her work was marriage and her place was in the home, tending husband and children and elderly parents, her own and her husband's. The idea made me cringe, so once I was fully aware that this was my future, I began to plot my escape.

It came in the person of Aunt E. J., Eliza Jane Wilder Thayer, my father's energetic sister, a female homesteader who had courageously proved up her Dakota claim, then worked for several years in Washington, D.C., before marrying (at the outrageously advanced age of forty-two!) a prosperous rice farmer and moving to Crowley, Louisiana. Now in her early fifties, Aunt E. J. was an indomitable woman, fearless, unfailingly optimistic, bright, and bossy. I think she saw something in me that reminded her of herself when she was my age. She called me her "Wilder Rose" (which I thought very clever) and offered me a way out of Mansfield, at least for a year.

"Come live with me and you can go to high school," she said.

"Oh, yes!" I cried ecstatically. I had no idea what kind of place Crowley, Louisiana, might be, but I was sure that it would be better than Mansfield, and we would have to go there by train. By train!

"Absolutely not," my mother declared firmly. She didn't like Aunt E. J., who had been her schoolteacher when she was a girl in De Smet. (Later, in the manuscript she called "Pioneer Girl," she confessed to being the author of a nasty bit of doggerel that included the memorable line, "We laugh until we have a pain, at lazy, lousy, Liza Jane." In a private note to me, she added that she had no excuse for such a terrible thing and that she should have been whipped.

I also believe, looking back, that my mother feared losing me completely; once I was able to escape her control, I might never come back. It had been a year of escalating battles between the two of us. I was considered wild by the Mrs. Grundys of Mansfield—those personifications of conventional morality— and my mother was always warning me of the dangers of being "talked about." Silly rumors swirled about my acquaintance with a certain Latin tutor, who was fat and greasy and smelled of cheap cigars, while they might have swirled about my friendship with George Cooley, which was the more credible threat to my reputation.

My mother rarely met a situation she couldn't manage, but even she was ready to admit defeat. I would never have known that, except that I overheard her telling Mrs. Moore that she had come to her wits' end with me and didn't know what she was going to do. Mrs. Moore counseled patience, for I was "at that difficult age" and would surely straighten out in time.

"They do, you know," she said. "You just have to maintain the upper hand."

My mother sighed and allowed that she wasn't sure she could maintain the upper hand that long, however long it was going to take. "And I don't trust Eliza Jane to discipline Rose," she added. "She needs close watching."

"It does take a mother to manage the wild ones," Mrs. Martin allowed. "Have I showed you the pattern for my new spring sprigged lawn?"

Taking advantage of the situation, I argued and begged and wept for another year of school, and Papa (who was no fonder of his bossy sister than Mama but was desperate for some peace in his household) intervened. Faced for once with his resolve, my mother gave in. It was decided. I would be the only girl of my generation to leave Mansfield to further her education. Becky and Josey (she of the patent leather shoes) were seized with envy—but only momentarily, for they had neither the imagination nor the will to escape. Both would marry town boys and bear town children, and while Josey would later leave Mansfield, Joplin was as far as she got.

The year in Crowley was educational in many ways. I not only triumphed over Caesar and Cicero and solid geometry, but I also helped Aunt E. J. hand out political leaflets and listened, awestruck, to her impassioned arguments on behalf of Eugene V. Debs, the Social Democratic Party's presidential candidate, thereby becoming a young Socialist myself. And I made time for my first beau, an "older man" of twenty-four from the University of Chicago, who was exceedingly handsome (as I remember him, but who trusts such memories, magnified through a dozen retellings?). He drove a phaeton with red spoke wheels and polished his manners until they glittered.

I graduated at the top of my Latin class in 1904, offered the class poem, and then returned to the relentlessly narrow life of Mansfield. But only briefly. In mid-summer, my parents took me and my carpetbag to the depot, where I caught the train for Kansas City. I was embarking on a journey that would take me almost to the ends of the earth.

After I left, Mama Bess and Papa moved back to Rocky Ridge, which by dint of work and saving and an inheritance from my Wilder grandfather now amounted to nearly a hundred acres. My father was still working off the farm as an agent for the Waters-Pierce Oil Company, and there was money coming in. My mother desperately wanted a nicer house than the little two-room affair with a loft, so she drew up the plans and over the next few years, it was built by Ezra Dennis and his nephew Orel, two local carpenters, with my father's help and under his watchful eye.

To the little two-room frame house with its loft, the Dennises added a downstairs bedroom, a washroom (which became an office after the bathroom went in), a living room with an alcove for bookshelves, and three porches. Upstairs, they added two bedrooms and a sleeping porch. In the kitchen, Mama Bess asked for the counters to be built low, to her height; in the parlor, she wanted a great many windows, window seats, a beamed ceiling, and paneling and flooring made from native oak cut on the farm and planed at the town sawmill. And at her insistence, Papa had the fireplace built of slabs of local stone, instead of the brick that would have been easier to manage. She objected emphatically to the brick, she confessed in one of the articles she later wrote for the *Missouri Ruralist*. "I argued; I begged; and at last when everything failed I wept." My father yielded to her tears. My mother got her fireplace: two sturdy slabs of Ozark rock, topped by a thick wooden mantle.

By 1913, the house was finished and painted white. To help pay the mortgage, Papa sold the hay from the bottomland and Mama Bess filled the upstairs bedrooms with city people who were visiting the mineral springs around Mansfield, on a paid board-and-room basis. And at last, some twenty years after we three left South Dakota, poor as a trio of church mice, my mother had the showplace she dreamed of, a comfortable, romantic-looking farmhouse that belied the hard, inflexible realities of the farm itself: the daily work, the apple trees' declining production, the invading scrub timber that had to be constantly kept at bay. The fact that a living could be wrestled from it only with great labor would not have been apparent to those who came from the city, or who read my mother's articles about the joys of life on a small farm. And perhaps not even to my parents, or at least to my mother—which is understandable, for as hard as she and Papa had worked, she had to insist (because she believed it) that their struggles were meaningful, were worthwhile. She had to deny their failures and, especially in her farm journal articles, enlarge every small success into a major victory. The house was the symbol of their victory over hardships and hard times.

But the farm could only be maintained by endless physical labor, hard, backbreaking labor. And by 1928, Papa was seventy-one and increasingly lame. Mama Bess was sixty-one and mentioned their health in nearly every letter, tweaking my guilt. Neither of them was capable, any longer, of the work it took to produce even a meager living. The farm was more than Papa could handle and the farmhouse too much house for Mama to manage. Mansfield had an ice plant, but there was no ice delivery in the country and my mother still relied on the springhouse in the ravine to keep the milk and butter and eggs cool. In the summer, the wood-fired cook stove turned the kitchen into an oven. In the winter, with only the coal heater in the dining room, the place was an icebox—and of course, Papa had to cut and split and stack wood and haul coal and ashes. In every season, there was the constant, day-in-day-out feeding of animals: the chickens needed their laying mash, the pigs their slop, the cows their hay, the horses their oats.

And my parents needed electricity, central heating, hot water, indoor plumbing, a refrigerator, and a bathtub where Papa could stretch out and soak his crippled legs and feet in hot water. They needed that modern cottage I had in mind, although in retrospect, I wonder if I needed to build it for them more than they needed to receive it. Perhaps the little house was an emblem of my success in the world of newspapers, magazines, and books, just as the farmhouse was for my mother, in her world. Perhaps that was why she resented the cottage, and me, and refused to even consider the idea.

Convincing Mama Bess to live anywhere other than the house for which she had argued, begged, and wept was going to be a challenge.

Looking back, I don't know why I thought it could be done.

The tenant house—the first part of my plan—was a relatively easy matter.

Papa agreed that it was impossible to get reliable farm help without a house for the hired man and his family. Mama Bess balked at the cost (less than a thousand dollars, I calculated), but she knew that Papa had to have help, and when she saw that he favored the idea, she finally agreed. He picked a site down the hill and the project got underway. Once the four-room house was finished, Papa hired Jess Wiley to live there, do the chores, and work the farm. Jess's wife's name was Angela. They had one child and another on the way.

But the cottage I wanted to give my parents—the "retirement house," Mama Bess called it with a disdainful sniff—was another story, and my plan was stopped flat by her refusal.

"Why?" I asked plaintively. "*Why*, Mama Bess?"

We were discussing it—again—at the breakfast table on a chilly, gray May morning, with the rain sluicing down the windows and the room so dark that I had lit the kerosene lamp. "Wouldn't it be so much better to have electric lights and an electric hot water heater, so you didn't have to heat bathwater on the stove? I could live here and rent this place from you—I'll pay sixty dollars a month for it, which will amount to a nice little annual income, don't you think?" Sixty dollars a month was twice what they could get for the place as it was, if they advertised it for rent. I would be glad to pay it, even for the months I planned to travel. It would be a base of operations.

Her blue eyes darkened and she set her mouth in that hard, strong-willed way that means she doesn't want to hear another word on the subject. Her roan-brown hair—short, now, and softly waved—was already liberally streaked with white and her once-fresh face was lined, the skin sagging, testimony to the age I wanted to ease.

"But *why*?" I persisted. "Papa is willing—he's told me so. In fact, he's enthusiastic about the idea." That was an exaggeration, but not by much. Papa knew that the new house would be easier for her to manage. "Really, if you don't want to think of yourself, Mama Bess, think of Papa and how much he has to do every day to keep this old place going. He's sometimes so lame he can barely get to the barn and back. I have the money and my Palmer account is growing like all get-out. I'd like nothing better than to do this for you. I'll furnish it, too, and even hang the curtains. You won't have to do a thing except walk in and take off your coat."

It was true. I would like nothing better than to do this. But her mother had trained her never to be beholden to anybody. She hated to accept generosity, even or perhaps especially from her daughter, for whom it is as much an obligation as a generous gesture. (And in this case, a guilt payment.) She accepted my annual subsidy because they couldn't manage the taxes and doctor bills without it, although every acceptance was accompanied by the familiar "I don't want to be a burden, Rose." The house, the house *I* wanted to give her, was an expensive luxury, and a different matter entirely.

But just at that moment, there was a loud crash in the shed at the back of the kitchen, where the firewood was stacked.

"What in the world—" my mother exclaimed.

"Sounds like something fell over," I said. "I'll go see."

I was getting to my feet when Papa pushed open the back door and limped into the kitchen, leaning heavily on his cane and dragging his crippled foot. My father is a short man, no taller than my mother, and frail, his white hair thinning, his face lined and leathery from long hours in the sun. His Airedale, Nero, trailed anxiously at his heels. Fumbling, he pulled off his dripping coat and hung it on the peg by the door. Then he hooked his cane over the back of his chair and dropped into it.

"Whew," he said, his voice cracking. "That last load of stove wood just about finished me, Bess. Dropped the whole damned armful on the floor." He wiped his face on the sleeve of his work shirt. "Knocked over the water bucket, too."

I gave my mother a "there-now-do-you-*see*?" glance. "Let me pour you some coffee, Papa," I said. "Then I'll go mop it up."

Mama Bess said nothing at all, and she was very quiet for the rest of the day. After that, I caught her paying surreptitious attention to Papa, watching him as if she wondered whether he was going to drop another armload of wood or fall over on the floor right in front of her.

But she held fast through June. That's when Troub arrived, driving a Buick she had named Janet, with Mr. Bunting, our Maltese terrier, in the front seat beside her. I was overjoyed to see Troub and made quite a fool of myself in front of my mother, who looked away from the sight of two grown women, crying with delight in each other's arms. She was distracted when little Bunty, fierce for his size, picked a fight with Nero, who was four times his weight. It didn't take long to see that the two dogs couldn't be trusted in the same room, and we had to adopt strenuous measures to keep them apart.

Three weeks later, in early July, Genevieve Parkhurst, an editor at *Pictorial Review,* came to stay for a week on her way to Reno, where her daughter was getting a divorce. We put Genevieve in Troub's room, and we all sat up late every night on the sleeping porch, talking and smoking and playing dance music on the new battery-operated Radiola I had ordered from the Wards catalogue a few weeks before. After Genevieve got on the westbound train, Mama Bess decreed that there would be no more smoking in her house, whereupon Troub remarked to me that she loved me, but she hated to be *bossed.* Perhaps it was time for her to leave, too.

The tension was so electric it crackled, and I was in the middle, between their two poles. To ease the situation, I ordered a big green tent. We pitched it at the edge of the ravine, where there was a breeze. Troub could read and write there, and we could smoke and listen to the radio and indulge in our Albanian coffee ritual, and all of it as late as we pleased. We could even sleep out there if we liked, and we did.

That didn't suit, either. The tent was a "reproach" to her, Mama Bess grumbled, especially because people might see it as they drove by and think that she had exiled Troub and me from the house. We would all be (gasp!) "talked about." But Papa said he was glad to have the living room to himself again in the evenings, without a flock of hens clucking nineteen to a dozen all around him.

"When's the next one aimin' to come?" he asked. When I said that Catharine Brody planned to visit as soon as she could get away from New York, he retreated behind his newspaper and Mama Bess turned her head away. She didn't like Catharine, whom she considered flighty and fast and who seemed likely to write books that had S-E-X in them. (She hadn't read past the first few pages of my Jack London novel for that reason. Jack London had S-E-X.)

And then, a week after we pitched the tent on the hillside, Mama Bess changed her mind about the retirement cottage. It might have been the combination of Troub and Genevieve, or of Mr. Bunting and Nero, added to her recognition that Catharine and Mary Margaret and who-knows-how-many other East Coast women were likely to step off the train at any moment, singly or in noisy combinations, giving Mansfield an endless source of gossip about what was going on in the Wilder house, right in front of poor Mrs. Wilder's eyes—unless she tried not to look, in which case it would go on behind her back.

Or maybe it was Papa, who had found a building site he liked over the hill on the Newell Forty, where there was an easy slope and a wide view over green bottomland. He liked the picture of the house I showed him, too, although he thought it would be better to build from scratch, rather than take whatever quality of building materials Messieurs Sears and Roebuck felt like shipping us, and I agreed. (I would have agreed to anything he wanted, just to move the project along.) He suggested using local fieldstone for the exterior walls, too, instead of wood shingles.

"A whole house made out of gol-durned rock ought to make her happy," he said. I wondered if he was thinking of the fireplace she had wept over.

Or maybe it was Mama herself, imagining life in a brand new, distinctively styled house with electricity and central heat and hot water—and no cigarettes or late-night dance music or who-knows-what hanky-panky going on upstairs. I had left the drawing of the house on the table where she could see it. Perhaps she studied it and thought of how her friends from Mansfield and Hartville would admire it and envy her, with all her new furnishings, an electric stove, even an electric refrigerator. The Wilders would be "talked about"—and written up in the newspaper—in the very best way. And Papa's workload would be much, much lighter.

At any rate, one Tuesday afternoon at the end of July she suggested—in a casual, offhand way, exactly as if it had been her idea all along—that she and Papa go to live on the Newell Forty. I joined the pretense that this marvelous notion was hers and proposed that we go straight over there and see if we couldn't find just the right spot for a house. It was an easy walk along a pleasant footpath, bordered with buttercups and Queen Anne's lace and lively with dragonflies. From the top of the ridge, the valley below was green and gold, dappled with purple cloud shadows. My mother admired the view, pronounced herself satisfied, and on Thursday, she and Papa picked out the spot for the house. A week later, I hired Mr. Johnson as the architect and Mr. Garbee as the contractor, both from Springfield, and the project got underway quickly.

Mama declared that she wanted to be surprised, so she wouldn't take part in the construction—her way, I thought, of disowning any construction mistakes, or perhaps a kind of passive resistance to what was now Papa's and my project. But her withdrawal allowed Papa to choose the materials and oversee the workmanship and gave me a free hand, which perhaps was not a good thing. Where houses are concerned, I am my own very worst enemy. As I wrote to my longtime friend Dorothy Thompson (recently married to Sinclair Lewis): "Without houses, who knows? I might have been a writer."

I'm afraid it was true. All spring and most of the summer I had been working steadily—short stories that were snapped up by *Harper's Magazine, Country Gentleman, The Writer*, and *Ladies' Home Journal*. Carl Brandt sold "One Thing in Common" to the *Journal* for a thousand dollars, my best price yet from that magazine. And I had the proofs of *Cindy* to correct, which Harper & Brothers was putting out as a book in September. Altogether, it was a productive few months that produced a steady and steadily rising income. And, of course, the stock market was going great guns.

But after the work began on the house—the Rock House, Papa and I were calling it—I managed to get only one more story written, "Gypsy Trail," which Carl sold to *Ladies' Home Journal.* The house lured me away from the typewriter, and instead of producing stories, my creative energy went into conjuring walls and floors and windows and shingles and, yes, electricity. It turned out that we could get electricity and a telephone out to the new house, but only if I would agree to pay for the power poles and lines, which of course I did because I also wanted to wire the Rocky Ridge farmhouse, where Troub and I would live.

And the construction brought dissatisfactions. I wasn't entirely pleased with the stonework, which looked too much like a crazy quilt to suit me. But Papa declared that he liked it, and what was done couldn't be easily undone. The chimney seemed out of plumb to me, although Mr. Johnson and the chimney man both pronounced it straight. Papa hated the rough texture of the plaster; I didn't awfully like it, either, and the plasterers didn't even try to get the color right until I made a fuss. I altered Mr. Johnson's plan for the bathroom, which made the plumber scowl. The flooring was the wrong width and had to be returned—and when the right flooring was laid, the wrong finish was applied. Five men worked an extra four days, sanding and refinishing the floors. And Missouri Power and Electric dragged their feet about the power lines until I threatened to sic a lawyer on them. The electricity finally came on at four thirty on the afternoon of the day before Mama Bess and Papa moved in.

And all this while, of course, the bills kept piling up. Sears and Roebuck would gladly have sold us the plans *and* the building materials for twenty-two hundred dollars. I originally expected to get it built for four thousand dollars—which would make barely a dent in my Palmer account. Mr. Johnson squinted at the plans and said he reckoned it would cost around six thousand dollars, to which of course his fee would be added, tacking on another thousand or more—and then there was the contractor's fee on top of that. I had promised to furnish the house and splurged wildly on furniture, draperies, appliances, and an Electrola-Radiola, so Mama Bess could play her records and listen to the radio. By the time I paid the last bill, the total had come to something like eleven thousand dollars.

But money wasn't an important issue—not then. The Palmer account had more than doubled that year, and I didn't want to draw on it. I remember telling Troub that every dollar in the account would be worth at least two by the end of 1929. So to avoid pulling feathers from the goose that was laying the golden eggs, I borrowed some money from her and took out a loan at the Mansfield bank from Mr. Kerry, a family friend. The house was finally finished and ready to move into on the Saturday before Christmas—my present for the parents and an expensive I'm-sorry for the claim shanty I had burned down all those years before.

But no matter. My father was touchingly pleased to have his own bedroom, a comfortable chair beside the living room fire, a hot bath to stretch out in, and the new furnace, which made the whole house toasty with a fraction of the work. My mother, who burst into tears when Mr. Johnson presented her with a bouquet of fresh flowers as she stepped in the door, declared herself delighted and grateful, although there was a little scene in the kitchen later that gave me to understand that her gratitude was colored by a great reluctance. As I said, my mother hates to accept anyone's generosity.

Our own Christmas, Troub's and mine, was sumptuous. She drove to Seymour to get a new casing for a leaking water pump and came home with a new 1929 Buick sedan. She gave me a globe for my December 5 birthday—"So you can start planning our next global excursion"—and for Christmas, she gave me a barometer. We couldn't make out how to read it, but we hung it in the living room and consulted it frequently. I gave her a Scottish terrier pup I purchased by phone from the Ewing kennel in Webster Grove. Named Sparkle, the puppy arrived on the morning train on December 18. Troub's ecstatic yelps warmed my heart.

It was a golden time, perhaps the best in our years together. Now that the parents were comfortably settled in their new house, Troub and I could sit by the fire in the evenings with our feet on the furniture, dance music on the radio, sipping cups of hot Postum and smoking our cigarettes while Sparkle napped on Troub's lap and Mr. Bunting, no longer challenged by Nero, went gaily in and out, his little white tail a triumphant flag. We felt liberated from my mother's censorious glances and her cautions about "talk." We were glad to be alone.

But there was work to be done, too. That week, we embarked on a furious orgy of housecleaning, furniture arranging, floor scrubbing, window washing, and painting of walls and ceilings that took us into every single crack and cranny of the house. But no matter how hard we scrubbed, there was something of my mother left behind, the scent of lavender, an aura, perhaps, or a shadow, a ghost in the house reminding me that she had dreamed this place and built it and lived in it, and it wasn't *mine*. Still, I was happy. Troub and I had our place in the country.

My parents were settled, and my father had a hired man. I had accomplished my plan.

After several exhausting but exhilarating days, we collapsed in front of the fire for another weary late-night supper of sandwiches and canned soup. I was absently eyeing my mother's old draperies and wondering whether the new ones ought to be green or red (to pick up a color from the Albanian rug we had laid on the floor) or perhaps gold (to match the new chair I intended to buy) or a neutral beige against which the other colors in the room would not compete. Troub was listening to the radio while she ate her soup. She suddenly looked up.

"My gosh, Rose," she said, awed, "just listen to that. It's Guy Lombardo and His Royal Canadians. They're playing 'Auld Lang Syne' at the Roosevelt, in Manhattan. It's New Year's Eve—and we nearly missed it!"

As the year had turned over into 1928, Troub and I had been in Albania, uncertain and unsettled. And now we were *here,* in our own home with Mr. Bunting and Sparkle and good work to do and good times ahead.

I raised my cup of Postum in a toast. "To 1929," I said.

"To 1929," Troub echoed happily and blew me a kiss. "All in all, 1928 was swell. But 1929 will be better."

"Yes," I said, believing it. "Nineteen twenty-nine will be the *best.*"

4. "THIS IS THE END": 1929

Thinking back, I find it odd that we had so little inkling on that New Year's Eve of the cataclysm to come. The country was on the cusp of irrevocable change and no one seemed to suspect a thing. I've often thought about that, wondering what signs of impending disaster we missed, what *everyone* missed. The whole world sailed on, gallant and gay, like a four-masted schooner with a band playing on the foredeck and flags flying and all canvas set, into an ocean marked ominously on the map, "Here Be Dragons." And lo! A dragon rises out of the depths and swallows the ship, masts and flags and all hands on board.

Troub and I might have been isolated at the farm, but we weren't entirely cut off from the outside world. We had the *Mansfield Mirror* and the *Wright County Republican,* although their coverage of the national news was limited. The *Kansas City Star* and the radio news broadcasts did a better job updating us on the world's daily doings. Some of them were memorable. On Valentine's Day, in a Chicago garage, Al Capone's gang gunned down seven members of Bugs Moran's gang in a dispute over control of the bootlegging business in Chicago. In early March, Herbert Hoover was sworn in as president; in response, sales of my reissued 1920 biography, *The Making of Herbert Hoover,* rose in a brief, happy flurry, then subsided as the president settled into the business of governing and the rest of the world went on with whatever it was doing. Amos 'n' Andy broadcast their first comedy program on NBC radio, and on the Mansfield square, men could be heard muttering, "Holy mackerel." The first all-color talking picture, *On With the Show*, opened in New York, memorable only for the song, "Am I Blue?" Babe Ruth hit his five-hundredth home run, the first Academy Awards were held, and Charles Lindbergh got married. Wyatt Earp died, and his death somehow seemed a symbol of the closing of the Western frontier, although it had been closed for decades. But shortly thereafter the first regular coast-to-coast air service began and a new frontier of time and space was inaugurated: you could travel by plane and train from New York to Los Angeles in the astonishingly short time of three days.

But there were no such memorable doings at Rocky Ridge, where the months of this last comfortable year slipped by in a swirl of small-town activities, agreeably mind-numbing. At least once a week and sometimes more often, Troub and I went with my mother to her club meetings—the Bridge Club, the Embroidery Club, the Interesting Hour Club, the Athenians, and the Justamere Club (which was exactly what it sounds like: just a mere club)—where the local hierarchy was on display and in fine feather. Mama Bess invited the clubs to her new home, where she served her famous gingerbread and I contributed French pastries. Mama's friends were open-mouthed at the luxury of central heat, the indulgence of electric refrigeration, and the distinctive textures and Mediterranean colors of the rough-plastered walls, which were nothing at all like the faded pink cabbage roses of their parlor wallpaper.

Although I had grown up in Mansfield, I was always an observer rather than a participant in these gatherings, and the conversations gave me plenty of story material. Books were seldom discussed and politics rarely, unless it was a local politician or prominent church member who had somehow disgraced himself and was being "talked about." But there were always conversations about children, needlework, recipes, flowers, and friends, observations about the last often couched in snide but unoriginal asides. I once heard Mrs. Stevens tell one of her friends, "If you can't say something nice about her, dear, come sit over here by me and *whisper* it."

And there was Mildred Hill, who frequently remarked in a tone of vague tolerance (as if all my present sins were rooted in our shared past), "Oh, I remember our wild Rose *when*," and went on to wonder, with a critical *click* of her tongue, "I just can't imagine how a body can make as much money as she does by simply putting words on paper." *Click click.* And in a lower voice, dark with discontent, "Don't seem right, someway." *Click.*

Or Hazel Thomas, who gazed over her drugstore spectacles at Catharine (lighting a cigarette) and shrilled, "Why, I never saw a *lady* smoke before." And Troub responded, with innocent astonishment, "Really, Mrs. Thomas? How queer. Where *can* you have been all your life?"

Mrs. Thomas had been all her life in Mansfield, of course, where only men and chimneys smoked, *ladies* never. But then everyone knew that Catharine Brody wrote books about S-E-X, so she was clearly no lady. And I wrote books about people like Charlie Chaplin and Jack London and President Hoover and lived in Greenwich Village and went to Communist rallies and traveled with men (*foreign* men, with guns!) in the remotest mountains of Eastern Europe, so I was no lady, either. No wonder that, for Mildred Hill and the rest of my mother's friends, I was a wild Rose.

But the world was intruding into Mansfield's isolation. Radios brought in the news from Chicago and New York and San Francisco. The livery stable and the blacksmith had been replaced by an automobile repair shop. The Bonny Theater showed talkies and put up posters of cigarette-smoking flappers on the wall out front. The town band played dance music at the bandstand on the square, and the young people (except for the Baptists) defiantly danced the Charleston and the infamous "Baltimore Buzz":

> First you take your babe and gently hold her,
> Then you lay your head upon her shoulder.
> Next you walk just like your legs are breaking.
> Do a fango like a tango,
> Then you start the shimmy to shaking.

The Mansfield Grays played other area teams on the town baseball field, and Mr. Pierson, who ran the pool hall, made surreptitious book on the games. Under the influence of the world-famous golfer, Bobby Jones, the men who could afford it (like Mr. Kerry of the bank) had gone golf crazy, and there was a new golf club and golf course, north of town on newly paved Highway 5.

The paving of the local roads, however much ballyhooed, led not to the hoped-for prosperity but to a disappointing decline. Instead of shopping in Mansfield (population 870), people hopped into their Fords and Buicks and Oldsmobiles and drove to Mountain Grove for groceries or to Springfield for clothes and tools and a fancy restaurant dinner. Not even the *Mansfield Mirror*'s repeated exhortations to "buy from your local merchant to keep him in business" could stem the enthusiastic tide of outward-bound commerce. And it wasn't just shopping trips. Everybody who had a car (and there wasn't any excuse for not having one, with credit so easy to get) spent Sundays sightseeing, to the point where the pastors of the town's churches felt they had to preach against the sin of skipping church just to go pleasure driving.

There were a few hot days in July, but the weather was fine for most of that last easy summer, and we whiled away the time with simple pleasures. Troub and I took the parents driving and ate dinner and supper with them at the Rock House or invited them to Rocky Ridge. We picnicked at the Gasconade River, where Sparkle and Mr. Bunting chased birds and lizards and Troub and I took off our shoes and danced barefoot in the shallows and giggled when the minnows nibbled our toes. We braved the bee-laden bushes to pick blackberries and raspberries for jam and bought peaches for canning from the Erb Orchard at Cedar Gap. In August, my new Mansfield friend Lucille Murphy and I drove to St. Louis for shopping and then west across the state to Kansas City before heading back home. In September, I canned corn relish and Troub and I went to the Springfield Dahlia Show and to the Wright County Fair and Stock Show, where a man lit his clothes on fire and jumped into a flaming tank, while awed spectators gasped and trembled at the foolhardiness of the deed.

Troub and my father had gone to Mexico, Missouri (which called itself the "Saddle Horse Capital of the World"), where Troub bought a Morgan gelding. She named the horse Governor, after Governor of Orleans, a Morgan my father had once had at the farm. Troub's Governor was a big horse and almost too much for her. I was concerned, but she bravely persevered and rode him nearly every day. She also bought a little black mare named Molly and a pony named Topsy. Our guests were encouraged to bring trousers so they could ride with Troub along the country lanes and woodland paths.

We had plenty of guests in that easygoing year. Genevieve came for several short visits, to work on her book. Catharine Brody arrived in March and stayed for two months, then returned later in the fall. Her first novel, *Babe Evanson*, had come out in 1928 to mixed reviews; her 1932 novel, *Nobody*

Starves, would be a best seller and she would be hailed as one of the "new realists."

Catharine made news in Mansfield, but not for her books. She was a small woman with brown hair and thick glasses, who "looked Jewish." This latter observation was passed along to me by my mother, who made sure that I was informed about the reception my friends enjoyed (or otherwise) among *her* friends.

Troub was writing, too, so for a while, there were four type-writers clattering away at Rocky Ridge. We enclosed the upstairs sleeping porch against the rain, and there was plenty of space to work—a pleasant space, too. The porch overlooked green trees and a grassy slope and caught the breeze. In the evenings, there was chess, jigsaw puzzles, books read aloud, stories shared, and conversation—real conversation, stimulating conversation, about politics, culture, books, films. Since we were the liveliest group in town, acquaintances from Mansfield sometimes joined us, although only one—Lucille Murphy—had a mind that was broader than a bridge plank. Lucille, who with her husband Eddie ran the Mansfield laundry, was pretty and full of fun and serious questions about life and love, and she enjoyed playing chess. As the year went on, Troub and I saw more and more of Lucille and less and less of Eddie.

Oh, there were dark moments—I can see them, feel them again, as I read back through the intermittent journals and the regular Line-a-Day diary I kept through those years. Diaries and journals are dangerous because they tend to crystallize passing feelings of discouragement and bewilderment that would oth-erwise evaporate in the progression of life events, and if they are read by others, by outsiders, they may lead to misunderstand-ings. "I have to *get away* from here," I wrote after a day spent in dismal company, and "Sick from vulgarities" after an evening at the Mansfield senior class play, even though in general, I was more or less content. After one of my mother's club meetings, I wrote, "What I am hungry for is an idea—to simply hear an *idea* discussed again, instead of all this trivial gossip." On the other hand: "I am very happy when I'm not working," an ironic acknowledgement of a universal human truth.

But happy or unhappy, I made time to work, producing my usual short magazine fiction, stories that readily sold to *Country Gentleman, Ladies' Home Journal, Redbook,* and *Pictorial Review.* I also wrote a serial—"An Albanian Romance," a serious effort at which I worked all through the summer. It sold nowhere, which made me very blue. As usual, I was writing because, while there was plenty in the Palmer account, I was in constant need of money (*cash cash cash*). There was the electric bill and the rent to pay to my mother every month, and salaries for Jess (the hired man) and our cook-housekeeper, Mrs. Capper, whom Troub had found in a work-wanted ad. Mrs. Capper stayed all week (she slept downstairs in the room that had been my parents') and took the bus back to Springfield on weekends.

And we weren't quite finished with our remodeling and landscaping. In June, we installed an electric water heater so we could have hot baths without carrying water; in September, a new lawn; in October, an automatic steam-heating system with an oil burner that was supposed to keep the whole house warm. My mother and I both had expensive dental work to be done. And I was planning to go to New York in December, where I would stay with Genevieve and see Carl Brandt and my editors and friends, and shop, of course. *Cash cash cash.* At the end of August, I withdrew ten thousand dollars from my Palmer account—not because I was worried about the security of the market but because I wanted to catch up on my obligations.

Ten thousand dollars—oh, if I had only had the wisdom to withdraw all of the money and close the account right then and there, things would have been very different. I could have paid all my bills and tucked the rest under the mattress.

But I didn't. None of us were wise where the market was concerned. We might have heard a few uncomfortable warnings in the newspapers or on the radio, if we had known how to look and listen. But we continued to crest the wave of national exuberance and, like everyone else in America, didn't pause to look beneath its surface. The minor breaks in the market—in August and September—didn't worry us: they were explained as "technical adjustments," like the other little ups and downs and zigs and zags we were used to. There were disquieting moments, like the mini-crash in March, when people who had bought on the margin got panicky. And there were a few like Roger Babson, who published a respected investment newsletter and uttered the gloomy prediction, with the Dow at its all-time September high of 381: "Sooner or later a crash is coming, and it may be terrific."

But the philosophy of the Twenties held that "later" was a long time away. Babson's pessimism was countered by the optimism of other economists, like Irving Fisher, who helpfully explained that stock prices had reached a "permanently high plateau" and that the "ever-ascending curve of American prosperity" was sturdy enough to survive whatever small breaks might interrupt it. On September 11, the *Wall Street Journal* published its thought for the day, Mark Twain's wry wisdom: "Don't part with your illusions; when they are gone you may still exist, but you have ceased to live." We held on to our illusions until the end of October, scarcely knowing that this was what we were doing.

On Tuesday, October 22, Carl telegraphed that *Redbook* had bought my short story—"Village Maid"—for a thousand dollars, a new high in their payment for my work. To celebrate, Troub and I drove to Springfield on Wednesday and I bought a splendid blue velvet dress and stylish suede pumps for my trip to New York. On Thursday, October 24, I wore the dress and pumps to the Embroidery Club meeting at Mrs. Hooper's house. They were envied by Becky and Josey, the town girls who had worn those beautiful dresses and patent leather shoes in school, when I, a country girl, was wearing calico and going barefoot.

That was Black Thursday. That night, listening to the radio news announcer reporting the day's heavy losses, I said to Troub, knowing it but not quite believing it: "This is the end, you know."

Troub, who was reading and eating an apple, looked up from her book. "The end of what?" she asked, blinking.

I threw up my hands. "The end of money," I said. "The end of easy magazine sales. The end of the good life."

Troub took a bite out of her apple and went back to her book. "Don't be an idiot, Rose," she said with her mouth full. "You know how it goes, up and down, up and down and sideways. This is just another little bump in the road."

But it wasn't. On Black Monday, the Dow dropped by 13 percent. On Black Tuesday, the pace accelerated. In those two days alone, the market lost more than thirty billion dollars.

When Troub read this news aloud at the supper table, I said again, "It really is the end, Troub. Palmer is finished—or he will be, soon. Our accounts are gone."

This time, she didn't argue.

PART TWO

5. KING STREET: APRIL 1939

"Was it?" Norma Lee asked, from her seat on the front porch steps.

Mrs. Lane's voice had trailed off into the spring evening silence. There was only the *creak-creak* of the porch swing and the croaking of tree frogs.

"The end, I mean," Norma Lee added. "Of the good life—at least for you and Troub."

Norma Lee herself had been fourteen the year of the Crash, old enough to be aware of her parents' pain, etched still in her memory with the sharp pen of bewildered disappointment. In 1927, her mother had received a five-hundred-dollar legacy from her aunt. On the advice of a banker friend, her father had invested it in the stock market. By August 1929, the account had tripled and her mother and father had discussed selling the stock and using the money to pay off the mortgage on the family home in Trenton, the small town in northern Missouri where Norma Lee grew up. But they decided to wait until there was enough money to buy a new car—a Buick, her father thought—so they could drive out West for the family vacation. Then they would pay off the mortgage, and with the money that was left, they would buy an electric refrigerator to replace the smelly old icebox.

Norma Lee and her younger sister Judy had chattered for hours about the places they would go in that magical new Buick and the sights they would see, plotting them on a map spread out on their bedroom floor. That is, until the end of October, until Black Thursday and the next, even blacker Monday and Tuesday and the weeks that followed after that, when the family knew that there would be no Buick and no refrigerator and no money to pay off the mortgage. Their dreams would have to be postponed indefinitely.

Norma Lee's mother mourned for days, and the banker friend, who had lost a very great deal of money, went into the woods and shot himself. But in one important way, the family had been lucky. Norma Lee's father, a conductor on the Rock Island Railroad, had held onto his job, and the family managed to survive the Depression without missing any meals or mortgage payments. Norma Lee had gotten a scholarship and gone to college, although, of course, she'd had to work. She was determined to get a degree and master a skill that would make her employable. Writing was that skill, she thought; magazine and newspapers were that business; and Norma Lee was not the kind of girl to miss a single opportunity. In her considered opinion, Mrs. Lane's willingness to help with her writing and introduce her to editors was the key to her professional ambitions.

The light from the living room window slanted across Mrs. Lane's face. "The end of the good life?" She seemed startled, as if she had forgotten where she was and that there was someone else with her, someone who wasn't Troub. She pushed the porch swing with her foot. "It was, yes. But we didn't know it then. Nobody really knew it, until later. After the good life was gone."

Mrs. Lane had started her story after supper, after Russell had walked to the lake for an hour's fishing and while she and Norma were doing the dishes. They had finished the kitchen work and gone to sit on the porch as the sky turned from lemon-and-pink-colored to a platinum gray. Now, the darkness was draped like a shadowy curtain over the trees around the house. Russell had cleaned his fish—three nice-sized perch—and gone upstairs. He turned up the volume on the radio, catching Fred Astaire in the middle of "Nice Work If You Can Get It."

"I suppose it took a while for the shock to sink in," Norma Lee said. "Was Mansfield much affected?"

"Not really," Mrs. Lane replied. "At least not at first. Crop prices had been terribly low for four or five years, so farm families were already used to getting by without a lot of extra cash. The people who had jobs held onto them for as long as they could. The people who didn't—" She shrugged. "They just kept on as best they could. They got by with help from their families, from their churches. The way everybody does when times are hard." Her tone changed. "That was before the days of the government handouts, of course."

Nice work if you can get it. And if you get it, won't you tell me how?

Norma Lee took her cigarettes out of her skirt pocket and lit one, the match flaring briefly against the dark. "That little scene in the kitchen, the day your mother moved into the Rock House," she remarked. Mrs. Lane's relationship with her mother intrigued her. "What was it? What happened?"

Upstairs, the song ended and Russell carried the jaunty tune on, whistling, the thin treble thread wrapping itself around them, brave in the dark.

"I'm not sure I know exactly," Mrs. Lane replied, after a moment. "She wasn't . . . herself that day. It might have been the accident. My parents were driving into Mansfield to pick up Mrs. Kerry and take her to see the house, and my father ran off the road and into an oak sapling." After a moment, she went on. "But it might have been something else. My mother has always been a mystery to me."

"And you to her, I imagine," Norma Lee murmured, thinking how hard it must have been for Mrs. Wilder to understand her daughter, even to imagine where in the world she was, what under the sun she might be doing.

Mrs. Lane chuckled. "Yes. A daughter who roams the globe, gets herself lost in the Arabian desert, is shot at during a revolution, speaks outlandish languages, reads unintelligible books. A pride, perhaps, an accomplishment of sorts, like being the only woman in her bridge club brave enough to raise a tiger cub. But an eternal uneasiness, too, for it means that her daughter is her*self,* separate from her. Separated, unlike her. Baffling. Inexplicable." She looked down at Norma Lee and said, playfully, "I suppose you're a mystery to your mother, too. Are you?"

Norma Lee wasn't startled by the question. It was something she had thought about often since she had left home.

"In some ways, yes, I suppose. I'm not like her at all. Leaving Trenton, going to college, moving to New York, getting my writing published in magazines that people actually read—my mother never wanted to do those things herself, so it's hard for her to imagine one of her daughters wanting to do them. But while she might be baffled, she's always said, quite bravely, that she's glad I have the freedom to do what I want."

After a moment she went on, choosing her words carefully. "I don't mean that my mother doesn't *care.* She comes from an openly emotional family and she's never withheld her affections from me or my sister—or her gratitude, when we do something for her." She heard the implicit criticism in her words, but Mrs. Lane didn't seem to be offended.

"Affection," Mrs. Lane said in a speculative tone. "Well, I'm sure the women in my mother's family *felt* affectionate toward one another, but they didn't show it. My grandmother, my aunts, my mother—there was always a kind of stern reserve, a holding back. Perhaps it was the fear that giving in even a little bit would lead to a total collapse of all the barriers, and they would be swept away by feeling. My mother reminded me once that a person—she meant herself, of course—couldn't live at a high pitch of emotion. It was a matter of self-preservation, she said."

"So it's better not to have any feelings at all," Norma Lee murmured ironically. "Or to show them. Not even occasionally."

Mrs. Lane might not have heard her. "Or perhaps it was the idea that affection somehow 'spoiled' a child. That life was real, life was earnest, and too much coddling insulated us from that essential truth, which would shortly be visited on us by cruel experience." Her sigh was barely audible. "But now that I'm older, I think perhaps that they were just tired, they were exhausted. The lives the women led in that time were hard and narrow. The work they did, it was simply relentless. They almost never sat down, and when they did, their hands were busy and their laps were full—shelling peas, mending shirts, darning socks, knitting mittens. There was no time, no room for a child. And they had so *many* children. My Ingalls grandmother bore five. My Wilder grandmother bore six."

Norma Lee pondered this for a moment, remembering her mother's capacious lap and her grandmother's lilac-scented embrace and feeling that Mrs. Lane had missed something essential when she was growing up.

"Your mother," she said after a moment. "Did she ever say thank you for the house you built for her? Do you think she enjoyed living there?"

"My mother is frugal," Mrs. Lane said with a little laugh. "'Thank you' is as costly as 'please.' No, she didn't say it, not in so many words, not then, not ever, really. But she gave every appearance of enjoying the house, even if it was more an emblem of my success as a writer than hers as a farmer's wife. I was, after all, her daughter, tiger cub or not, and she could claim my tigerly success as her own. She certainly liked to show off the house to her club friends, and when the grand opening was written up in the *Mansfield Mirror,* she bought several copies and cut out the story and sent it to her sisters, to Grace and Carrie. She knew it was better for Papa—less work and more comfortable—and I'm sure that pleased her, especially in the winters." She pulled her knitted sweater tighter around her. "It's getting chilly. Aren't you tired of listening to me ramble?"

"Oh, not at all, Mrs. Lane," Norma Lee said, unwilling to let the evening end. She clutched at a detail. "You said you bought a new dress for your trip the day before the Crash. Did you go to New York, anyway, in spite of what happened?"

"Of course I did. Why wouldn't I? I spent the first three weeks of December there."

"What was it like? I mean, people must have started to worry about what was going to happen—their investments, their jobs, their futures. Were they glum? Angry?"

Mrs. Lane hesitated. "Some were dismayed, I suppose, those who had any inkling of what it meant. And most were dispirited by the loss of their money—even though the money wasn't real. That is, it was just numbers in their brokerage statements, not actual bills snatched out of their pockets."

"Yes," Norma Lee murmured. "I can see the difference."

"And almost everybody assumed that this was just a bigger dip than usual, that the market would turn around in a few months. They were determined to be gay while they waited it out. When I saw Mr. Palmer, our stockbroker, he handed me a *New York Times* article headed "Bankers Believe Liquidation Has Now Run Its Course and Advise Purchases." She laughed. "He said I should snap up a few bargains."

"Did you?"

"No. Instead, as usual, I spent too much money on clothes and hats and shoes." She chuckled wryly. "I was only following the advice of President Hoover. He kept urging people to spend all they could to support retail businesses. And, of course, it was wonderful to be in the city and to get a shampoo and a manicure and dress up for friends. It was like a three-week party, really."

"So you saw lots of people," Norma Lee prompted. She liked it when Mrs. Lane dropped the names of her writer friends. She filed them away in her mind in case she needed them at some point in the future. You never knew when an introduction might come in handy.

"Oh, yes," Mrs. Lane replied. "I saw Dorothy Thompson again and met her husband."

"That was Sinclair Lewis?"

"Yes. She calls him Hal. Even before the Nobel, he was legendary—*Main Street,* of course, and *Babbitt.* I hadn't expected to like the man. I cared so much for Dorothy, you know. We met in the American Red Cross office in Paris and went together on a walking tour from Blois to Ambois. She had a bad first marriage, a disaster, really, and I couldn't imagine why she would marry again. But Hal's cosmopolitan charm completely won me over, and Dorothy and I were able to get away for some private time together. Now, of course, our politics . . . " Her voice trailed off.

Tactfully, Norma Lee said, "I suppose you went to the theater while you were there."

"Oh, yes, yes, of course. Mary Margaret McBride and Stella Karn and I saw *Silver Swan.* It was a flop, but I rather liked it. Oh, and *Many Waters* and *Berkeley Square,* too. Stella gave a party for me at the Casino and Genevieve—I was staying with her—invited sixty people to a tea for me. So you see, we were all spending money as if we would always have bushels of it. And one weekend, I went to Croton to stay with Floyd and Marie Dell."

"Oh, Floyd Dell!" Norma Lee exclaimed excitedly. "His play, *Little Accident*—wasn't that made into a movie not long ago?"

"Yes, with Douglas Fairbanks Jr. Floyd and Marie and I went for tea at Lydia Gibson's, and Lydia gave me the portrait she painted of me in San Francisco in 1917. I shipped it home—it was Mama Bess's Christmas present that year. She hung it in the living room at the Rock House, but it's at Rocky Ridge now, on the wall over the buffet. Oh, and another weekend I went to Nyack, to visit Berta and Elmer Hader."

"The children's book illustrators?" Mrs. Lane had mentioned them before.

"Yes," Mrs. Lane chuckled reminiscently. "Berta and I told stories about being dead broke in Greenwich Village in 1919, living on split pea soup and fifty cents a day in a three-story house on Jones Street and wearing all our clothes, layer upon layer, to stay warm. But Berta made good, in a big way. That year—1929—she and Elmer had just published a children's book, *Two Funny Clowns*. The next summer, when I was working on my mother's autobiography, I thought of Berta's book and sent her some pages. That was the beginning of *Little House in the Big Woods*." She sighed. "Then it was nearly Christmas and I went back to Rocky Ridge. Anyway, I was out of money. New York isn't much fun unless you have a little loose change rattling around in your pocket."

"You haven't mentioned Troub. She stayed at the farm?"

Mrs. Lane nodded. "I wanted her to come with me, but Catharine was there and we didn't quite trust her to manage the farmhouse by herself. I bought Troub a pair of Bonwit Teller blue silk pajamas—they were lovely on her. And presents for the parents and a box of New York pastries and some cans of pâté de fois gras and nuts and marzipan. On Christmas Eve, Troub and I held a gala celebration around the Christmas tree for the parents and Jess—our hired man—and his family, and Lucille and Eddie. And Catharine, to my mother's dismay. The Mrs. Grundys of Mansfield were having a field day gossiping about her, and my mother was certain her tarnish would rub off on me." She smiled, recollecting, then sobered. "It was the last of the merry Christmases, I suppose. By the next year, everything was changed." She yawned. "Norma Lee, it's late."

"But you still haven't told me about your mother's books," Norma Lee reminded her.

"No, I haven't." Mrs. Lane got to her feet. "But not tonight. It's time for bed."

"We can go on with it tomorrow, though, can't we?"

"I suppose. If you really want to. If you don't think it's a waste of time."

"I *do* want to go on," Norma Lee said. "Of course I do." She got up, too. "Stories are never a waste of time, don't you think?"

"Well, then," Mrs. Lane said, going to the screen door. "In the morning."

Upstairs, on Russell's radio, Astaire was singing, "You Can't Take That Away From Me."

6. MOTHER AND DAUGHTER: 1930–1931

I made two New Year's resolutions for 1930: pay debts and save money.

Pay debts and save—both resolutions based on a supposition that there will be money coming in to spend and save. I should have known better, but I excuse myself by saying that it took awhile for the new reality to show itself in the magazine markets I depended on. In the meantime, Troub and I simply couldn't believe the worst, and our shared optimism carried us forward in a kind of unthinking momentum through the days.

I was still fueled with the energy of my trip to the city and because I needed money (*cash cash cash*), I kept on writing at my usual pace: seven short stories in the first half of 1930. In a normal year, all seven would have sold, for a thousand or more each. That year, Carl sold just three.

But even that took several months, and paying the monthly bills was a wretched exercise in subtraction. The weather was wretched, too, with January and February ice storms that pulled down trees, closed the roads, and knocked out the electricity for days at a time. The Ozark winter, in concert with the dismal financial situation that was reported in every newspaper, did nothing to improve our state of mind. Catharine had been with us since before Christmas, and Troub and I were finding that a little bit of Catharine went a long way. We were cooped up in the farmhouse with nothing to do but read and write and play chess and do jigsaw puzzles.

A jigsaw puzzle craze had swept the country that year. I remember thinking that the puzzles were more than just an all-absorbing way to fill the empty hours; they offered the fulfilling illusion of *work,* especially for those who were otherwise unemployed. Putting the pieces together, finding the one piece you needed, seeing the picture emerge out of a chaos of jagged, disconnected pieces—all this offered a fugitive sense of accomplishment, of completing something. The engrossing pastime (it wasn't really *work*) reassured people that they could control objects and events and allayed the fear that they were completely at the mercy of forces outside themselves.

For me, it was not an unfamiliar fear. I had once written to Guy Moyston that the trouble with my life was that it had no plot. Just when I thought there was something in the center, something to hold onto, the center was swept away by events I couldn't control. And as the days wore on and my New York visit shimmered into a half-forgotten mirage on the horizon, the farm felt more and more like a trap, a place of exile, a prison from which I could never escape. A late January note in my diary recalls, "This life is really nauseating"—and it was. I was in a blue funk.

Troub and Catharine helped to relieve the sense of isolation, and there were also the letters from friends. The letters were a substitute for the conversation that fed my soul and at the same time, a distraction from the work I knew I should be doing. I often thought that my truest self was not in my magazine work—I wrote to earn a living, and the fiction had nothing to do with *me*—but in my letters. I wrote to my New York friends, Mary Margaret and Genevieve and Berta, whose letters to me were full of news and notes about their lives and work and the literary scene. And

Dorothy, of course, whose career as the wife of Sinclair Lewis I had come to accept and with whom I discussed men and love and sex and all the things I wanted from life—in the abstract, since getting what I wanted was now beginning to seem utterly impossible. And Clarence Day, who'd stepped aside from his writing of *Life With Father* long enough to get married. After he'd done the deed, he wrote to ask, "Will my getting married change Troub and you? It won't me," and I thought to myself, what complete idiots men are. And always, oh yes, always dear Mr. Older, Fremont Older, whose interest in my work went back to the *San Francisco Bulletin* days, when he assigned me to the feature writing that led to my freelance work, and with whom I discussed politics and political philosophies and all the grand ideas that made the world go round.

In the letters, I could be funny and eloquent and confident and interesting because the *I* who wrote was not the *I* who had to continually deal with money (the need for it, the lack of it), housekeeping, dogs, gardens, chickens, writing, bad teeth, the weather, and my mother. The *I* of the letters was someone else—or rather, a multiplicity of someones, a particular persona for each of my correspondents.

This was something of a hazard, in fact, because anyone reading the letters might suspect that I was pretending or posing or even lying. But that was not it, not at all. It was rather that the personality to whom I was writing brought out a particular personality in *me,* in the way that a play brings out an aspect of an actor's self that can emerge only in that context—and then the next play brings out another self, and then another and so on. The letters connected me to the people who were living active, animated lives—*real* lives—in the swirling universe of events and ideas. The letters were lifelines, conduits, channels, and the energy that flowed through them invigorated me and reminded me that I might be exiled to Rocky Ridge, but I was still a citizen of a larger world.

The weather warmed in early March, and Catharine went back to New York. The next week, she wrote that most of our friends were in a blue funk, too. Some had been let go or had their hours drastically reduced, and the rest were wondering if they would have a job at the end of the month. In early April, Genevieve came for a short visit, bearing more dismal news. From her desk at the *Pictorial Review,* she saw what was going on in the magazine world. Advertisers were cancelling their contracts, publishers were reducing the number of pages of editorial content, and editors were using stories and articles they had already bought and stockpiled—or worse (where authors were concerned), reprinting pieces from previous issues. The fiction market was dead as a doorpost. George Q. Palmer was still sending his weekly Wall Street reports, but by mid-April, they sounded positively gloomy. Troub, saying that facts were facts and she had to face them, sold Governor. She got $125 for a horse that was worth four or five times that amount, but it was the best she could do. I think that my father, who loved the big Morgan, felt the loss even more than Troub did.

In the midst of all this bad news, Mama Bess brought me her autobiography.

My mother and I have had our differences, but I have always known that she was an extraordinary person, a never-give-up woman who pushed herself beyond the limits that hindered other women of her era. She urged my father to leave the Dakotas and begin a new farm in Missouri. She worked with him to clear the land and farm it, and she did whatever had to be done—selling butter and eggs, cooking meals for traveling salesmen, hosting boarders, writing farm journal articles—to bring in money. She organized women's clubs and farm clubs. She managed loans as secretary-treasurer of the Mansfield Farm Loan Association, a branch of the Federal Farm Loan Bank. She wrote for the *Missouri Ruralist*, and through her columns, she got a reputation as a persuasive booster for the family farm.

My mother came from a family of writing women. Her mother wrote letters, and when she died, Mama Bess inherited her pearl-handled pen, carved in the shape of a quill. Her younger sisters Carrie and Grace wrote for the *De Smet News* and her older sister Mary—blinded at fourteen by an illness—published poetry and hoped to write a book.

As far as I know, my mother's first sustained writing effort was the journal she kept on the six-week trip from South Dakota to Missouri in 1894. I remember her sitting beside the campfire at night, writing with a pencil in a five-cent memorandum book. She sent parts of the journal as a letter to the *De Smet News* and pasted the clipping in her scrapbook, with the words "First I ever published" penciled in the margin. Years later, she showed me the journal and asked if I thought I could "fix it up" enough so that it could be published.

But by that time I had begun my own career and didn't have many extra hours. In 1908, I went to San Francisco and began writing for the weekly Junior Section of the *San Francisco Call*. In 1909, I married Gillette Lane, a reporter for the *Call*. I was pregnant quickly but to my deep sorrow, the baby, a boy, didn't live. It's not true that you ever forget: the heart pain is as scalding now as it was the day I lost my child. But you learn, in time, that loss and grief are a part of life, and you get on as best you can with the daily business of living.

After the baby, while Gillette pursued a number of advertising schemes across the Midwest, I was reporting for the *Kansas City Post* and the *Kansas City Journal*. I was learning the trade, covering crimes, accidents, scandals, county fairs, and flower shows—anything, everything I was assigned to. The next year, I went with Gillette to the East Coast, where he contrived more promotion schemes and we lived a hand-to-mouth life one fast jump ahead of the bill collector. Then it was back to San Francisco, where we moved into an apartment on Leavenworth and went to work for Stine and Kendrick, a major real estate company. California was booming. The old ranches were being subdivided and sold as small farms. Sales were quick, commissions good. But then the European war began, the land boom fizzled, and so did our marriage, although Gillette and I would not be divorced for several more years.

I went back to writing. A friend, Betty Beatty, was editing the woman's page in the *Bulletin,* and in early 1915, I began as her assistant for $12.50 a week, plus space-rates for other pieces I wrote. It wasn't long before Fremont Older, the *Bulletin's* legendary editor, took me under his wing. Almost before I knew it, I was getting some very good serial story assignments. One of the early assignments, for example, was a story on Art Smith, the young daredevil pilot who was appearing at the Panama-Pacific International Exposition. The story ran for four weeks and was published as a book. Through similar assignments—interviews with Charlie Chaplin, Henry Ford, and others—I learned how to spin narratives at the rate of fifteen hundred words a day, keeping the story going for weeks at a time. I learned how to capture and hold readers, keep them turning pages and buying newspapers. Newspaper writing then was much more sensational than it is now, and more entertaining. It was aimed to excite readers' emotions, and I worked hard to learn the trick of telling a compelling, emotional story.

My mother had been writing, too, and the practice took her far beyond the little journal she had scribbled on the way to Missouri. Her writing grew out of talks she had given to farmer's groups on improving the lives of farm women, as well as raising chickens and other farm topics. Between 1911 and 1915, she wrote eight pieces (including a poem and two articles she wrote under my father's name) for the *Missouri Ruralist*, a paper that had a circulation of about fifteen thousand and paid ten or fifteen dollars for each piece—good money for that kind of writing, at the time. But more importantly, Mama Bess was putting her writing to work. She was learning the craft. She was also anxious to break into the magazine market I was writing for, so I tried to include ideas and suggestions in every letter home.

I always told my mother that she could be a good writer if she would put the time into it—if she would let some of the chores slide, or pay a neighbor to pick the cowpeas, or take the clothes to the Mansfield laundry instead of doing the washing herself. Looking at her work from an editor's point of view, it would have to be said that she was better at managing anecdotes and short, simple stories than longer narrative, and that grammar, punctuation, and spelling were not her strong suits. But she had an eye for nature, a knack for developing a moral lesson through a simple story, and a sense of the importance of everyday things. She couldn't submit handwritten copy to the *Ruralist*, of course; I remember urging her to go to Springfield and buy an Underwood that she could pay for on the installment plan. She took my advice and taught herself to type, although she preferred not to.

After I went to work for the *Bulletin*, I saw the chance to be of some significant help. I invited her to come out to San Francisco and stay with me for six weeks or so during the Panama-Pacific International Exposition in the fall of 1915. I paid for her train ticket and gave her some money to make up for the extra work my father had to do while she was away. When she was with me, I helped her with a couple of pieces about the Exposition for the *Ruralist* and we blocked out several stories she could work on at home.

At the same time, I was writing a series of articles about Charlie Chaplin (I was hoping to syndicate them), so she got a glimpse of my life as a working writer. She didn't like it at all, especially the amount of time it took. "The more I see of the hours you have to put in," she told me, "the better satisfied I am to raise chickens. I want to do some writing that counts, and I want to earn more money as a writer. But I could never let myself be *driven* the way you are, Rose. I don't see how you do it."

It was, I think, a moment of truth for her. Writing isn't magic, it's work; earning money as a writer means showing up at the typewriter every day, whether you feel like it or not. Still, after she went back to Rocky Ridge, she did begin writing more regularly for the *Ruralist,* at the rate of two pieces a month, which—considering all the other work she had to do—must have required a great deal of effort. I found her stuff a little stilted and preachy, but she got looser as she went along, and I'm sure that her *Ruralist* readers appreciated her moral lessons. No, I *know* they did because they wrote to tell her so.

Aside from making time to write, my mother's biggest problem was coming up with things to write about. I tried to get her to think of writing the way I thought of it—as a commodity to be sold and resold, whenever possible—and I helped by sending her story ideas and sharing my stuff. Recycling a piece of writing was a common practice and collaborations were the name of the game at the *Bulletin*. There, the editorial staff constantly exchanged story ideas and copy and rewrote other writers' stuff, often from beginning to end and sometimes without the approval of the original writer. Sole authorship was a rarity.

The pieces I sent did help her, I think. For instance, I gave her a copy of a little piece I wrote called "Quarrels of the Proverbs" that was published in the *Bulletin* in early 1915. Three years later, when she was running short on ideas for her *Ruralist* column, she gave the piece a new title ("When Proverbs Get Together") and recast it in a personal setting. Her writing was always stronger when she wrote in first person, the *I* voice. I urged her to include details of her life experience in everything she wrote, to make it richer, more concrete, more *hers*. And to tell the truth, I thought her proverbs piece was better than mine. It encouraged me to think that she might be ready, with a little help, to aim at the magazine market.

In 1918, at the end of the war, Mr. Older left the *Bulletin,* and I did, too. I moved to New York and began writing for *McCall's,* where Betty Beatty, from the *Bulletin,* was an editor. That's where I came up with what I thought was a perfect writing opportunity for Mama Bess, exactly fitted to her experience as a farmer's wife. Unfortunately, it wound up causing trouble between us. At my suggestion, Betty had agreed to give my mother a chance at an article on life as a farm housewife for a series called "Whom Will You Marry?" I told Mama Bess that she should sit down and read *McCall's* carefully before she began writing, so that she could mimic its breezy, colloquial style. But the piece she sent was her usual *Ruralist* style, stiff, moralistic stuff. If I hadn't gone over it pretty thoroughly, Betty would have turned it down. The article came out in the June 1919 issue, and the check arrived in my mother's mailbox. But she was unhappy.

"It's not the article I wrote," she lamented.

"It's your article, *edited*," I told her, trying to smooth her ruffled feathers. But that wasn't true. It was a substantial rewrite. I had moved paragraphs, cut a big section, and created a new introduction and conclusion. But if I hadn't done it, she would have lost the publication—and the payment.

The same thing happened a few years later when the *Country Gentleman* was publishing a series of my Ozark stories. The editor wanted a pair of companion pieces—one called "My Ozark Kitchen," the other "My Ozark Dining Room"—both to carry my mother's byline, each to earn $150. Mama Bess wrote the pieces, but—like her *McCall's* article—they required a substantial rewrite, which upset her in exactly the same way.

And there we were, at loggerheads again. It was another battle of wills: she defending her original writing, I defending my editorial work. My advice was based on a decade of experience in writing for the newspaper and magazine market, but she just wouldn't listen. She had been raised in a long tradition of mother-knows-best that simply didn't recognize a daughter's separate expertise. She was qualified to give me instructions when it came to churning butter or taking care of the chickens. But if she was going to move into my world, she would have to accept my help, even if she didn't want to.

After a few years, Mama Bess ran out of enthusiasm for farm topics and stopped writing for the *Ruralist*. She was still looking for things to write about, though, so I encouraged her to go back to what she once called the "story of my life thing"—an autobiography that she had been working on for some years. Grandma Ingalls had died in 1924 and Mama Bess regretted not asking her to write down some of the family stories. So she wrote to Aunt Martha Carpenter, Grandma's sister, asking for a family record and any stories she might remember. She even (and this surprised me) offered to pay Aunt Martha to hire someone to take down her stories and told her that I was interested in using them, too—family history that we could share.

Aunt Martha replied with some details about the domestic side of pioneer life, but as it turned out, Mama Bess didn't need much prompting. She possessed a store of her own recollections about her family's covered wagon travels, their log cabin in the Big Woods, their dugout in Minnesota, and the building of the town of De Smet. As a child, I had heard these stories over and over. They were a part of our family's pioneer legacy.

And now, settled in her "retirement cottage" with no chickens to take care of or garden to weed and plenty of time on her hands, she had written her "story of my life thing." That was what she brought to me in early May 1930, not typed, but handwritten in orange-covered Fifty-Fifty school tablets that she had bought at the grocery in Springfield.

She called it "Pioneer Girl."

My mother and I had been discussing "Pioneer Girl" off and on ever since I returned to Rocky Ridge. I suggested that she write from her own viewpoint, seeing the events and people just the way she saw them as a child. It would be an easy, natural voice for her—she could simply write the way she spoke. I also suggested that she stay with the order of events as she remembered them, tell what happened without trying to make a "story" of it, and include everything she could recall. I thought her project might have a chance as a nonfiction serial in one of the women's magazines, and I offered to type it and send it to Carl Brandt for his opinion when she was finished.

But that was before. Before the Crash. Things were different now. The magazines weren't buying anything, and if they were, autobiography wasn't it. But here it was, three hundred and twenty-six handwritten pages, ready, she said, for me to type.

She sat down at the kitchen table, frowning at the stack of orange tablets. "I hope you can fit this in with your other projects, Rose. I don't want my work to get in the way of something that earns money."

I got out tea bags and the porcelain teacups and turned on the electric burner under the kettle. After Rocky Ridge was wired for electricity and before the money went away, I'd had an electric stove installed in the kitchen. It was a blessing in hot weather.

"I'm between projects," I replied. "I mailed 'State's Evidence' to Carl the day before yesterday. He's sending it to *Country Gentleman*. But I don't hold out a lot of hope. Things are slow just now."

Mr. Bunting scratched at the screen door and I went to let him in. He'd gotten into the habit of running off, and his white coat was matted with grass burrs—heaven knows where he'd been.

"Oh, *Country Gentleman*," my mother said, with her cheerful little laugh. She sat down at the table, arranging her hands. Her hair had turned almost completely white in the last year and she wore it in crisp, careful waves. "Don't worry, Rose. They'll buy it. They love your work. They can't get enough of it."

I envied my mother's cheery certainty. I had been writing for *Country Gentleman* since 1925, and the editors had published sixteen of my stories. But they could love my work and still not have the money to buy it.

"It's different these days." I slid a meaningful glance toward the stack of tablets on the table. "The magazines aren't buying much."

"I'm not surprised," she agreed with a sigh. "The Palmer reports are very gloomy." She had opened an account with Mr. Palmer about the same time I opened mine and had sent him whatever she could save from my stipend. Her money had disappeared, just as Troub's and mine had, although she had kept a stiff upper lip about it.

She brightened. "Just the same, I'm hoping that Mr. Brandt will like my story enough to feel that he can send it to the magazines. Who knows? It might earn a little something." She looked away and added, delicately, "You're carrying a bigger load, now that there are bills to pay for two houses. I want to help."

Bills to pay for two houses. Perhaps she didn't mean it as an indictment, but that's how it sounded. *If you hadn't spent all that money building the Rock House, Rose, we wouldn't be in this fix.*

I bristled. But I only said, "I'll get started on this tomorrow, but don't get your hopes up, Mama Bess. Genevieve says that nothing is selling. The magazines don't have any money."

She squared her shoulders. "Well," she said, predictably, "where there's life, there's hope, as Ma always said." She smiled. "And where there's a will, there's a way."

That was on Wednesday. On Thursday morning, I took the manuscript upstairs to my desk on the sleeping porch. Troub was there, drinking coffee, eating an apple, and marking up a story about Mr. Bunting that she was hoping to sell to the *Atlantic Monthly*. Her eyebrows shot up under her bangs when she saw the stack of pages.

"My golly, Rose. What's *that*?"

"Mama Bess's 'Pioneer Girl,'" I said, sitting down at my typewriter. "The story of her life thing. She wants me to type it."

Troub rolled her eyes. "That's going to take a while, dear. And you won't be typing, you'll be editing, too." It wasn't a question. She knew my penchant for editing everything that came within reach of my pen, and she had read Mama Bess's writing. "Your mother can tell a good story," she added, "but she can't write for sour apples."

"I'll probably edit some," I conceded. "I'm going to send a sample to Carl Brandt to see what he thinks about it."

"She'll fuss about the edits," Troub predicted and went back to her work. "She'll fuss a *lot.*"

I settled down to work, rough-editing as I typed. Troub was right, generally speaking. My mother is not a polished writer. But as I worked, I was captured by the narrative itself, by the physical hardships and dangers the Ingalls had lived through. Crossing a flooded river in a flimsy wooden wagon pulled by swimming horses. Surrounded on all sides by a wild prairie fire, saved only by a narrow strip of plowed earth. Surviving a brutal winter in a starving town, no roads in or out, no railroad, no food, no fuel. And disease—scarlet fever, measles, influenza, consumption, the threat of infection—so mysterious and frightening, especially to a child.

Over the years, I had heard almost all of the stories, told by my mother in her soft, uninflected voice as we sat before a comfortable fire, where I could look up at her and know that she had survived, unharmed, to tell the tale. But I certainly hadn't experienced them in a single, continuous narrative, one episode after another after another, as I did now. "Pioneer Girl" was not artful, by any measure, but that seemed to me to make it even more compelling. It was *raw* story, *real* story, the bedrock truth of what had happened, unmediated by any effort to make it pretty. I knew my mother's story, but I hadn't fully comprehended the events that were part of her experience, and by direct inheritance, mine. In a peculiar, almost eerie way, it was as if I were meeting her for the first time, not as my mother, but as the girl she had been.

So I began to type her handwritten pages, smoothing out the awkwardness as I went, recasting sentences, reordering some of the material so that the times and places were coherent, altering the paragraphing, and expanding a few scenes. I also straightened out the insertions and deleted her private comments to me. At one point, she said that anybody else reading this would think she was making it up, but it was true. At another point, she said that she and Mary caught a rash at school and had to be smeared with sulphur and lard. They weren't allowed to touch the baby. The baby was her brother.

Her *brother?* Until now, I hadn't known that my mother had a brother! Or that he had died: "Little Brother got worse instead of better and one awful day he straightened out his little body and was dead." I stared at the words until they blurred, their despair clutching like a tiny fist at my breaking heart.

Was my mother remembering her brother as she wrote this? Or her own infant son, *my* brother, who died before they could give him a name? Or perhaps even my son, dead at birth? My grandmother's child, my mother's, my own—three little boys who would never be men; three dead boys, never spoken of but never forgotten. That afternoon, I put her story aside and went for a long walk along the edge of the ravine, where I could weep alone, not only for the sons but also for the mothers who had never known them.

On Friday, I sent Carl a few rough-edited pages as a sample. On Monday, I was surprised and cheered by his telegram saying that "State's Evidence" had sold to *Country Gentleman* for twelve hundred dollars and that the sample pages I had sent him were "very fine."

I telephoned Mama Bess to tell her and went back to work. By the next Saturday, I had produced a hundred and sixty rough-edited, typed pages. I sent the package to Carl for his opinion, although I already knew what he would say. He would tell me that the story was fascinating, but that it needed a great deal more work before he could send it out. Both statements would be accurate. It *was* a fascinating story. And it needed a great deal more work before anybody else had a look at it. What I sent was for his eyes only.

I didn't do any serious writing of my own for the next few weeks. Mama Bess's teeth were causing her a great deal of pain, so we made several trips on the train to St. Louis, where one dentist pulled the rest of her teeth and another fitted a new set of dentures for her—expensive but necessary, and she felt (and looked) much better when it was done. She could smile now, and she did, showing off her pretty teeth.

The weather that summer was horribly hot—the worst since 1901, according to the *Kansas City Star*—with temperatures topping one hundred for day after debilitating day, with almost no breeze. I bought electric fans for both houses and set them up to blow over bowls of ice cubes (thank heaven for the electric refrigerator), and I sat at the typewriter with a damp towel over my head and shoulders.

But I was too exhausted by the heat, too stupefied, really, for serious work or even serious thought. During the long, languid days, I wrote letters and read and watered the rhododendrons and visited with Catharine, who came in July for a long visit. In the cooler evenings, Lucille drove out from town and the four of us—Troub and I and Lucille and Catharine—had moonlight suppers on the garage roof, where we might hope to catch a breeze. We played bridge and Troub and I told stories about our wild adventures with Zenobia, the Model T Ford we had bought in Paris in 1926 and driven through France and Italy to Albania. *Albania*. It seemed like a dream, like another existence, another incarnation.

And as if in another dream, far away across the moonlit ridges, we could hear the hounds crying joyously on the trail of the elusive fox that, in Ozark foxhunting tradition, would be brought to bay but never killed. The dogs were always called off with a hunter's horn and the canny fox that fooled them was free to repeat his fleet performance another night. Briefly inspired by this wild night music, the immense night sky, and the clamoring dogs, I wrote a piece called "Reynard Runs," which immediately sold to Elsie Jackson, editor of the *North American Review.*

But even if it had been cool enough to do serious work, I wouldn't have. There were only so many magazine markets, and Carl already had a substantial backlog of my stories, which he would sell when he could. And as I said, I write for money: when there's no money to be had, there's no point in writing. The check arrived for "State's Evidence," but it went quickly, and by the middle of June, I was down to seventy dollars in the bank and worried to distraction about the bills. I slept badly and dreamed of being pursued down a dark alley by a menacing creature named Debt, like a monstrously misshapen figure in a Thomas Nast cartoon.

A month after I sent "Pioneer Girl" to Carl, he returned it. It had been turned down by editors at *Good Housekeeping, Ladies' Home Journal, Atlantic Monthly,* and *Country Home.* In its present form, he said, it had no future.

I was furious, *furious.* Of course it had no future in that form! The typescript I had mailed him—for his opinion about the story itself, not the telling of it—was only lightly edited, a quick first pass through my mother's manuscript. I hadn't asked him or expected him to send it out: that was only inviting rejection. He should have shown better judgment. By sending it out too early, he had jeopardized the whole project.

And now I had to tell my mother.

7. "WHEN GRANDMA WAS A LITTLE GIRL": 1930–1931

She was devastated, of course.

She looked at me across the little table in her kitchen. "I did so hope it was ready to send out," she lamented and added sadly, as would any disappointed writer, "I spent *so much* time on it, Rose, weeks and weeks. All wasted."

"It's not wasted," I replied consolingly, picking up my teacup. "You can't give up yet, Mama Bess. I've had more rejections than I can count, and I've learned not to take no for an answer. What I sent to Carl Brandt was just your manuscript, typed and rough-edited. It wasn't ready for submission. If it's all right with you, I'll run it through my typewriter again." I gave her a smile. "Okay?"

Her mouth tightened and I remembered what Troub had said about her fussing over the edits. But "Pioneer Girl" *had* been rejected. If she refused to let me run through it again, it was the end of her project. She had to decide.

After another moment's thought, she replied, warily. "I suppose I wouldn't mind if you could fix it up a little." She wrinkled her nose. "Just don't turn it into fiction, like your stuff, Rose. I want my story to be *true.*"

I drained my teacup and put it down. "Tell me, Mama Bess," I said. "If it came to a choice, which would you, as an author, rather have—money or prestige?"

"Your father and I could use the money," she said, and added primly, "I certainly never want to be a burden to my daughter."

I winced. How often had I heard that refrain?

She reached for the teapot. "But I wouldn't object to a little prestige." She refilled my cup. "Why are you asking?"

"Because part of the material—the section about the Big Woods—might work as a children's book. I was thinking of sending it to Berta Hader. She might be able to use it as the text for one of her picture books. Berta says that several of the publishing houses have developed juvenile departments—and she knows the editors. It likely wouldn't be worth a great deal of money, but there might be some recognition, especially if it won a contest. Shall I send it to Berta? And maybe ask Carl about contests it would be eligible for?"

"I suppose," she said, and poured another cup of tea for herself. After a moment, she added, "I'm glad you thought of that, Rose."

It was as close as I was going to get to "thank you." As I walked home through the hot August afternoon, I wished with no little irony that I had enough money in the bank to allow *me* to write for recognition—or even just to write something that pleased me, rather than my editors.

Recasting my mother's material for children took ten full writing days. I pulled out the section that was set in the Big Woods and rewrote it from the original first-person narrative into a third-person story for children that I was calling "When Grandma Was a Little Girl." My mother looked it over and gave her approval. On August 18, I sent the twenty-two-page typescript to Berta.

By that time, *Good Housekeeping* had bought one of my backlog of stories for twelve hundred dollars, enough to pay immediate bills and give Mama Bess the first half of her overdue 1930 subsidy. Feeling better, I settled down to work on the rest of her project: a wholesale rewrite of "Pioneer Girl."

The day after Labor Day, the work was done. I had spent another nine working days on the rewrite, creating dramatic scenes from some of the narrative material, expanding and adding dialogue to many of the events, and building a stronger story line. The typescript now came to a little more than two hundred pages. Mama Bess said she liked what I had done, although I thought it was still flat and not nearly dramatic enough. But Genevieve, who had arrived for a brief stay, read it and was enthusiastic.

"This really ought to sell, Rose," she said. "I wonder about Carl Brandt, though. He just doesn't seem to have any oomph left. Mary Margaret told me last week that several of his writers have left him."

And with that, I made up my mind. A week later, I told my mother I was going to New York. I wanted to look for a new agent.

I had been with Carl Brandt's literary agency since 1920. The year I signed with him, I was on my way to Europe and needed an agent to handle my Herbert Hoover biography and deal with editors while I was abroad. Over the course of the decade, our association had always been pleasant, and he had sold a lot of work for me at good prices. But as Genevieve said, the difficult market seemed to have taken the starch out of him. The mistake he had made with "Pioneer Girl"—sending it out when it clearly wasn't ready—was really bothersome. It was time for a new agent, someone more aggressive, more alive to the changing situation.

On October 15, I got off the train at Penn Station with my trunk and my typewriter, nearly broke. But in one of those wonderful nick-of-time happenstances, I had just taken off my hat in Stella and Mary Margaret's Greenwich Village apartment when Carl's office called. *Country Gentleman* had bought "Paid in Full," which I had written in a ten-day, all-out stint after I finished the rewrite of my mother's manuscript.

Now happily supplied with pocket money, I began a round of lunches, teas, dinners, and visits with old friends—Dorothy, Genevieve, Berta, Elmer, and Frank America, a friend from my Paris days, a coworker at the Near East Relief Agency. The city was a manic mix of frenzied gaiety in the nightclubs and speakeasies and the misery of the unemployed men on the street, lined up for cups of hot coffee and soup. Hoover is doomed, I thought when I saw them. No president could survive this kind of national disaster.

I hadn't yet told Carl I was shopping for a new agent. When I dropped in at his office, he advised me not to try to sell "Pioneer Girl," but I persisted, showing the newly rewritten version to several editors. Graeme Lorimer, the editor of the *Saturday Evening Post,* looked it over, shaking his head.

"Interesting story," he said. "But as it stands, too flat, not enough flesh on the bones. Why don't you take this in hand and rewrite it as fiction, Mrs. Lane? Do that and we'd be glad to have another look."

And Thomas Costain, the *Post's* fiction editor, handed the typescript back to me and said that he might be willing to read my *father's* pioneer stories, if I worked them up. "I should think that your mother's experiences would be better suited to a woman's magazine, rather than the *Post,*" he remarked dryly over the pipe stem he held in his teeth.

But the women's magazines were interested only in fiction, and light, romantic fiction, at that. I'm sure Mama Bess was disappointed when I wrote to tell her that "Pioneer Girl" and I weren't having any luck.

I was still looking around for an agent when something entirely unexpected happened. Dorothy Thompson's husband, Sinclair

Lewis, won the Nobel Prize for literature, the first American to receive it. Dorothy wanted to go to Stockholm with him, so she asked me to stay in their Westport house and oversee the care of their six-month-old baby until they got back, around the first of March. They had a maid, a chauffeur, and a baby nurse, so it wouldn't be an onerous duty. My job was simply to make sure that the household held together and report any problems to Dorothy. Westport was within easy commuting distance of the city and I would be able to come and go as I wished. It would mean that Troub and I would not be together at Christmas for the first time in years. We would miss each other, but that couldn't be helped.

And in the meantime, thankfully, I had found more work. Lowell Thomas, a roving journalist best known for his film of T. E. Lawrence, *With Allenby in Palestine and Lawrence in Arabia*, knew of me in connection with *White Shadows in the South Seas*, the book I had ghostwritten in 1919 for Frederick O'Brien. (An ill-fated project for me—I didn't get the royalties I was promised—but a very successful one for O'Brien. The book became a best seller, largely on the strength of my rewrite, and was made into an Academy Award-winning movie.) Thomas was publishing a series of first-person "true adventure" books. He needed a ghostwriter.

Hack work, yes, of course. But there were no other projects in sight, it was work I could do while I supervised the Lewis household in Westport, and I needed the money. Thomas was paying a thousand dollars a book for the two manuscripts he had in hand, and he had more lined up after those were done. What's more, he held out the very attractive possibility that he might send me to Venezuela or Singapore to do some research. That scheme would eventually come to nothing, but while I thought it might, it was a powerful enticement. Altogether, the project had a golden glimmer. Instead of going home empty-handed, I'd be taking *cash cash cash.*

I ghosted one of the Thomas books in November and December, another in January and February, and got a start on a third in early March. I won't pretend it was easy to keep at it because the manuscript material ranged from very bad to utterly wretched. But I spent long days at the typewriter, feeling ironically grateful that Hal's Nobel Prize for literature had awarded me the time and space to do this distinctly nonliterary work. Genevieve came to Westport for a weekend, and I had to conceal the evidence of my cottage industry. It wouldn't do for her to know that I was ghostwriting for Lowell Thomas. I was perfectly aware, though, that other writers were doing the very same thing, when they were lucky enough to get the work. It was a secret every ghostwriter intended to keep.

As it turned out, it was a good thing I stayed, for something very important happened a few weeks before Dorothy and Hal got back. The previous August, I had sent my excerpt, "When Grandma Was a Little Girl" to Berta Hader, with the idea that she might want to use it as the text for a picture book. She and Elmer had written and illustrated a children's book called *Under the Pig-Nut Tree,* which Knopf had published the previous May. Their editor was Marion Fiery, who had begun her career in the children's section of the New York Public Library, moved to E. P. Dutton's new juvenile department in 1925, and was hired by Knopf in 1928 to start a new juvenile program. Berta had shown "When Grandma Was a Little Girl" to Fiery, who liked it—with reservations.

In the middle of February, Berta arranged to introduce me to Marion Fiery at a Sunday afternoon get-together at the Haders' beautiful, hand-built stone house on River Road in Nyack, overlooking the Hudson. It was a congenial gathering of artists and writers, and afterward, Marion and I (by this time, on a first-name basis) rode the bus into the city. I took her to the Brevoort Hotel for supper and an evening's talk. She said she liked "Grandma" because it covered a period of American history about which almost nothing had been written for boys and girls. But she was thinking of it as a story for young readers, eight to ten years old, rather than as a picture book for children. If she bought it for that market, it would need to be lengthened to about twenty-five thousand words and retitled.

The next day, back at Westport, I wrote to Mama Bess, who had already received a letter from Marion confirming Knopf's interest. She didn't have a copy of the version I had sent to Berta, so I told her where to find my carbon copy in the filing cabinet beside my desk on the upstairs porch. "It's your father's stories," I told her, "pulled out of 'Pioneer Girl' and strung together." Currently, the story was set during the winter, so to get the additional words Marion wanted, I suggested that Mama Bess expand it to include the other three seasons, a full year, adding as many details of pioneer life as she could remember. I told her that if she would rather write in first person (always easier for her), I would change it to third when I typed it.

"Just get another tablet," I wrote, "and start putting down whatever comes into your mind, in any order. When I come home, I'll go through the whole thing. Then we'll send your book off to your editor and get the contracts signed." I added that I hoped she was pleased because it would be quite a feather in her cap to have her book published by Knopf, a major publisher.

Her book. This was a tricky letter. I had made a great many changes in my mother's original material. I wasn't sure how carefully she had read the rewritten pages I sent to Berta or even how well she remembered her original work. I also knew that in order to have the confidence and the motivation to go on writing, she needed to hear that it was *her* book that would be published. On such fictions our confidence, our relationships with others, and even our lives, are often built.

Another thing. I had not corrected Marion's impression that what she had read was entirely my mother's work. As far as she knew, it was produced by a natural, untutored talent. She wanted it that way, of course. Marion made no secret of the fact that there was a certain nostalgic appeal in the idea of a sweet, sixty-something farm housewife sitting down at her desk, alone, to write the remembered tales of her pioneer childhood. It was the kind of human interest drama that any publishing house would make the most of.

And something else, too. I didn't consider my work for Mama Bess to be the same thing as my ghostwriting for Lowell Thomas. She was my mother and I was obliged to help her—and I wasn't getting paid. But if Marion Fiery had any idea how much I was involved, *she* might consider it ghostwriting. She might just toss off a mention in an editorial meeting: "Oh, by the way, Mrs. Wilder's book is being ghostwritten by Rose Lane, so there won't be a lot of editorial work to be done on it." Word would get around, and I didn't want that.

Would I have felt differently if I had known that this one book was only the first of an eight-book series? Would I have asked for recognition and a share of the royalties if I had known that each book would take two or three months away from my writing projects and sap whatever meager store of energy I might have for my own work?

Perhaps. But at the beginning, I had no way of knowing how many books there might be, or that they might win literary prizes, or that the royalties might be quite substantial. And even if I had known all that, it probably wouldn't have made a difference, not then. All we had for sure was *one* book and that's all I was thinking about. In fact, I was feeling grand about it, for my mother's sake, and I wanted her to feel the same way.

Was this a deception? Yes. I was deceiving Marion Fiery by omitting the fact of my contribution—but she didn't want to hear it.

Did my mother see this as *her* deception of Marion Fiery, and of Virginia Kirkus and Ida Louise Raymond, her later editors? And after them, her readers? Was she uncomfortable when she was asked about "her" books? I would like to think that she was, at least a little—and even more, perhaps, as the years went on and the children became real to her, as readers, in a way that they weren't in the beginning.

But, as I said, my mother is a mystery in many ways, at least to me. Everyone *said* they were her books, so perhaps they were entirely so, in her mind. Or perhaps (and I think this is nearer the truth), she managed to persuade herself that whatever I did to the text mattered so little that she could overlook it altogether.

In any event, neither of us could see into a distant future that held eight books instead of just one. We would go forward as we began.

And so the decision, such as it was, was made.

The rest of that winter in the city was a blur of people and events. At the beginning of March, Dorothy and Hal returned from Stockholm, bearing the Nobel medal and a large purse full of Swedish *kroner*. I moved back to the city, where I took a room at the Tudor Hotel. I saw Marion Fiery for lunch at Henri's, had dinner with Mr. Palmer (who mourned the state of our stock accounts), and said goodbye to Carl Brandt.

For my new agent, I settled on George Bye, who had established his literary agency some seven years before. He was Lowell Thomas's agent. And we had another connection: before the war, both of us had been reporters for the *Kansas City Star*. We met at his office and he agreed to take on my work, and my mother's. "She has a contract coming from Knopf," I told him. "I'd appreciate it if you would handle it." I left my rewritten version of "Pioneer Girl" for him to look over.

And then, because I still owed Lowell Thomas that third book, I left the pleasures of friends and the city's infinite variety and took the train home to Rocky Ridge. My diary notes that I arrived on the 10 a.m. train. I was met by my father, my mother, Mr. Bunting, and Sparkle.

And Troub, dear Troub, dearest Troub.

8. LITTLE HOUSE IN THE BIG WOODS: 1931

While I was in New York, I learned from a friend that Guy Moyston was married.

The news wasn't a shock, exactly, or even much of a jolt: Guy and I had said our half-sad, half-relieved goodbyes three years before, when I came back from Albania. I reminded him of the lines from Frost's poem, "The Road Not Taken," from which I had borrowed the title of my almost-autobiographical novel a decade before, a book about diverging roads, about going on alone:

> *Two roads diverged in a wood, and I—*
> *I took the one least traveled by.*
> *And that has made all the difference.*

"I didn't write that," I said to Guy at the end, when we kissed goodbye, "but I live it."

I had said the same thing to Guy in the beginning—that I didn't want a relationship that held me down, held me in—and at the time, he'd agreed. We had met in San Francisco during the Great War. He was an Associated Press correspondent with publishing house connections and helped me place my book about Henry Ford with Century and the Charlie Chaplin book with Bobbs-Merrill.

"You're off to a great start, Rose," he had said. "I'll be watching to see what you do—and expecting good things. See that you don't disappoint me."

The next year, we both went abroad. Guy was posted to the AP's London bureau, then dispatched to Ireland to cover the Sinn Fein rebellion. It was a dangerous assignment, for a bitter civil war was brewing. He tried for weeks to arrange a meeting with Eamon de Valera, the leader of the revolt. Finally, on the appointed night, he was blindfolded and shoved into the back seat of an automobile. He said he could feel the shoulders of his two burly guards as the car careened through Dublin and knew he was a dead man. Many informers had been taken out like this, their bodies found with the IRA death warrant pinned to a sleeve. But Guy was taken to de Valera's hideout, where he got his interview.

I was in Paris then, in the delicious spring of 1921, recovering from the breakup of a year-long romance with Arthur Griggs. Arthur was an agent for the Agence Littéraire Française, whom I'd met when he was looking for an English translator for three of Sarah Bernhardt's stories—I translated them and Arthur placed them in *McCall's*. I was miserable, of course, but tremendously relieved, for Arthur had proved to be emotional chaos, a hurricane fueled by alcohol that threatened to suck me into its vortex.

In May—ah, Paris in May, nothing lovelier!—I moved into an apartment at 8 Square Desnouettes and began to assemble *The Peaks of Shala* from my Albanian travel pieces. Guy came to Paris to see me and we went walking together in the Loire Valley; a little later, I joined him in London. I needed love, all kinds of love, friendship, affection, physical passion. But I also needed freedom, craved independence, and I hadn't yet learned—would never quite learn, I think—how to reconcile the two. After a few months, I was no longer wildly romantic about Guy. But he gave me a warm place to keep my heart while I went about doing my work.

For the next several years, as Guy and I traveled separately around Europe, we wrote regularly and saw one another when we could. Then in 1925, when I went back to the States, to the farm, he dropped in for a few days. He stayed for three months. After that, we went East together and had another three months in Croton-on-Hudson, collaborating on a magazine serial and working on his play, *Smoke.* For me, it was a good time, one of the happiest in my life, with trips to the city and rambles in Guy's Ford and walks around the countryside. Troub was back in the States then and joined us when she could, bringing a new kind of energy and lightness. It was the beginning of our friendship and time together—mine and Troub's, I mean. When I went back to Rocky Ridge, she went with me.

But those three months in Croton seemed to change things, or rather, Guy changed and I didn't. I suppose he might have been a little jealous of my friendship with Troub. Whatever the motive, he began to want a closer connection, permanence, even exclusivity. I had to tell him that, while I cherished our time together, I didn't want to be married. I wasn't a wife. I had said the same thing to Gillette, when we ended our marriage, and to Arthur Griggs. And now, in the Ozark spring of 1931, all three of these lovers had found and married other lovers, and I had taken a different road.

What was this road? It was a question I asked myself as I unpacked from the trip, for it was also the anniversary—the twenty-second—of my marriage to Gillette. My letters to Guy had been returned to me and I had brought them back to Rocky Ridge. I reread them now with a kind of wistful longing, not at all for Guy or even for the person to whom I had written (these two were perhaps not the same). I was longing, instead, for the feelings I had then, wishing I could love with that sweetly giddy, self-forgetting exhilaration just once more in my life and knowing, somehow, that I wouldn't. I was, I think, longing for my younger self, full of optimism and joy and impatient for life, for adventure, for risk. As I looked in the mirror at my graying hair, at the unlovely lines around my mouth, I felt all of my forty-four years like a sodden weight.

But there wasn't time to linger over the past, over paths untaken. After several weeks of daily, fingers-to-the-typewriter-keys work, I finished my third ghostwritten book for Lowell Thomas and sent it. Unfortunately, it turned out that the Great Adventurer was as hard up for cash as the rest of us and I had to write several times for payment—and then wait a while longer, since he would pay me in post-dated checks.

In the meantime, George Bye wrote that he wasn't "warmed" by my mother's "Pioneer Girl," which he described as a mild tale told chronologically, without "benefit of perspective or theatre" by a fine old lady in her rocking chair. I knew he was right: the material needed the real-life dramatic tension of fiction. But when I talked this over with Mama Bess (who had settled down to produce another fifteen thousand words for Marion Fiery), she was adamant.

"I want to tell the *true* story," she said firmly. Her blue eyes darkened and her mouth set in that hard, stubborn line that I knew very well. "I'm sorry if it's not exciting enough to suit those editors in New York, but I'm not going to make up lies to make it more exciting."

"Nobody's suggesting that you tell lies," I replied cautiously. "But sometimes we need to use fiction to tell the truth. Sometimes fiction tells a truer story than facts."

She wasn't listening—and even if she had listened, I'm not sure she could have made the distinction. Not then, anyway. That would come later, when she had more experience as a writer.

"Lies," she said now, sniffing as if she smelled something unsavory. "I may not tell all of the truth, but I am not going to tell any *lies*." And that was that.

The Ozark spring was its usual frolicking, abandoned self, with an abundance of dandelions to be dug out of the lawn, an exuberance of apple blossom, an enthusiasm of birdsong—all very lovely, if you have the heart for it. I planted nasturtiums; moved the tulips, grape hyacinths, jonquils, and Madonna lilies to the iris bed; and transplanted wild flowers and ferns to the rock garden. Troub and I took the parents on Sunday afternoon drives to Ava and Mountain Grove and Bagnell Dam, which was still under construction. We went to a fiddlers' contest, went to movies, and told stories in the dark. Mrs. Capper was cooking for us, and Mama Bess and Papa and Lucille and her husband Eddie came for a Sunday leg of lamb or Saturday corned beef and cabbage. I played chess with Troub and bridge with Lucille; had a brief contretemps with my mother and a neighbor, Mrs. Moore, about eavesdropping on my telephone conversations on our party line; attended club meetings; and renewed the note at the bank, paying $108 interest. I worked on a short story, thought about money, and asked myself if this was going to be my life from now on, day after day, year after year, just this. Perhaps, if I could have looked into the future, I might have been glad to have so much.

One dreary afternoon, I was looking for a notebook to capture a story idea and came across my diary for March and April 1921, written in Albania. I turned the pages, realizing with some surprise that it was just ten years (ten years? a decade? it seemed a lifetime!) since my first trip to Albania, when I was gathering material on postwar Europe for the Red Cross's publicity effort and writing a series of travel articles for the *San Francisco Bulletin*. In April, I met two American women, Betsy Cleveland

and Margaret Alexander. They were going into the mountains of northern Albania to look for locations for new schools.

I jumped at their invitation to go along and we set off, across mountains that were meant to be looked at, not walked or ridden on, with two *gendarmes*, an interpreter, a pack train of sure-footed donkeys (they had to be, to cross those impassable peaks) and four guides in colorful turbans and sashes. And Rexh, a bright-eyed, capable Moslem boy in a defiant red fez who was very near the age of my own son, if he had lived. Rexh's fearless insouciance in the face of dangerous circumstances laid immediate claim to my heart, and over the years, he became a surrogate son, the child I had lost and found again in the blue, snow-crested Dinaric Alps. I saw to it that he was enrolled in a vocational secondary school in Tirana and then—when it became clear that he had a strong academic bent—I helped him go to Cambridge. I treasured his affectionate ("Dear Mother") letters, always hopeful and thoughtful; I nagged him about his health, chided him about his studies, and sent him more than I could afford—in the past twelve months, nearly thirteen hundred dollars.

I thought now with a shaft of intense longing of those brave, beautiful days in that wild landscape, the distance measured not in miles but by the time it took to walk across the wild mountains and by our meetings with the gentle people who lived as uncounted generations before them had lived, in villages built before men began to remember, two hundred miles and twenty centuries from any life we knew.

"How did you come here?" the villagers would inquire politely. It was a ritual greeting, asked of any traveler.

"Slowly, slowly," we would answer, which was literally true since we had come over the mountains, where anything faster than a crawl might result in a fatal tumble. "Slowly, slowly, and little by little."

"Glory to your lips," they would reply with a deep bow, as if we had said a very wise thing. "It is so."

With the sadness you feel when you know you have left something precious behind and will never see it again, I closed my journal and put it away.

The diverging road, the road taken. How had I come here, over what mountains, to Rocky Ridge?

Slowly, slowly. Little by little.

I thought of New York and the people and the pulsing energy and the ideas that sparked other ideas, and the vigorous, vital, vibrant change that made things happen. I looked out the window at the unyielding gray skies and unchanging green hills, where day after day, nothing ever happened.

Nothing, nothing at all.

Mama Bess had been working on the additions to her book: descriptions of smoking the venison, butchering the pig, and making bullets, as well as spring, summer, and autumn material. The writing was easy for her and pleasant, for she remembered her parents' work with a nostalgic fondness. We discussed the additions when we were together or by telephone, and she sometimes gave me short sections to read. The first week of May, she came over for tea with her material for the last seven chapters of what we now called "Little House in the Woods." I turned to it after I finished the story I was working on, which *Country Gentleman* had returned as "too grim." It would be 1934 before that one—"Vengeance"—saw print. I'm sure that the bleakness of the story was a reflection of my mood and the mood of the nation, as it came to us on the radio, in the newspapers. It was a dark time.

My rewrite of "Little House" took just a week. The language was simple, the descriptions straightforward, and there was virtually no character development—nothing much for Mama Bess and me to disagree over. I added dialogue and action, smoothed out the sentences and paragraphs, and carved chapters out of her continuous story. She came over twice to read my revisions, and then I packaged the typescript for her to mail to Marion Fiery and typed a cover letter for her to sign.

I wrote a separate note to Marion, letting her know that George Bye had agreed to handle the business details, if the book was acceptable. If the manuscript needed more work, I asked her to write directly to me, since my mother and father were leaving for a long motor trip. I skirted the issue of my involvement with the vague comment that my mother "naturally" had "consulted" me about her writing and invited her to drop in for a visit if she came out this way.

"We're only four hours from St. Louis by train," I added. "We have saddle horses and dogs and if you come we'll take you on an Ozark foxhunt—a thing unique in all the world."

My parents' motor trip was a three-week summer vacation expedition, with Papa driving, Mama Bess navigating, and Nero riding on the Buick's running board. My mother had taken the train to Dakota when Grandpa Ingalls died in 1902 and to San Francisco in 1915, but this was the first time that the she and Papa had gotten away together since they settled in Missouri. (It's hard to leave when there are chickens to feed and cows to milk. Now, of course, they had Jess, the hired man, and the garden and what was left of the chicken flock were both under my charge.) They planned to go to De Smet, then on to the Black Hills to visit my mother's sister, Carrie. They could afford the trip because they had the sixty dollars a month I was paying for the Rocky Ridge farmhouse and because Lowell Thomas had finally come through with a check for five hundred dollars, half of what he owed me. I gave that amount to my mother, my subsidy for 1931.

While they were gone, I had the fourth Thomas ghostwriting job to do, the adventures of an Arctic explorer named Hubert Wilkins. Thomas needed it quickly since there was a chance that *Collier's* might take an excerpt. Between that job and everything else, it was a difficult month. Two of our dogs were sick. Mr. Bunting (who refused to stay at home and ran off every chance he got) developed a terrible eye infection and I took him—on the bus—to a vet in Springfield. Peter, the mongrel pup we had adopted, had a canker in his ear. For the second summer in a row, the heat was unrelenting, with the temperature climbing past a hundred and no rain. The springs dried to a trickle and the garden began to die for want of water.

The garden wasn't the only thing that was dying: things weren't going well between Troub and me. Her income, like mine, had almost completely evaporated. She had been trying to write an adventure story, but she was never diligent for very long and she hadn't been able to keep at it. She was spending most of her day on horseback with Lucille or at the movies with Julia or swimming with Linda, three of her Mansfield friends. I couldn't go with them: I was working long hours on the Thomas book. I suppose I was jealous of her freedom, and perhaps of her friends. I know I was tired to death and out of patience, and I snapped at her when she went off for the day and left her share of the housework to me.

It's hard to know now which of us was at fault. Likely both, and it's certainly true that the searing heat ignited our tempers and made each of us flare up, quickly and uncontrollably. One evening when Troub came home late after an outing with Lucille, she announced that I was the only reason she had come to Rocky Ridge and the only reason she stayed. If I didn't care for her anymore, she intended to leave and go back East.

"But I believe there's still a chance for us, Rose," she added, very seriously. "It's this place that's turning us inward, making us crazy, both of us. It's too isolated. We're too far away from the rest of the world. I want to get out of here. And you *have* to come with me."

Troub's words were frozen in a terrible finality. She was right. It was the place that was making us crazy. But while she was free to leave, I wasn't. If she wanted to get away, all she had to do was get in the car and go. I couldn't.

It's hard to understand why I felt so paralyzed. At the time, I explained it to myself in terms of money, but that couldn't have been all of it. My parents' health seemed stable, at least for now. I might have rented out the farmhouse—or let the parents move back to Rocky Ridge and rented out the Rock House. We might have gone to New York, where Troub and I could have rented a cold-water flat and lived very cheaply. I could have finished ghosting the Thomas books and found other work. I could have . . .

But the actual details of our escape somehow eluded me. I couldn't imagine getting away. I think I must have been simply overwhelmed—by the unforgiving heat, by the worsening economy, by my own deepening depression, by sheer bafflement.

And Troub didn't leave, either. Not then, anyway. We held one another and cried and went to sit on the garage roof with our cigarettes, watching the fireflies dance across the meadow and listening to the melancholy music of the baying hounds, ranging the moonlit Ozark hills long into the night in pursuit of their elusive fox.

And when my parents returned from their free-and-easy vacation with a banal "East, west, home is best," I noted in my diary, with a bitter irony, the utter complacency of that threadbare old adage. East, west, anywhere, everywhere seemed better to me than Rocky Ridge, and one night I dreamed of telling them that Troub and I were leaving the very next day. I was escaping. They could do whatever the hell they liked with the damned houses.

But it was only a dream, and when I woke, I said nothing. I did nothing but plod, in place, through the next day, and the day after that and the day after that.

But no, that's not quite correct. I did *think* something. I remembered the music of the hounds across the silvered Ozark hills and thought: *I need to write about Missouri—it's untouched story material that I understand and can work with. And any story material can be used to say whatever can be said about the world.*

It was a thought that I would remember and act on, a thought that would carry me away from Rocky Ridge at last. But not for several years.

It was the middle of September before we heard from Marion Fiery that Knopf had accepted the revision of *Little House in the Woods*. The book business had become so uncertain that my worry over my mother's book had been mounting all summer, and Marion Fiery's letter came as an enormous relief. I wrote in my diary that I was feeling grand about the news, and we celebrated with a jubilant Sunday dinner, my mother and father and Troub around the table at Rocky Ridge.

But there was a surprise. When George Bye forwarded the contract, it covered not one but three books: the first one and options on two additional books. I had not expected this, given the tenuous economic situation. Mama Bess was astonished, pleased, and apprehensive.

"Another book?" she asked faintly. "But what in the world shall I write about?"

Another book. *Two* other books. Did I think about what this would require from *me*, what kind of difficulties we might run into in a continuing collaboration? I didn't, although, looking back, I know I should have. I only thought how happy I was that my mother was at last successful as a writer and that she might be earning a little royalty income from more than one book.

"You could expand some of the material from 'Pioneer Girl,'" I suggested. "How about the Indian Territory episode in Kansas?"

She shook her head firmly. "I wasn't three years old yet, much too young to remember anything but the stories Pa and Ma told about it. I put everything I know about that time in 'Pioneer Girl,' which wasn't much. To fill a book, I'd have to make up a lot. It would be more like fiction, and you know I don't want to do that."

That's where we left it—until a few days later when she telephoned to tell me what she had decided. "*Little House in the Woods* is all about me," she said. "I don't want your father to feel left out. My next book is going to be all about him—about his life on his father's farm in New York state. I'm going to call it *Farmer Boy.*"

I was pleased. I had heard Papa's stories often and loved them: they were as real to me as Grandpa Ingalls's tales were to my mother. "You could follow the same scheme we used in *Little House,*" I said. "Begin with winter and then cover the seasons, spring, summer, and fall. I'm sure Papa will be able to provide plenty of descriptions of the things he remembers. *If* you can pry them out of him."

We shared a knowing chuckle. My mother sometimes called my father "The Oyster." He only talked when he felt like it: the rest of the time he was shut up tight, perhaps the consequence of living with two very talkative women.

"I'll try," Mama Bess said. There was a silence on the line. When she spoke again, her voice was determined. "Now, Rose, I need to tell you something. I liked what you did with *Little House*. But this time, I mean to do all the writing myself. I'm glad for the help you gave me, but I know I've improved a great deal and I don't want to take any more of your time than necessary. I'll bring you the pages when I'm finished. All you have to do is type them."

I knew that wasn't going to work, but I didn't argue—not then, anyway. She was eager to get started and I was just as eager to see her writing, if only because it kept her from dropping in for endless gossip and cups of tea. I wrote to George Bye to thank him for taking the time to work with the Knopf contract. I didn't expect his 10 percent of the royalties to amount to much—hardly enough, I was afraid, to offset the bookkeeping cost. He had stopped sending out "Pioneer Girl." That project, it seemed, was dead.

But I had come up with an idea. The previous October, when I was in New York, Thomas Costain, the fiction editor of the *Saturday Evening Post,* had rejected my mother's "Pioneer Girl." But he had told me that he would like to see my *father's* story.

"I don't necessarily mean your father," he had said thoughtfully, filling his pipe with tobacco. "But a man's story. Pioneer life, the farming life—it must have been hard. Had to be a test of a man's courage, his endurance, his physical stamina. I'd like to see what you'd do with that, Mrs. Lane."

I remember telling Clarence Day that I had heard pioneer stories all my life and while I readily admitted their admirable qualities, they didn't particularly interest me. Or words to that effect. But a writer who ignores an editor's expressed preference for a particular kind of story is missing a chance. And working with my mother's material had made our family's pioneer experience much more real and compelling to me. It had given me something to think about.

The next day, October 7, I walked over to the Rock House for tea and told my mother I was thinking of using some of the elements from "Pioneer Girl" as the basis for a magazine serial. A young newly married couple, homesteading in the Dakotas, the grasshoppers eating the wheat crop, the young husband walking back East to find work, the young wife staying on the claim with their baby through a long, hard winter, like the winter of 1881. Would she object?

"Why should I?" she replied. "Those are family stories—you've heard them all your life. And, of course, you'll change everything up so much that all the truth will be cut out of it. You always do, for those magazine stories you write." She sniffed, disdaining fiction as a lesser form of art.

Then she changed the subject, telling me at length what people were saying about a friend's daughter who had been seen smoking in public on a Mansfield street.

"It makes a girl seem tough," she said primly, taking great care not to look at my cigarette. I finished my tea and left, contemplating what I might become in twice ten years if I stayed in this place.

When I got home, I sat down at the typewriter, lit another cigarette, and typed the word "Courage" at the top of the page. My new story. I gave the characters the names of my Ingalls grandparents, Charles and Caroline. The events of the narrative would be nothing like the events of their lives, but using their names was a way to honor their bravery and to anchor my fiction in their reality. I was glad to be working again.

The cooler autumn weather had come and it seemed that things were looking up. My mother was still celebrating the sale of her book, and I was delighted when George Bye placed two of my stories with *Good Housekeeping* and *Ladies' Home Journal*. What's more, I had succeeded in wringing another five hundred dollars out of Lowell Thomas by cashing his post-dated checks.

But our rejoicing was abruptly cut short in early November. I was hanging the new living room draperies I had made—a neutral beige because we had other lively colors in the room—when the mail arrived. Among the bills was a handwritten letter to me from Marion Fiery.

I dropped what I was doing, sat down to read, and felt that the bottom had just dropped out of everything. Knopf had been pinched by a drop in bookstore sales. It was closing its children's department and letting Marion go. Her work would be done by a secretary, which meant that *Little House* would be published on the adult list with no editor to watch over it. This was very bad news, and Marion wrote that she was heartbroken. But luckily, my mother hadn't yet signed the contract. Marion suggested that Mama Bess hold off and ask George Bye to offer the book elsewhere. It was an unusual letter for an editor to write—testimony, I thought, to my good relationship with her. I guessed that it was handwritten because she hadn't wanted her secretary to see it.

I wrote my thanks to Marion and wished her well in her job search. Then, to gain time, I wired Knopf over Mama Bess's name that the contract was unsatisfactory and that she wouldn't be signing it. Then I telephoned my mother to give her the news.

She was utterly distraught. "I don't see why you've refused the contract," she wailed. "I'd rather see Knopf publish the book than not to have it published at all. I don't *care* about the royalties."

"You don't want your book published without an editor to look after it," I said firmly. "I hate to ask George Bye to send it around—he doesn't know anything about the juvenile market. I've asked Marion Fiery whether she knows another children's editor who might be interested in it." I'd had to phrase that very carefully in my letter since it's terribly improper for an editor at one house to slip a book to an editor at another house, especially a book on which a contract has already been written.

"And while we're shilly-shallying, Knopf may decide they don't want it," my mother said frostily and put down the receiver, hard. Before I hung up, I heard a dry cough on the line. Mrs. Moore, two houses down the road toward town, was listening in again. I wondered what she made of the conversation—and how long it would take her to begin spreading the news that Mrs. Wilder and her daughter were having an argument about Mrs. Wilder's book (which Mrs. Lane was trying to keep from being published) and that Mrs. Wilder had hung up on Mrs. Lane. Five minutes, maybe?

Just when I thought things couldn't get much worse, they did. Another crisis hit, even more disastrous than the news from Knopf. Since the Crash, George Q. Palmer had somehow managed to keep his stock brokerage firm afloat, promising that our losses could still be recouped when the market recovered. But now Palmer was bankrupt. Everything, all the stock that Troub and I owned, even Troub's small inheritance—every cent was gone.

Palmer's letter—a form letter, sent to all his clients—arrived on a chilly, rainy afternoon the week before Thanksgiving. I had a pot of bean soup on the stove and Lucille and I were playing chess in front of the fire when Troub brought in the mail. She opened the letter, read it, then handed it to me and went to sit on the sofa, dumbstruck and white-faced, for the rest of the afternoon. Lucille was naturally curious and hoped we'd tell her what was going on. She stayed for soup, *croque monsiers* (a toasted cheese and ham sandwich that I learned to make in France), and two more games of chess.

It was after eight by the time Troub and I could take our cups of evening hot chocolate and sit down in front of the fire, Sparkle and Mr. Bunting asleep on the rug at our feet. I reread the letter. It seemed that Mama Bess's money might still be safe, but both my account and Troub's were definitely gone.

By this time, Troub had recovered enough to be mostly matter-of-fact. "I don't have a penny to my name," she said, "so I need to make some money, fast. I could stay here and write. If I kept at it, I'm sure I could sell enough short fiction to pay my share of the bills. Or I could go back East and look for a nursing job. I could stay with Dad for a while, I guess." She paused, tilting her head and wrinkling her nose the way she always did. "What do you think, Rose?"

I already knew what I had to say. She had been trying to settle down to writing for months and hadn't produced more than a dozen pages. Ironically, her inheritance had kept her from being a writer, Now that it was gone and she had to take her writing seriously, she might make a success of it. But while we had partly repaired our frayed relationship, we both knew that it was time to let each other go. Still, Troub was Troub: she wanted me to tell her what to do.

"I think you'd be in greater demand as a nurse than as a writer," I said, speaking as honestly as I could. "At least, right away. You should probably take the Buick and go back East while I still have the money to buy the gas. If you want to sell the car, you can apply my share of whatever you get to what I still owe you for the house loan." It was about twenty-eight hundred dollars, I thought. I softened my voice. "You can always come back, you know, when things get better. And they will." I didn't believe that, somehow—that things would get better. Or that she would come back. But I had to say it.

She stared into the fire, where a log shifted and sparks flared up the chimney. After a moment, she turned back to me with a smile that trembled at the corners of her mouth.

"Of course I'll come back," she said brightly, blinking back the tears. "Whenever I can. And when you come East, Rose, you can stay with me. By that time, I'll have a job and an apartment. We can do the shows together—it'll be great fun." She paused, watching me. "And maybe you will decide to stay. Just . . . stay with me."

"That will be grand," I said, around the lump in my throat. "Let's do plan on it, Troub."

But we both knew we wouldn't. We'd had nearly seven years together, most of them good years, interesting, exciting years. We had shared experiences, expenses, travels. We had cared for one another, in all the ways we knew how, in all the ways that mattered. But we had never laid any claim to one another, we hadn't clung, we hadn't clutched. We had prided ourselves on enjoying each other, without obligation. And now that we had reached the end, neither of us gave way to tears—not then, anyway.

The uncertain situation with my mother's book was resolved in another week in a much more satisfactory way. Mama Bess (citing the "bird in the hand" adage) was still angry with me for canceling her arrangement with Knopf. But on Thanksgiving Day, she and Papa joined Troub and me at Rocky Ridge for a holiday dinner, with roast turkey and stuffing, baked sweet potatoes, home-canned green beans, pumpkin pie, and cider. We were just sitting down to eat when Mr. Roper, who delivered for Western Union, drove up the hill, bringing a telegram from Marion Fiery. Virginia Kirkus, the children's editor at Harper & Brothers, had agreed to take *Little House.*

"Thank God," I breathed.

"That's grand!" Troub exulted, with a grin that nearly split her face. "Congratulations, you two!"

I raised my glass. "Congratulations, Mama Bess."

"All's well that ends well," my mother sighed happily, as we toasted her and her book with glasses of Thanksgiving cider.

We learned later that this happy turn of events was the work of Marion Fiery herself. In an unusual move, she had asked Virginia Kirkus to tea at the Biltmore on a Friday afternoon. She had given her the manuscript and the weekend—just two days—to decide whether she wanted it. On Monday, Miss Kirkus had let Marion know that she would recommend the book—which would be retitled *Little House in the Big Woods*—for the spring list at Harper. Two weeks later, Mama Bess received Miss Kirkus's letter of acceptance and, ten days after that, another letter announcing that the Junior Literary Guild had chosen the book as its April selection. I was enormously cheered. Mama Bess was thrilled. We could breathe easily again.

Troub left one gray, chilly morning in early December. Bunty and I stood on the porch and watched her drive away with Sparkle on the front seat beside her, the Buick crammed with her belongings. Shivering, bereft, I picked up Bunting and held him tight against me, then went into the empty house, where the silence rang in my ears. In two days, it would be my birthday. I had been thirty-eight when Troub and I had begun our journey together. Now I was forty-five. The roads had diverged again. She had taken one of them, going on without me. I had stayed behind.

I got a wire from Troub four days later, letting me know that she had arrived safely and that the Palmer account in which my mother had invested—on my advice—had indeed been closed. Mama Bess and I went to the bridge club meeting at Mrs. Kerry's that evening, and I told her.

"I'm truly sorry," I said as we got out of the car. "It's all my fault, every bit of it. If I hadn't encouraged you to invest with Palmer, you'd still have the money."

"Well, of course, it's too bad," she said in a philosophical tone as we walked to the Kerrys' house. Snowflakes had been falling all evening and the path was icy. She took my arm. "But it's *not* your fault, you know, Rose. And it doesn't do to cry over spilt milk. Least said, soonest mended, you know." She lifted her chin. "Anyway, there will be some royalties coming from my *Little House*, don't you think?"

Hearing her, seeing how brave she was, I felt as I had when I was not yet three years old, watching our little prairie house burn to the ground, knowing that I had caused the fire.

And now, this. My mother had lost all the money she invested on my recommendation. I would never be free from the debt.

PART THREE

9. KING STREET: APRIL 1939

"But you hadn't *really* caused it, had you?" Norma Lee asked. "The fire, I mean." She pulled the hoe toward her, making a shallow furrow in the freshly turned earth of the garden, along the length of string that marked the thirty-foot row. From the house came the sound of Russell's handsaw. He was upstairs this morning, working on Mrs. Lane's bookshelves. "You were so young when it happened," she added. "Surely such a young child could not possibly remember—"

"I have an excellent memory," Mrs. Lane broke in sharply. She bent over the furrow, dropping the dry, wrinkled seeds of the peas at two-inch intervals.

"I'm sorry," Norma Lee said hastily. "I didn't mean—"

"Of course you did." Mrs. Lane straightened, pushing up the sleeves of her old green sweater, bulky over the blue cotton housedress and rickrack-trimmed apron she was wearing. Her voice softened. "I can remember far back into my childhood. You've seen the picture of me on the walnut dresser upstairs? It was taken when I was very young. I remember that the photographer kept putting my right hand on top of my left, and I kept putting my left hand back because I was wearing my carnelian ring. Aunt Grace gave it to me. I wanted to show it off." She dropped the last pea, slipped the seed packet into the pocket of her apron, and straightened up. "There. You cover that row and I'll mark the next."

Norma Lee plied the hoe, pulling the soil over the seeds. "Another battle of wills. You defeated that photographer, I noticed." She chuckled. "I saw the ring in the picture. It's pretty."

"Of course I defeated him." Mrs. Lane pulled up the stick that was fastened to one end of the string and moved it a foot to the left to mark the new row. "I remember how good that little victory felt, too. But that's not my point, Norma Lee. The point is that I *remember* the day that photograph was taken. The fire was just a few months later. I remember that, too, very well. And I remember making it happen. I opened the stove door and shoved in too much slough hay. It flamed up and fell on the floor and we lost our house and all that we owned." Her voice dropped. "Because of me. My fault."

"But it was an *accident*," Norma Lee protested. "And you were a little child. You didn't mean—"

"No, I didn't. But actions—intentional or not—have consequences, and we have to live with them." Mrs. Lane walked to the other end of the row and moved the second stick, pulling the string taut. "It was not long after my baby brother died, and my mother was still in bed that morning. I intended to help her. Instead, I burned down our house. We lived in my father's shanty for a while after that, but for my parents, it was the last straw."

Norma Lee stared at her for a moment, thinking that— whether Mrs. Lane's story was based on actual fact or was the product of a child's dramatic and troubled imagination—she had just learned the motive behind the building of the Rock House, behind the books, too, perhaps. By such extraordinary efforts, the daughter had repaid her guilty debt to her parents.

"I am so sorry," she said softly. "Calamity upon calamity."

"Those were hard times," Mrs. Lane agreed in a matter-of-fact way. "I was just a small child, but I remember how my parents suffered. There were prairie fires and drought and the crops failed and my baby brother died. Hard times." She pointed at the stick that marked the end of the new row. "You start there with the hoe, Norma Lee, and I'll plant behind you."

Norma Lee began making a furrow. "And then?" she prompted.

"It was hard, but we came through. People do, you know, if they have heart. If they have courage. 'One man with courage makes a majority, ' Thomas Jefferson said. I had to write that over and over in my penmanship book in Miss Barrows's class in De Smet, along with 'Sweet are the uses of adversity. ' Both of them are engraved on my spirit."

Norma Lee thought of her own childhood, her father's steady work on the railroad, which allowed her mother to hire a girl who came in every day to scrub the floors and do the wash and cook the meals. There had not been much adversity, except that they had lost the electric refrigerator and the new car they'd never had. Did that mean that she—and her mother and father—possessed less courage? There was a stretch of silence as she finished opening the furrow and Mrs. Lane began dropping in the seeds.

"I've never been captured by the myth that the prairie was somehow the Garden of Eden," Mrs. Lane went on. "You know, Emerson and Thoreau's idea that the wilderness was the book of God. I suppose there's some virtue in the idea that fallen man can redeem himself and the wilderness through his hard labor. But it's also a hellish project, and the government made it worse with the Homestead Act. I saw that early in my life, when my parents were trying to survive on 320 acres of so-called free land, struggling against the weather to make a crop."

"Courage," Norma Lee said thoughtfully.

Mrs. Lane made a noise in her throat. "Adversity," she said. "Sweet are its uses. And sweeter still its contradictions." She straightened up and they stood for a moment, looking at their work. "Making good progress, don't you think? Tomorrow, we'll put in some carrots and radishes, if you're still game—oh, and spinach. And when it warms up, we'll plant corn and beans and squash. The weather willing, I'll grow enough vegetables this summer to feed myself—and you and Russell, too."

"Is that your pioneer spirit asserting itself?" Norma Lee asked with a little laugh, using her hoe to pull the earth over the seeds Mrs. Lane had planted.

"Maybe," Mrs. Lane replied. "But I rather think it's my instinct for self-preservation. And my refusal to buy food crops that are subsidized by FDR's New Deal government. Farmers could do better if the government didn't meddle and the free market was allowed to take its course. And we could all grow at least some of our food, if we invested a bit of work. And faith."

"Faith?" Norma Lee was surprised. Mrs. Lane was not a religious person.

"Not that kind of faith, my dear. Faith in the natural order of things. Faith that these seeds will sprout—in this climate, anyway. I wouldn't bet on it in Dakota." Mrs. Lane pointed toward the row of berry bushes on the other side of the garden. "I gave the blackberry and raspberry bushes a severe pruning a few weeks ago. They needed it—hadn't been pruned in years. Culling the old dead canes and cutting back the live ones makes the bushes tougher, stronger, more productive. I have faith that there'll be enough for pies—and plenty left over for jam." She grinned. "Sweet are the uses of adversity. Even the simplest story in McGuffey's *Reader* had to have a moral, you know. Patience. Faith. Courage. Although I rather imagine that these days, the moral of most stories would not be so clear—if you could find one at all."

Norma Lee had reached the end of the row. "Courage," she said, leaning on her hoe. "That was the working title of your book about Caroline and Charles, wasn't it? I think I like that title better than *Let the Hurricane Roar*."

"That's because you don't know the song," Mrs. Lane replied. In a throaty contralto, she sang:

> Then let the hurricane roar!
> It will the sooner be o'er!
> We'll weather the blast,
> And land at last,
> On Canaan's happy shore!

"But as a title, *Courage* would have done as well," she added briskly. She paused, frowning, holding out her hand and glancing up at the sky, which had clouded over since they had begun their work. "Speaking of blasts, was that rain?"

"Oops!" Norma Lee exclaimed, as more drops splattered into the dirt at their feet.

"Then it must be time for a cup of tea," Mrs. Lane said, picking up the spading fork. "And then we can get started on that cake for Russell. It won't be ready by lunchtime, but we can have it for dessert after supper tonight. Oh, and bring the hoe. I don't want that wooden handle to get wet." They hurried to the house, leaving their tools on the back porch.

"*Let the Hurricane Roar*," Norma Lee said, getting out the cups and the tea canister as Mrs. Lane put on the kettle. "I read the serial, you know, when it came out in the *Saturday Evening Post*. I was still in high school then. My English teacher brought the first installment to our class and said your story was the best thing she had ever read about pioneer life."

"Really?" Mrs. Lane asked, sounding pleased.

"Truly. She said the characters were so real, and they faced so many hardships. It was realistic and optimistic at the same time."

"Optimistic," Mrs. Lane said. Her voice changed. "Yes, it was optimistic, especially the ending. Too optimistic. That's what a Kansas wheat farmer told me, anyway."

Norma Lee was going on. "I went straight home from school and read it for myself—gobbled it down, as a matter of fact, and then went back and read it again. After that, I couldn't wait for the next week's installment. I thought it was marvelous, and everybody in our family thought so, too. All over town, people were talking about it. There was even a piece in the *Trenton Republican-Times,* saying how good it was. I would love to hear how you came to write it." She put the cups on the table. "And what about your mother's book—the second one, *Farmer Boy?* You haven't told me yet how that was written."

"My dear child," Mrs. Lane said, with a rueful laugh. "Has anyone ever told you that you are *persistent?*"

"I intend to be a reporter. I'm practicing on you." There was more to it than that. Norma Lee was already seeing that this was a story worth remembering—and retelling, some distant day in the future. But perhaps Mrs. Lane and Mrs. Wilder didn't want the truth told—about Mrs. Wilder's books, anyway.

Chuckling, Mrs. Lane opened a cupboard and took out what was left of the cinnamon rolls they'd had for breakfast. She put two on small dishes and set them on the table. "Let me tell you, Norma Lee. Writing *Hurricane,* and *Farmer Boy,* too, was the nearest thing to hell you can possibly imagine."

"I want to hear it," Norma Lee said urgently. "Please."

"Well, then," Mrs. Lane said with a small sigh, and began again.

10. *L*ET THE HURRICANE ROAR: 1932

Not long ago, I read back over my diary for the first half of 1932 and was stunned by the amount of writing I actually produced in those months. I made some money, too, over five thousand dollars—more than I expected, but not as much as I needed.

For the first four months of that year, through the end of April, I concentrated on the ghostwriting I was doing for Lowell Thomas. The Hubert Wilkins book, about an Arctic explorer who was with Ernest Shackleton when he died on the South Atlantic island of South Georgia in 1922, was difficult because it was so entirely factual. The Tex O'Reilly book, *Born to Raise Hell,* was at the other extreme, filled from start to finish with wild fictional adventures that I struggled to make sense of. Getting Lowell Thomas to pay up proved to be a struggle, too, an ongoing one. I vowed not to write for him again unless we were starving—and since we had the garden, the chickens, and the cows, that wasn't likely to happen.

I also managed to squeeze in the time to read and correct the proofs of *Little House in the Big Woods* and write three stories. George Bye sold two fairly quickly, one of them—"Old Maid," which I had finished at the beginning of January—to the *Saturday Evening Post,* my first sale there. I was disappointed in the price, only seven hundred and fifty dollars, when I was expecting a thousand dollars. The next year that story would be selected as one of the O. Henry "Best Short Short Stories," alongside pieces by F. Scott Fitzgerald, Erskine Caldwell, and Conrad Aiken. I was in good company.

But I was underpaid. "Skinflints," I complained to George about the *Post*. But he replied that seven hundred and fifty dollars was the best he could do, under the circumstances. "This is an awfully dark hour," he lamented. "Everybody's feeling it."

An awfully dark hour—and dark days, dark weeks, dark months.

I followed the international news with alarm. Early in the year, Japan invaded China and took control of Manchuria, and Lowell Thomas let me know that the Singapore trip he had proposed was cancelled. I had been in Berlin during the doomed days of the Weimar Republic and witnessed the flood of inflated currency that drowned that government. Now, in Germany, six million were unemployed and the Nazi Party controlled the Reichstag. I was in Albania when the Italian dictator Mussolini took aim at that defenseless country. Now, he was raising his Fascist fist everywhere, and no one—not even the pope—dared oppose him.

The national news was grim, too. On the first of March, Charles and Anne Morrow Lindbergh's baby was kidnapped from his crib, and although Colonel Lindbergh paid a ransom, the child—chubby and winsome, another lost little boy—was found dead two months later. Heartsick, I followed the tragic story in the newspapers, but it was only one of a rash of kidnappings-for-ransom and robberies. Everywhere, armed gangs robbed banks at will. The largest: the Barker Gang's robbery of $267,000 from a bank in Minneapolis. Even the local Bank of Mansfield had been robbed. The lone bandit forced five employees into the bank vault at gunpoint and made off with as much cash as he could carry in his hat. The *Mirror* didn't specify what kind of hat he was wearing, but Mr. Kerry said it likely didn't hold more than a couple of hundred dollars. Now, the townspeople bolted their doors and scrutinized every stranger walking down the street.

And then, in the late spring and early summer, the newspapers were full of the Bonus Army. Twenty thousand destitute former soldiers and their families converged on Washington to demand the bonuses that Congress had already promised them for their military service. They were violently evicted by federal troops under the command of General Douglas MacArthur, Major George S. Patton, and Major Dwight D. Eisenhower. MacArthur dispatched troops to Anacostia Flats, where they fired teargas on the occupiers. Their makeshift Hooverville of combustible shacks, tents, and cardboard box dwellings caught fire—some said that MacArthur had ordered it torched. Two babies died and the hospitals were filled with casualties. All over the country, the people's hearts were with the veterans, most of whom were unemployed. Herbert Hoover's hopes for a second term, if he had any, went up in flames with the veterans' Hooverville.

And to make a bad year much worse, the weather was simply unendurable. After the warmest U.S. winter on record, spring tornadoes raked the South, killing hundreds, injuring thousands. In the Midwest—and at Rocky Ridge—the warm spring turned into a summer of record-breaking heat and heart-breaking drought. Weeks of hundred-degree days dried up the crops that the grasshoppers didn't get, and dust storms began to boil across the sky. The ruthless, implacable weather accentuated people's sense of utter powerlessness against iron-fisted dictators, lawless thugs, a ruthless military—and nature.

But George Bye was thinking about the publishing business when he made that remark about an "awfully dark hour." I heard from my writer friends that the publishing houses had cut their lists by half, the magazines simply weren't buying, and even the best writers were in trouble. William Faulkner and Erskine Caldwell took jobs as scriptwriters in Hollywood. Mary Margaret wrote that she had found some work as what she cheerfully called a "demi-ghost": she received byline credit for "as-told-to" articles about people like Prince Christopher of Greece and philanthropist Marion Tully. The work, when she was able to get it, paid good money. But her roommate Stella lost her job as a publicist and they had to give up their beautiful apartment and move into a hotel.

I replied, commiserating, and added that I had five stories out, as good as anything else I had published, and not a sale in sight. "I try to put on a brave front," I wrote. "I am my blithe, gay self—on the outside. But I will confess to you (because you're a freelance writer and will understand) that down in my gut I am scared. Really, truly scared."

"Of course you're scared. We're all scared," Mary Margaret replied. "New York is a kind of Jericho for journalists and writers these day." And with the wry humor that would make her a famous radio show host by the end of the decade, she added, "All we have to do, you know, is remain invincible."

I muttered that to myself in the darkest hours. If I'd had a Spencerian copybook, I would have written it more than a hundred times, two hundred, three hundred. *All we have to do is remain invincible*—which assumed, of course, that we had been invincible in the first place. Which I was beginning to doubt.

At Rocky Ridge, the warm winter brought almost no snow, and spring brought no rain. The large farmhouse was empty and resoundingly silent without Troub, whose gay chatter had always filled the days with a distracting but comforting music and whose constancy had made a place for itself in my heart. She wrote cheerfully that she missed me but that she had found a good-paying job as a private-duty nurse and asked me to mail her nurse's cape. A few days later, she sent a box of oranges, grapefruit, kumquats, and tangerines, with her love. The fruit arrived prepaid express, and a good thing, too. I had just paid the monthly bills and wired money to Rexh for his Cambridge expenses and didn't have a penny.

I shared the fruit with my mother, who had gotten in the habit of dropping in, unannounced, three or four times a week, for breakfast, tea, or supper (with my father), or for the evening. I resented the morning and afternoon interruptions—they broke up my work—but I knew she was lonely. She made no secret of the fact that she felt Rocky Ridge was more enjoyable now that there were just the two of us. She came frequently, laden with local gossip, idle chatter, and scraps of her writing.

But as the spring wore on, there were often three of us since Lucille Murphy had also gotten into the habit of dropping in. While Mama Bess had tolerated Troub, she made no secret of her disapproval of Lucille, who came often in the evenings to play chess with me or work jigsaw puzzles. Lucille sometimes stayed overnight, too, especially when her husband Eddie (quite a loudmouthed boor, I thought, and felt sorry for her) went foxhunting with his friends.

Lucille was a plump, pretty blonde, earthy and robust, with the common-sense manner of someone who has grown up around working people. She had initially been Troub's friend more than mine, and she and Troub had gone riding together many afternoons. But I quickly came to enjoy her easy company, her lack of pretension, her scorn for pretenders and stuffed shirts, and her appreciation of the absurdities of small-town morality. She'd had a year at the University of Missouri and liked to read. I shared my newspapers and magazines with her, and as a result, she was always ready to discuss current affairs and politics.

But best of all, Lucille pulled me out of my unhappy stewing about things and made me laugh. She was far more willing than Troub to pitch in if there were peas to pick or floors to be swept, and she genuinely liked to cook. She enjoyed needlework, too, and we started a hooked rug for the living room, working on it together whenever she came over.

It was a spring and summer of illnesses. One morning, Mama Bess phoned me in a sheer panic, crying that there was a fire and it had gotten into the barns. I ran straight over to the Rock House, yes, ran all the way. But there were no fires anywhere—hallucinations, Dr. Fuson told me, although he couldn't say what caused them. Papa caught a bad cold and was in bed for days, and his crippled foot became extraordinarily painful. Mrs. Capper still came in to cook and clean five days a week, but she was always limping about and muttering about her bad leg, which would one day be one leg, the next day the other. I tried to let her go, but she begged to stay on. I gave in, although I could have managed without her and couldn't really afford the expense of her salary.

And then sweet Mr. Bunting—whom I couldn't keep at home, short of shutting him in the house—came down with the mange. It made the poor little dog miserable and whiney and required multiple visits from the local vet. As for myself, I was miserable and whiney, too. I had the flu, my teeth were in awful shape, and I was suffering from an off-and-on depression.

Now, looking back over my diary entries and thinking about everything that was going on in those months, I'm not at all surprised when I read phrases like "utterly miserable" or "another lost day" or "submerged in fear." The times were terrible, yes. I was ill, I was stuck in a place that had begun to feel like a prison, and there was a national depression. People everywhere were losing their jobs, their homes, their health. Any sane person would be frightened and despondent. Or, to put it another way, anyone who was constantly cheerful and optimistic must have been suffering from some mental disorder. No wonder I felt "submerged in fear."

But despite the darkness, I sat down at the typewriter almost every day. I was working concurrently on the two ghostwriting jobs, switching from one to the other as Lowell Thomas mailed me material. Then, one gray afternoon when I was wearily slogging through yet another bewildering chapter of O'Reilly's wildly crazy fantasies, my mother brought me her second book, *Farmer Boy*.

It was cold that day, only twenty degrees above zero, too cold to work on the sleeping porch. Swathed in sweaters, with an afghan over my knees, I was working in the dining room, where the oil burner kept the floor warm enough so my feet didn't freeze. My mother took off her hat and coat, put the stack of orange-covered tablets at one end of the table, and went to get teacups out of the cupboard. As she poured hot water over the tea in the cups, she told me, once more, that she wanted this book to be all her own.

"I am sure I've improved an awful lot since I wrote 'Pioneer Girl,'" she said in a warning tone, "so I don't think you'll have to do anything much to this book. Of course, I'd be glad if you would fix up my spelling and punctuation where you see a mistake. But I just want you to type it, that's all. Please, no other changes."

I thought of "Pioneer Girl." If *Farmer Boy* was anything like that, it would need more than a little cosmetic work. "I'm sure you've improved a great deal, Mama Bess," I said cautiously, "but I do hope you'll let me use my—"

"No." She put the teakettle back on the stove. "Please just type it, Rose, so you can get back to your own work. Your writing will earn much more money than mine, and the time you spend on my stuff will only slow you down. I don't want to be a burden."

I don't want to be a burden. The old refrain set my teeth on edge, as it always did, and I started to protest. But she raised her hand.

"Let's don't argue about this, dear. I don't want to have to depend on you." Her voice was sweet, but very firm. "I want to stand on my own as a writer. I want *Farmer Boy* to be my book."

We were teetering on the brink of that old conflict, and I stepped warily away. I was too weary and dispirited to engage in another battle of wills, and I genuinely didn't want to upset my mother. As a writer, she was doing the best she could. And she could be excused for feeling confident about *Farmer Boy*. Bubbling with excitement, she had called me a few days before with the news that she had just received a check for three hundred and fifty dollars from the Junior Literary Guild. It was the most she had ever earned from her writing, and she saw the money as an affirmation of her skill as a writer. I couldn't bear to bring her down to earth. And if I tried, she simply wouldn't believe me. I was still her little girl. She was my mother. And Mother always knew best.

But when I began to work on her manuscript, I saw how serious the problems were. We had talked about setting the book within the four seasons of the farm year, and she had done that. But there was too much extraneous material, often delivered in indigestible chunks of expository prose. Instead of advancing the action or defining the characters, these anecdotes stopped any forward movement and had nothing at to do with characterization. Some of the material wasn't appropriate for children. Most of it felt clumsy and amateurish. And the settings—well, they just didn't seem *real.* I understood why: my father had no great powers of description and my mother had never visited upper New York state. She grew up on a treeless prairie. She had no idea what the Wilder farm and its surrounding landscapes looked like, still less how they had looked some sixty years ago. *Farmer Boy* was supposed to be a book about a boy growing up on a farm, but it lacked any real sense of the land.

As I said, she came over often for breakfast or tea. Each time I tried to show her the problems, but each time she refused to listen. I tried on the telephone, too. Once I even got as far as saying, "Mama Bess, I really like the stories you've put into *Farmer Boy* and the loving way you depict the Wilder family. But this story at the very beginning, about the schoolmaster—"

"Oh, thank you, Rose," she interrupted. "It always does my heart good to hear you say that you love my writing. And that story about Mr. Corse is your father's favorite. But I want to read you the thank-you letter I got from your Aunt Grace."

Aunt Grace was ill, and she and her husband, Nate Dow, were destitute. Back in February, she had written what my mother called a "begging letter." Mama Bess had sent her what she could afford at the time, and I had chipped in what I could. When my mother had finished reading the letter (and adding the comment that it was a sad day in America when folks couldn't get by on their own), I tried again to bring the subject back to the book.

"As I said, Mama Bess, I'm enjoying *Farmer Boy*. But I really think there are a few adjustments that need to be made, especially in the beginning pages. That's where Mr. Corse gets out a blacksnake ox whip and lashes one of the boys until his clothes are cut to pieces and the blood is flying. Then he kicks him—literally kicks him—out the door. Do you really think this is something that children—"

"I'm sorry, but your father wants me," she broke in cheerily. "Just be a dear girl and squeeze in my typing whenever you're not busy with something else. There's plenty of time. I don't have to send it to Harper until August." And she hung up.

To my relief, Lowell Thomas sent an additional packet of manuscript material for the O'Reilly book and I had a legitimate excuse for putting *Farmer Boy* aside. Bunting was sick again, too, so I alternated between taking care of the little dog and subduing the reckless, recalcitrant O'Reilly. I finally finished the book in the middle of April and sent it off with the passionate hope that it would be the last job I would do for Lowell Thomas.

I had no sooner put the O'Reilly package in the mail than I heard from George Bye that Graeme Lorimer, the editor of the *Saturday Evening Post,* was still interested in "a piece from Mrs. Lane about pioneers."

"Dear Rose," George wrote, "can't you come up with *something* that will make our friend Lorimer lust for your work?"

I thought immediately of "Courage," which I had started in October and then laid aside, heartsick at the Palmer bankruptcy and Troub's leaving. I had picked it up again for a few days in January and worked on it enough to know that it was going to turn into something good. But I could see that it was a large project, so I put it away in favor of the short stories that might produce a quicker return and the ghostwriting for Thomas, which had a deadline. Now, I was anxious to get back to it, on the chance that it might work for Lorimer and the *Post.*

But Harper needed *Farmer Boy* at the end of August and my mother was impatient for me to get to work. So as soon as I finished the O'Reilly book, I went back to her manuscript, typing her handwritten pages, aiming to produce a chapter a day.

It was frustrating work, since I wasn't master of the material. It was her book and without her agreement, I couldn't do the kind of serious cutting and editing and rewriting that was needed. At one point, early in June, she dropped in for breakfast and I showed her some of the changes that I wanted to make.

She only smiled, tilted her chin, and said, very firmly, "Just do it the way I have it, dear. That will be quite good enough."

I flinched. The tone of her voice was just as it had been all those years ago, when I was a girl. I would want to do something a new way, a different way, and she would say to me, reprovingly, "No, Rose. Just do as you are told, dear. That will be quite good enough."

That day, I noted in my diary that "the thing has me stopped." Stopped flat. It was an inconsequential little job, yes, but it was getting in the way of what I needed to do, what I *wanted* to do. It was getting in the way of "Courage," which had been growing in my mind all the time I was doing Thomas's work, and now my mother's.

Finally, toward the middle of June, I was nearly finished typing *Farmer Boy*. I had put in a full thirty days on a project that I had little heart for, and it was time to set my mother's stuff aside and work on mine. "Courage" was rising like pulsing yeast, and I had to get back to it.

The story was a simple one. Charles and Caroline, newly married, have homesteaded a claim and moved into a dugout, where their baby, a boy, is born during the winter. The next summer, their wheat crop offers astonishing promise, but drought and a relentless swarm of grasshoppers devastate it. The Svensons, their only neighbors, abandon their claim and leave, defeated by their losses. Charles must leave too, walking back East to earn money and planning to return before winter sets in. But he breaks his leg in an on-the-job accident, and Caroline stays alone with the baby on the claim through the winter, braving not only the storms outside but also the inner storms of fear and uncertainty. When the weather clears, Charles returns and the couple realizes that their success depends, as an old hymn suggests, on their strength and courage, on their determination to weather nature's storms.

I ended the book with Caroline's bright hope for her infant son, measured by the house and fields and horses he will own:

> Somehow, without quite thinking it, she felt that a light from the future was shining in the baby's face. The big white house was waiting for him, and the acres of wheat fields, the fast driving teams and swift buggies. If he remembered at all this life in the dugout, he would think of it only as a brief prelude to more spacious times.

A simple pioneer story, yes. But it was also a story of our times, I thought. "Courage" was my reply to the pessimists who told us that the Depression had wrecked all our dreams. It was a testament to my belief that while political leaders might flounder and fail, ordinary men and women would simply move on, bravely, indomitably, redeeming every disaster by their individual struggles. And even more, it was a personal tribute to my faith in myself. It was the first time I had written something from the heart of me, something I truly believed in. Somewhere along the way I had realized, with a kind of stunned, blinking awareness, that at last I had become a writer, a real writer, with an important message to deliver. Courage. Whatever the storm, we must remain invincible.

The project had turned into a long, three-part serial, and I worked steadily at it all through July, in spite of the devastating heat, over a hundred in the sleeping porch where I worked every day, in spite of problems with my teeth, in spite of interruptions by my mother and her friends. I was heartened by a note from George Bye who, sight unseen, said he thought the story would sell, then deeply disheartened by a letter from Graeme Lorimer, saying that the *Post* didn't have space for a serial because the issues were now less than normal size and they were trying to give their readers as great a variety as possible.

And I was truly terrified when I looked at my bank balance and realized that I had less than two months' living expenses. I had to tell Jess and Mrs. Capper that I could no longer afford to pay their salaries. Jess could work for the rent, at least for a while, but Mrs. Capper left the next Sunday. It was a terrible day. We both wept.

Such storms, I thought, after she had gone and I was alone. Such storms all around me, within me. I clenched my fists and thought of Caroline and her baby boy, surviving the longest, hardest winter in a prairie dugout, completely alone, with no one to help, no one to depend on. *Invincible,* I reminded myself. *I must remain invincible.* I went on writing.

The Sunday night before "Courage" was finished, I walked over to the Rock House for supper. I had already told my parents the basic outline of my story. That night, we sat outside on the porch and talked about the courage it took to defy the elements, to wrest a living from a hard and unforgiving land. My mother said it reminded her of a hymn that her family used to sing, "Let the Hurricane Roar." She couldn't remember all the words, but I was struck by the idea. Many Americans had sung that hymn since they were children. They would instinctively feel the powerful faith behind that simple phrase. They would understand what it meant—*all* that it meant, then and now.

I went home and retyped the first page of my story, heading it "Let the Hurricane Roar." That week, I sent the typescript off to George Bye, feeling alternately hopeful and despairing. It had to sell. It *had* to—but would it?

Now that "Hurricane" was done, I was obligated to finish typing my mother's manuscript. So, gritting my teeth, I went back to *Farmer Boy*. I had come to deeply resent the task, not because I had to do it, or even because it had been such an interruption. I resented it because I wasn't allowed to do it *right*—to do the editorial revisions that would have turned a weak manuscript into something strong and good. By the time it was finished, I could barely stand to look at it. When I gave the typescript to my mother to mail, I felt very sure that her editor at Harper would reject it.

I took a few days to recover from the constant, hard pushing that produced both my serial and my mother's typed manuscript. Then, desperate for cash, I started one story, gave up on it, and started another one—"Country Jake"—with a little more promise. Meanwhile, "Hurricane" was making the rounds of the magazines. I got a telegram from George Bye raving about it, then a plaintive note saying that *Women's Home Companion* wanted it badly but felt it was too long: they just didn't have the pages for it. The *Post* had already warned of that, and I was seized with a cold dread. It was possible, even entirely likely, that every magazine in town would want the story, and still it would end up with no place to go. *Invincible,* I reminded myself again. *Invincible.* I went back to "Country Jake."

And then, on the Tuesday after Labor Day, I got a wire from George Bye. Graeme Lorimer had decided that the *Saturday Evening Post* had to have it, after all. They were paying three thousand dollars and would publish it in two installments. George had tried to get them to go higher (it was easily worth ten thousand dollars, he said), but that was the best they could do. He was sure, however, that there would be a book publication as well; he had already talked to Maxwell Aley at Longmans, Green. Aley wanted the book for his spring list, both in the United States and in England. "Low bow of homage," George telegraphed.

I was so excited that I didn't get to sleep until 3 a.m. the next morning, and the sheer delight of it stayed with me for days. I had written "Hurricane" for the money, yes—but it was much more than that. I wrote it because I believed that ordinary people would always go on as my parents and their parents had gone on, with courage and fortitude. It was the first thing I had written that I truly believed in. And now, having written it, I could believe in myself.

Two weeks later, Harper rejected *Farmer Boy*. I made cinnamon toast and tea and Mama Bess and I sat at my kitchen table over Ida Louise Raymond's letter.

It was a hard, hard blow, and my mother kept saying, "But I thought it was such a good book, Rose! I wrote down the stories just as Manly told them—and you know how hard it is to get him to talk."

I felt sorry for her, of course, and I tried to comfort her. Rejection is never easy. But I also felt that this particular rejection was the best thing that could have happened, and I was grateful for Miss Raymond's detailed and decidedly firm revision letter, with instructions for reshaping the manuscript to make it acceptable. She had a sharp critical eye and she made no secret of her disappointment, sweetening her critique with only the mildest praise.

My mother had already heard some of the same criticisms from me, but she had danced away from them like a skittish colt refusing the halter. Now, she had to be still and pay attention because the revision instructions came from her editor, and her editor held the purse strings. If she didn't make the changes Miss Raymond laid out, she would lose not only *Farmer Boy* but also the third book in her Harper's contract. Without continuing support from the new books, the sales of *Little House in the Big Woods* would dwindle away to nothing. She had already begun to hope that, in the long term, these books would free her from her financial dependence on me—a hope we shared.

But she was faced with a hard, uncompromising choice. To become independent in the long run, she would have to depend on me in the short run. It was a bitter irony to acknowledge.

She tried to get around it by saying in a careless, offhand way, "Well, then, I suppose I'll have to go over it once more. When I'm finished, if you can spare the time from your work, Rose, maybe you could type it." She sighed. "Again."

"I'll be glad to," I said and looked at her squarely. "But I won't do it unless you let me make the necessary changes."

She looked away for a moment. By agreeing, she risked ceding—in her mind, at least—a portion of the ownership of her book. *Farmer Boy* would be mine as well as hers, even though my name would never be on it. She didn't like the thought—but she was beginning to see that she would have to live with it.

She met my eyes and looked away. Then met my eyes again. "Yes," she said, very quietly. "Yes. Fine. Whatever you have to do to make it acceptable."

"Good," I said and gave her the carbon of the typescript that had gone to Harper. I suggested that she go through and mark the sections that Miss Raymond wanted cut, then rewrite, paying attention to the other criticisms.

I made another suggestion, too. Miss Raymond had noticed, as had I, the lack of landscape descriptions in the book. My mother had never been to the Wilders' New York farm. She couldn't describe what she had never seen. And she wasn't the kind of writer who could imagine a setting she had never visited.

"It's an entirely understandable problem," I told my mother, wanting to reassure her. "I know that the task of making those 'word pictures' for blind Aunt Mary gave you the gift of description. But in this book, all you have to go on are Papa's descriptions, and he's not very free with his words."

She bit her lip, her blue eyes troubled. "If I were younger, I'd go and have a look for myself. But as it is, I don't see how I can manage. Your father would never leave right now, with all the autumn work to be done. And I couldn't—"

"I just got my check from the *Post*," I said, "and I want to go to New York City and see some people. Instead of taking the train, I could drive upstate to the farm where Papa grew up and take notes for you. It'll only mean an extra week—two, at the outside."

My mother sighed. "I hate to see you spend so much of your time on my project," she said heavily. "But I suppose it has to be done."

"I think it does," I said and poured her another cup of tea.

She went back to the cinnamon toast on her plate. "Thank you," she added in a low voice.

I couldn't be sure whether she was thanking me for the tea or for the offer of a week's research at the Wilder farm. But at the moment, it didn't matter. The words were sweet.

"You're welcome," I replied and smiled. It felt as if we had achieved some sort of truce.

Lucille Murphy, always eager for a new adventure (and certainly ready to get away from Eddie for a month or so) volunteered to come along. We left the next week. I was glad for the company and for someone to share the driving. Lucille was a good companion and I thought I was good for her, too. Our conversations often took her outside the bounds of her day-to-day experience, which I'm sure made her relationship with Eddie seem limited. I doubted if he ever read anything beyond the *Mansfield Mirror*.

Since one purpose for the trip was to gather material for *Farmer Boy,* we drove north and east to Spring Valley, in the southeastern corner of Minnesota, where my Wilder grandparents had settled after they left New York State. Papa and Mama Bess and I had spent eighteen months with them in the early 1890s, recuperating after the disastrous last days on the homestead claim. All the Wilders were gone now except Papa and his younger brother, Uncle Perley, who still lived in Louisiana. The grandparents had died long ago and Aunt E. J. and Uncle Royal, Papa's older brother, in the last few years.

But I found the farm and the church and a few people who still remembered us. I wrote to my mother with a message from Mrs. Landers, who (with a good-natured laugh) directed me to tell her to send back the pie tin she had borrowed, full of gingerbread, when we left there in 1891.

"She don't need to bother with the gingerbread," Mrs. Landers said. "Just the tin'll do." My mother, chagrined at having borrowed something so very long ago and failed to return it, immediately sent a pie tin from her own kitchen, with a note and a pair of crocheted doilies as an apology.

The trip was rather like a vacation. Lucille was lively and gay and for the first time in too long, I could relax and be cheerful—and why not? The air was crisp and the autumn trees flamed like crimson and gold torches against a very blue sky as we drove across the upper Midwest, then through Ohio, Pennsylvania, and New York. The check from the *Post* and the advance from Longmans, Green on the publication of *Hurricane* in book form meant that I was free from urgent financial worry for the moment, and we could treat ourselves to nice hotels and good meals.

It was a time for conversation, too. One or two nights into the trip, sitting late over apple pie and coffee at a candlelit table in a hotel dining room, Lucille said, "You know, Rose, I don't think I love Eddie anymore. Not the way I used to, anyway." She looked away. "And I feel guilty about it."

"I'm sorry," I said, not because she didn't love him—she had outgrown him, or outgrown her need for him, both of which were quite natural things but tragic in their way. I was sorry that she felt guilty. But that was a natural thing, too.

She sat still for a moment, her gray eyes sober, her soft blonde hair haloed around her face. She seemed very young, or I felt very old, or both.

"Has that ever happened to you?" she asked, almost timidly. "That you fell out of love with someone?"

"More than once." *Gillette,* I thought. *And Arthur. And Guy.* Or just Guy, whom I thought of quite often and sometimes even missed.

"Or perhaps it wasn't that I fell out of love," I amended. "Perhaps I simply understood that I hadn't loved in the first place. That I had only loved my image of the man, which was made out of myself, out of the best that was in me at the time."

Lucille frowned, understanding, but not quite. She picked up her coffee cup in both hands, her elbows propped on the table, the fabric of her dress falling away from her arms, plump and pale in the candlelight.

"Well," she said in a practical voice, "I don't much think that Eddie is the best of me." Her grin was lopsided. "The worst, maybe. Could that be?"

"But remember back to when you first loved him," I prodded. "Who were you then? And who was he?"

"Who was I?" She looked away, silent, musing. "I see," she said, after a moment. "Yes, I see. I was a kid then. I needed somebody brash and cocky, somebody I could belong to, who would tell me what to do. I'm . . . different, now. But he's still brash and cocky. And thinks I belong to him, and he can tell me what to do." She put her cup down, chuckling ruefully. "Funny, isn't it?"

"I wish it were," I replied, not smiling. "We marry to get what we think we want and need, and after a while we don't. But then there's still the marriage to deal with."

Somewhere a tray rattled and a waiter dropped a handful of silver. Lucille picked up her white napkin and began to pleat it in her fingers. "You were married once, Troub told me. What was he like?"

I thought of Gillette, his superficial culture, his energy and drive, his push to get ahead, his skills as a promoter, as a *self*-promoter. "He was a traveling salesman with an impressive line of goods," I said, as if that explained everything. Not quite, perhaps, but close enough. "And I was a foolish girl and lonely and very tired of working and eager to be impressed. And eager for a life that was something other than being on the job every minute. Both of us thought marriage was something it wasn't. We were made for each other, you might say."

"When did you know—" She stopped, looked away, looked inside herself. "That you didn't want to be married any longer?"

I heard the question behind the question and said what I thought would help her. "When I knew he didn't have anything left to teach me. When I understood that there was nothing more I wanted to learn from him. When I could find myself in myself, and not in him. When I saw how many things I wanted, and wanted all of them at the same time, and knew that *none* of them could come from him."

"Ah," she said, very quietly. I could see her mentally tabulating what I had said, considering it in relation to herself and the husband she no longer loved. "Was it hard . . . to get the divorce?"

"The divorce itself wasn't hard. But first I had to cut myself free from the clinging." I thought of something I had once written to

Dorothy Thompson. "We're not born to be ruthless, we women. But that's what it takes to hit the hands on the gunwale with an oar until they let go." I remembered something Gillette had wailed at me, "Oh, why can't you, just once, Rose, be *human!*" when what I had wanted, *all* I had wanted, was the most fundamental of human desires: to be free to live my own life.

She shivered. "I'm not sure I can be that ruthless. That heartless."

"I wasn't sure," I said. "You won't be sure, either, until you *are,* suddenly." I remembered myself at her age, facing her dilemma. "The thing to remember is that something will come to take its place. Something different, of course. But something better. Because whatever is ahead will be better than what you have now."

She gave me a skeptical look. "Do you really believe that?"

I laughed. "I believed it once. I wrote it, once, in a book. Perhaps I can believe it again, in the right circumstance."

"Well, then." Lucille picked up her water glass and tipped the edge of it to mine in a mock toast. "Here's to the right circumstance," she said.

A few days later, we reached the small town of Malone, New York, fifteen miles south of the St. Lawrence River and five miles or so from the village of Burke, where the Wilder farm was located. I sent my father a postcard view of a grand hotel, which in a rather curious fashion had been built around the Methodist chapel he had attended as a boy. We got a room at the hotel, had lunch, then drove out to Burke.

We found the old farm easily from Papa's directions. I was glad to see that the house was still standing and in decent repair. There were two large maple trees nearby, which might have been there when Papa was a boy. The weathered split rail fence along the road, though—that might have been there then. When I told the owner that my father had grown up in the house and that my mother was writing a book about the farm, she invited me to come inside and look around, and I did, breathlessly.

There had been some alterations, but the rooms seemed to be pretty much as they had been when my father was a boy. It didn't take much imagination to see him, going on ten, taking his bath in front of the kitchen fire or rocking the big barrel churn in the whitewashed cellar or blacking the stove—and throwing the blacking brush so hard at his sister Alice that it hit the parlor wall and left a big inky smear on the wallpaper. I looked, but there was no sign of that smear. And no sign, either, of Aunt E. J.'s repair, so perfect that Grandma Wilder had never even noticed. But that had been nearly sixty years ago. The wallpaper had likely been replaced many times since then.

Most of the barns, though, still existed as they had when my father was a boy, matching the sketch he had made for my mother. I made detailed notes about them and about the surrounding pastures where the cows had grazed and the fields my father had harrowed with the work team of big, gentle brown mares, Bess and Beauty. The schoolhouse the Wilder children attended was still standing, too, down a narrow dirt lane to the bridge on the Trout River, not far from the spot where Papa had said the sheep were washed before shearing, then along a path through a wood. Now that I had seen the place, I knew I could sharpen the vague descriptions and prompt my father into more detailed recollections.

Lucille stayed for a few days in New York, then left me there and drove back to Mansfield—and Eddie—alone, still unsure of what she intended to do. I stayed with Genevieve, and we made the old, gay rounds of people and places. But the city had a bleak, almost Dickensian feel to it, and there were encampments of homeless people in empty lots and along the riverbank in Morningside Heights, with men, women, and children huddled around campfires, trying to keep warm. I spent several weeks seeing friends (but not Troub, who was on a nursing assignment in Florida), talking with George Bye about the current writing market, discussing *Hurricane's* book publication in the United States and England with Maxwell Aley, and dropping in on editors. Everyone had read the serial in the *Post,* and I was heartened by their congratulations.

"I told you so," Floyd Dell said. "Entirely worthy of you, Rose."

Berta Hader put her arms around me and whispered, "Elmer and I *loved* it. We can't wait for your next one."

"A stunning piece of work," Mary Margaret burbled. "And a perfect ending. So good to read something optimistic when everybody is so down in the mouth!"

I was in New York on Election Day. Franklin Delano Roosevelt won in a landslide, carrying forty-two out of forty-eight states, the first Democrat since Franklin Pierce to win a majority of the popular vote. People were understandably nervous about Roosevelt's vague policy positions (What was a "New Deal"? What would he do about the banking situation?) and his health (Could the man *really* walk? Could he stand up to the demands of the office?). But they were ready to vote for anyone but Hoover. The president had become the scapegoat who bore the blame for the Depression, the butt of everyone's bad jokes—and worse. When his campaign train pulled into Detroit, the crowd was waiting with eggs and rotten tomatoes, chanting "Hang Hoover! Hang Hoover!" Even staunchly Republican Mansfield would turn against him, giving Roosevelt 362 votes to Hoover's 303.

Roosevelt was at the Biltmore on election night, and newspaper reporters were camped in the hotel lobby, anxious to hear the election returns as they came in. When Genevieve and I went out to supper, the streets in her neighborhood were filled with the swingy sound of "Happy Days Are Here Again," blaring from hundreds of radios in hundreds of windows. And it wasn't the *New York Times* that scooped the announcement of Roosevelt's win. Shortly after 11 p.m., Americans heard the news on their radios, everyone everywhere, all at the same time. For this former newspaper reporter, it was the end of an era, in more ways than one.

I took the train back to Mansfield, then collapsed into bed with a bad case of the flu. On Christmas Eve, family and a few friends gathered around the tree at Rocky Ridge and exchanged ten-cent presents. For Christmas dinner, Lucille baked a turkey with all the trimmings, and Mama Bess brought a mincemeat pie.

When the party was over, I went back to bed for the rest of the year.

It was late January when my mother gave me her new version of *Farmer Boy*. It had been raining for several days. The creek was up, the roads were muddy, and the sky was an unrelieved leaden gray. Catharine, who had come after Christmas to stay for several months, was in her room upstairs, having an afternoon nap. I was in the living room beside the fire, doing a pen-revision of "Vengeance," which *Country Gentleman* had rejected as "too grim" and which I wanted to send out again. I had brought in a tea tray and set it on the low table, thinking that Catharine might be coming down soon.

I laid my work aside when my mother came into the room. She put a stack of orange-covered notebooks on the table beside my chair. "I'm happy to tell you that I got a check from George Bye for $562.69," she said. "Royalties for *Little House*."

"That's wonderful!" I exclaimed, meaning it. "Congratulations! You must feel just grand."

"I do," she said modestly. "And I just this morning finished rewriting *Farmer Boy*. It's ready for you to work on."

"Good," I said. "I hope the rewrite wasn't too difficult." I got up and poured a cup of tea for her. There were cinnamon rolls on the tea tray, but she shook her head when I offered one.

"Well, I took out those things that Miss Raymond didn't like," she said, sitting down on the sofa. "And I used the notes from your trip to expand the descriptions of the farm and the buildings and such." She stirred sugar into her cup, not looking at me. "I've done the best I could, but it'll likely need a lot of fixing. I want you to do what you have to do so that Miss Raymond will take it, Rose."

I gave her a direct look and asked a direct question. "You're sure?"

She nodded. "I'll come over every couple of days and you can show me what you've changed and tell me why you did it." She pursed her lips. "A person is never too old to learn, as Ma used to say." I murmured something and she added, "And, of course, I want to learn as much as I can from you. I'm hoping I'll improve so much that all you have to do with the next one is type it."

I poured myself another cup of tea. The Harper contract specified three books, so she felt she was obligated to write a third. At least, *she* felt obligated—Harper wouldn't. There was no guarantee that they would accept a third book if the sales of *Farmer Boy* didn't meet expectations. Come to that, there was no guarantee that they would accept a rewritten *Farmer Boy*, especially given the economic uncertainty. I doubted that she was thinking of this, but it wasn't a good idea to say anything that might undercut her confidence as she began work on her third—and perhaps her last—book.

"While you're doing that, I need to start working," she went on. "It takes me so long to write anything because I never know where I'm going. I just have to let the story wander around until it begins to lead somewhere."

I stirred the fire and the coals blazed up. "I'm glad to hear that you're ready to get started. Have you figured out what you're going to write about?" We had talked about this before. If she went on writing, it would be easiest for her to use the story material in "Pioneer Girl" as a kind of outline.

"I suppose it should be the Indian Territory story." She sounded uncertain. "But the books will be out of order. I don't quite know how to handle that."

"Out of order?" I added another oak log to the fire and sat down with my cup of tea.

"Well, I didn't start 'Pioneer Girl' in Wisconsin because I wasn't old enough to remember the first time we lived there, and I didn't include the time we spent in Missouri. I started 'Pioneer Girl' in Indian Territory, which I don't exactly remember either, except through Ma and Pa's stories." She added sugar to her tea and stirred. "I was only a year and a half when we went there. And three and a half when we started back to the Big Woods."

The Ingalls family itinerary was complicated. My mother was born in northwestern Wisconsin. When she was still a toddler, her father and mother packed up their family (my mother and her older sister Mary) and headed for Indian Territory, for what my grandfather thought would soon be free land, opened up for settlement. He wanted to get a jump on the others who would be flocking to stake their claims. They lived there for a year and a half—that's where my mother's sister Carrie was born. Then they traveled back to my mother's birthplace in Wisconsin, where they lived for three years. From Wisconsin to Missouri to Indian Territory and back to Wisconsin again.

Mama Bess put her spoon in the saucer. "But you see, that's not the way it seems in *Little House in the Big Woods*. In that book,

I'm already four, and it seems like we've lived in Wisconsin ever since I was born. And Carrie is a baby. So writing about Indian Territory, where Carrie is born, is going backward."

I nodded, seeing her dilemma. She was still thinking that she was writing autobiography. "Just ignore the issue," I said. "Pretend that the second stay in Wisconsin was the first and go on with the story in Indian Territory."

"But I can't pretend," she protested, frowning. "That's fiction, Rose. That's what you write. I want my books to be the *truth*." Her frown deepened. "But it's awkward. I just don't know what to do about Carrie."

"I'm sure you'll come up with something that feels right," I said comfortingly. Time enough to discuss it later, when she had produced her manuscript.

I heard footsteps overhead. Catharine was getting up. My mother glanced toward the stairs, then drained her teacup and set it down. "I probably shouldn't tell you this," she began in a low voice, "but—"

"If it's about Catharine, please don't."

Another frown. "But I really think you should know that she is being talked about, Rose. She was seen exchanging pleasantries with one of the traveling salesmen in front of the pool hall."

Uh-oh, I thought. Growing up in Mansfield, I had been told that traveling men were bold and bad. Nice girls weren't supposed to speak to them, and if a girl did, well, she wasn't nice. Since the Crash, the number of salesmen had dramatically decreased, but they still occasionally came through town. The Mrs. Grundys of Mansfield might go to the movies and listen to the radio, but their view of traveling men was apparently unchanged. And while the Catharine I knew was anything but flirtatious, even a polite hello-it's-a-lovely-day would be enough to set them off.

My mother leaned forward, very serious. "You know I don't make moral judgments." Her tone was prissy. "But other people do, and their opinions of Catharine rub off on our family. On you, Rose. On me." She straightened her shoulders, took a breath, and paused. Then, with a sternly hushed emphasis: "People will say that the Wilders have gone *tough*."

I was exasperated. "You can't be serious, Mama Bess. Why would people associate you with what Catharine does? And why in the world would anyone object to a simple exchange of pleasantries on the sidewalk? Surely nobody thinks she's going to run off with the fellow."

But I was fighting a losing battle. My mother's compass swung to the poles of her friends' opinions. And of all my New York visitors, Catharine was certainly the most flippant, the most flirtatious, and altogether the sort of "new woman" that made the Mansfield matrons uncomfortable, armored as they were in their narrow morality. Her blonde hair, makeup, and tight skirts had already attracted their scrutiny. Anything she said or did would serve as a subject for tittle-tattle until a new scandal came along to keep their tongues busy.

"You mark my words, Rose." My mother gave her head an ominous shake. "That girl is going to come to no good end."

"Yes, Mama," I said dutifully.

Catharine was clattering down the stairs. My mother stood. "I must be on my way." She glanced at the stack of tablets and her face softened. "About *Farmer Boy*—I'm sorry I didn't let you do the revisions you wanted to do before I sent it in the first time, Rose. That would have saved us both some extra work."

It was a remarkable moment.

I had planned to start another story after I finished revising "Vengeance," but I put the idea aside and went to work on *Farmer Boy*. My mother had taken out most of the digressive material, added a few descriptions, and reworked some of the chapters. But there was still a great deal to be done, and I worked through the whole month of February, spending every day on it. I was resentful because it took me away from my own work. But at least this time, I had the freedom to add the dialogue and detail that would make the story interesting to a young reader. And since I had visited the Wilder farm and had seen the places, I could describe the settings with authority.

On March 2, I finished the manuscript and handed it over. I knew it was good, and Mama Bess must have agreed because she promptly sent it off to George Bye with the cover letter I composed for her. Two weeks later, Harper accepted it. Miss Raymond wrote that *Farmer Boy* "wasn't quite another *Little House*" but excellent in its own way, "different, sincere, authentic." But she only offered a 5 percent royalty rate, half what *Little House* was earning.

I wrote right away to George Bye, protesting that the reduction in my mother's royalty was a dangerous precedent, especially since she felt she was obligated for a third book. Beating the drum for her, I wrote to Bye that she was already working on that book, an Indian story that promised to be even better than *Little House*. Bye carried my concern to Miss Raymond and reported her reply. The juvenile market, she said, was at a very low ebb, and she had been ordered not to "go into debt" for *Farmer Boy*. She was willing to make an adjustment—5 percent royalty up to three thousand copies, 10 percent after that—but it was the best that she could do. In the end, I had to tell my mother that she was probably lucky that Harper was willing to bring the book out, given the current economic catastrophe. She signed the contract. *Farmer Boy* would be published in the fall.

And the economic situation really was a catastrophe, the terrible reports filling every newspaper and radio broadcast. The Crash itself had been bad, and the weeks and months that followed had been worse. But the months between Roosevelt's November election and his March 4th inauguration were horrible beyond description, with banks closing all across the country. Everyone was desperate for change, but what would the new president do? What *could* he do? Would anything make a difference?

With the cooperation of Congress, FDR immediately nationalized gold, making it illegal for Americans to possess gold coins or bullion and forcing them to trade it to the government for paper money at the rate of $20.67 an ounce. Thinking about the situation, and remembering an episode that had happened when I was in Baku eleven years before, I sat down and wrote "A Little Flyer in Inflation," retelling (and taking many liberties with the truth) an incident in which my friend Peggy Marquis and I had meddled with Azerbaijan's exchange rate. In my story, Peggy and I are hauled before a panel of Russian judges to explain how and why we had managed to bid up the ruble, thereby destroying its value. One of the judges exclaims, "This is chaos, chaos! People cannot live without some fixed standard, a firm standard of value." In the story, I wrote that "money is a matter of faith—as thirty-six inches are a yard only because multitudes agree to that measure of length and keep that agreement." If the agreement was broken, "faith was gone, and any tangible thing to eat, to wear, to shelter one's body from the weather was more valuable than any number of pieces of paper, which were only symbols of a lost faith."

"A Little Flyer in Inflation" was a parable, for me, of what was going to happen now that Roosevelt had effectively taken the country off the gold standard and given the government the right to create money. *Harper's Monthly* agreed. They bought the story immediately.

11. *A* YEAR OF LOSSES: 1933

The year 1933 was worse than 1932, and I would rather just skip it. But I can't tell this story without including that year—a long, dark year that was a long, dark night of the soul, not just for me, but for most Americans. Many were sick in mind and spirit, many were sick in body, and almost all were adrift in seas of bleak misery. Failed hope is a knife that slashes all moorings.

In 1933, thirteen million people, a third of the workforce, had no work. People who lost their jobs moved themselves and their families into makeshift housing with little to eat and no way to stay warm and dry. Dispossessed farmers stuffed their belongings into dilapidated jalopies and headed for California in pursuit of a dream of plenty, only to find a cruel desert. Homeless men hopped freight trains and rode the rails, aiming to hop off in a town where they could exchange work for food—although it was more likely that a railroad detective or the local sheriff would collar them and toss them in jail for vagrancy. But it was the children who suffered the most. Malnutrition and a lack of medical and dental care would doom them to a lifetime of poor health and bad teeth. I knew that from my own painful experience as the child of poverty-stricken parents.

Am I trying to lighten the darkness of those lost months in my life by framing them in the context of a black, black time in the lives of all Americans? Perhaps I am, although I'd rather think

I'm just trying to understand. Yes, of course, I suffered my own personal unhappiness, which spilled into my daily diary and the journal I kept intermittently. But I am more likely to write about my pain and grief in my journal than any fleeting pleasures, so the journal is bleaker by far than my lived life. I once wrote that I would be glad to die, although in the same entry, I noted that I was ordering garden seeds—a startling and slightly irrational intersection of despair and hope, it seems to me now.

Still, I saw clearly the relationship between my personal pain and the country's pain: I was not just *I*, but a metaphor. Trapped as I was at Rocky Ridge, ill, adrift, often unable to work—I was like many people, like all the others who were caught in situations over which they had no control. The sense of national helplessness created by the Depression was enough to blight the dreams of even the sunniest optimist. For me, it was also the awakening of a stronger and more determined political consciousness.

After the positive reception of "Hurricane" as a magazine serial, I was bitterly disappointed by what happened to the book early in 1933. It was published on February 21, to positive reviews. *The Bookman*, for instance, called the book a "rich and moving experience" that was so "natural, direct, and simple" that it might have come from a pioneer journal. Both George Bye and Maxwell Aley assured me that in any normal year, *Hurricane* would have been a best seller. But 1933 wasn't normal and the book wasn't a best seller, not even when its price was lowered from $1.75 to $1.50. People simply weren't buying books—and who could blame them?

During January and February that year, the country was in a panic. Interest rates had gone up, businesses couldn't borrow to pay bills, and the rate of bank failures, already high, spiked even higher. People rushed to their banks to pull out their money or trade their currency for gold, then hurried home to stuff it into mattresses and shoeboxes or bury it in their backyards. In January, President Hoover proposed a national bank holiday to gain control of the situation, but Roosevelt, awaiting his March inauguration, refused to cooperate, and the crisis continued to deepen. States were forced to declare their own bank holidays. In Cleveland, depositors thronging on sidewalks in front of banks were told that they could withdraw only 5 percent of what they had on deposit. In Mansfield, the banks stayed solvent but just barely. Fearing that withdrawals might be limited there, too, my mother withdrew eight hundred dollars and paid off the mortgage on the farm (a better use for the money, both of us thought, than sticking it in the mattress). Everywhere, factories closed, retail shops shut their doors, and nobody, *nobody*, bought books. All this could have been avoided if Roosevelt had cooperated with Hoover, it was said, but FDR was willing to let the whole banking situation go to smash so he could be credited with saving the banks and take advantage of the situation to expand his executive powers.

Roosevelt's inauguration took place at the end of the week following *Hurricane's* publication. In his address, he declared (to cheers and applause) that we had nothing to fear but fear itself, but just in case, he would ask the Congress to give him war powers authority. Almost immediately, he declared a bank holiday. Both of Mansfield's banks were closed for the duration, and if you didn't have enough money in your pocket to buy food or gasoline or pay the electric bill, you were out of luck. There was talk that scrip would be issued either nationally or locally so that there would be money when the banks reopened (if they did), but nobody knew how this would be done or who would do it or how it would work.

Roosevelt gave his first radio talk the next Sunday night. Lucille and I went to the Rock House to listen with the parents, but their radio wasn't working, so all four of us piled into Papa's car and drove to Mrs. Moore's house to hear it. The president's talk seemed to quiet the panic, and people began taking their money back to the banks.

Over the next few weeks and months, FDR cut quite a popular figure, especially because he was also moving to repeal Prohibition. "Beer by Easter!" the newspapers bannered. Roosevelt reminded some of Moses leading the Israelites out of bondage in Egypt, although a few speculated that it might take more than forty years to get the country out of the Depression. It seemed that the American people wanted their government to do something, *anything*, as long as it was done with a confident vigor. Will Rogers remarked, with his usual cynical humor, "The whole country is with him, even if what he does is wrong, they are with him. Just so he does something. If he burned down the Capitol, we would cheer and say, 'Well, we at least got a fire started anyhow!'"

I wasn't cheering. I was reminded not of Moses but of Mussolini, whose growing power I had watched with alarm during and after my years in Albania. And my alarm only grew when the farm bill—the Agricultural Adjustment Act, the AAA— was introduced in a flurry of New Deal bills within days of the inauguration. It was supposed to balance supply and demand for farm crops so that farmers got a decent price for their produce. Under the act, they would be paid to stop growing corn, wheat, rice, and peanuts, among other crops, as well as stop producing milk and butter and raising pigs and lambs. The Supreme Court would declare the AAA unconstitutional a few years later, but in the meantime, the government would pay a million farmers to plow up ten million acres of cotton. Oats and wheat would be burned, even though this year's winter wheat crop had failed. And millions of hogs and cattle would be bought from desperate farmers, then shot.

Across Missouri and Kansas and Oklahoma, across the Midwest and the South, farmers were incredulous. They and their families had worked long and hard to raise their crops and livestock, and it hurt like hell to see them plowed under or killed—especially when the meat simply went to waste. AAA payments might be the farmer's only source of income and the federal buyout of his crops and livestock might have saved him from bankruptcy or even starvation. But he hated the AAA and Roosevelt and himself and crept away in shame with the money in his hand.

In farm communities everywhere there was open rebellion. In Mansfield, even people who had voted for FDR were heard to mutter darkly, "No government is gonna tell me what to grow." Or "Taking money from the government to stop farming is just the same as going on the dole. I ain't a-gonna do it!" My father was dead set against the idea, and for weeks, that's all he talked about, threatening to shoot any federal agent who tried to shoot his cows. Mr. Olds, managing editor of the *Springfield Leader,* told me that a revolution was coming and advised me to stock up on food: "A thousand dollars in canned goods is better than a thousand in currency, Mrs. Lane—although you couldn't scratch up a thousand dollars in currency anywhere. Not even ten dollars. Banks've been tee-totally cleaned out."

I didn't fool myself, though, that an earlier solution to America's banking crisis would have helped *Hurricane.* People who had money were holding on to every nickel, and people who stood in soup lines couldn't afford to fork over $1.50 to read a book. It would enjoy a modest sale of more than ten thousand copies, even going into a fourth printing in midyear. But that was months away, and by that time, my hopes for a decent sale for my first serious piece of writing—writing that came from my heart—had withered and died. I felt the way a mother must feel when her child, in whom she has invested all her love and care, is rejected. I understood why, but understanding didn't ease the sense of loss.

But I was beginning to think of another project, for which *Hurricane* might be a kind of prologue. It would be a multivolume series of historical tales that together would make up one large novel, the connected dramas of American settlement, ranging across the continent from east to west. I wanted to make this a popular novel, a sales success, but also a *serious* novel, and I thought seriously and ambitiously about it, even indulging myself in drawing up the grand scheme with the same enthusiasm with which I once drew up schemes for Albanian houses.

However, it wasn't long before I saw with something like despair that I wasn't brave enough to do this kind of epic work, to risk such a vast expenditure of time and effort. I simply didn't have the courage. Realistically speaking, I didn't have the time, either. A grand, beautiful novel of this scale would take years, and I didn't have years to think and plan and write. I had to produce stuff that would *sell*. And I had to do my mother's work, as well.

At least, that's what I told myself. Or perhaps it was that I was simply afraid of attempting big work, afraid of making a fool of myself, of appearing ridiculous. It's a cheap vanity never to attempt big work, so that I never have to say I've failed.

All this was going through my mind during the month I spent on *Farmer Boy*. I felt a sulky exasperation at having to do this—for a second time—instead of my own work. I told myself that the royalties would certainly ease my parents' financial situation. And I was giving my mother a generous gift of my time—I ought to be able to take at least a little pleasure in that. But even that was difficult because having to accept my help was so difficult for *her*.

Perhaps that's why she tried to diminish some of my pleasure in the small success of *Hurricane*. I had given her my advance copy of the book, signed, of course, and I thought she might even read it, since some of the episodes were built on paragraphs from "Pioneer Girl." But when she came over for tea one day and happened on the trade advertisement for *Hurricane*, she pretended to be puzzled about the setting and the characters.

"Caroline and Charles don't belong in that place—in the Dakotas—at that time." She was frowning at me over her reading glasses. "They were in Wisconsin when they married. And when they lived in the dugout, they weren't newlyweds. They already had three children—Mary and Carrie and me."

Really, I shouldn't be hurt by this silliness. I should have simply laughed and shrugged it off, since she was so obviously missing the point. I wasn't writing about Charles and Caroline: I had chosen those names to honor my grandparents, not to tell their story.

But *her* point was something very different. She was letting me know, once again, that my fiction was less truthful, and hence less significant, than her true-life stories. And later, I heard some talk in town that she resented my use of a few fragments of "her" family story, although I had grown up hearing them and they were my stories, too.

Of course, town gossip always magnifies family disagreements, and I doubted that my mother—so circumspect, even secretive, about her private affairs—would publicly air what she would consider a family disagreement. Still, my disappointment in *Hurricane's* sales had made me raw, and her undisguised disregard for my work was another turn of the screw. It was the same kind of thing that had made me so miserable when I was a child and she found fault with my efforts to help her. Do any of us ever outgrow those old childhood hurts, or do they gnaw and fester in our spirits the whole length of our lives?

But of all the desperate losses of those dark, terrible months, there was one that hurt more than all the others put together. In February, on a day when the radio was full of bad news, the skies were an unforgiving gray, and the temperature barely climbed above zero, Mr. Bunting was hit by a car. Catharine was with me then; she found him crawling up to the house, covered in blood. He died later that day and we buried him on the hill, where he had loved to bark at the birds. His was a worse loss than any I had experienced since the loss of my child, and I couldn't seem to get over it. There were moments I felt a kind of dull relief because he was gone: he was often muddy, frequently sick, and always running off. But any relief, if that's what it was, was immediately smothered by a terrible longing for his gay, gallant, fearless little self. And then by an even more terrible loathing of *myself,* for my lack of tenderness, of love, of attention. If I had been more watchful, if I had taken better care of him, if I had loved him more—

But that was wrong, just wrong. Perhaps I hadn't been watchful enough, but I *had* loved him, loved him with a hard, fierce sweetness, as I would have loved my child. And he had loved *me.* He had run into my room every morning as I was dressing to lick my bare toes. He had snuggled in my lap every evening, as I read or played chess. Now he was gone and it wasn't just the little dog I mourned, but the loss of that love, mine and his. Would I ever love again? Would I *dare?* I couldn't stop crying. For months, it seemed, I couldn't stop crying—not just for Bunty but for *all* of it. For all I had lost, for the little dog, for the book, for Troub and Albania and our lost, beautiful dream.

After Bunting's death, the days and weeks were unrelievedly dark. The final portion of the *Hurricane* advance arrived and was paid out in bills, and there was no more coming. Thinking to relieve the situation, my mother, who always said with a long sigh how much she hated to depend on me as her "sole source of support," brought me two money-saving schemes, little dramas of self-sacrifice, of martyrdom.

The first involved cutting off her electricity. She proffered this sacrifice with the brave, playful reminder that she had managed perfectly well without it for most of her life and could manage perfectly well without it now. Cutting off the Rock House, she pointed out, would reduce my electric bill by half. (Never mind that her furnace wouldn't run without it, not to mention the refrigerator and the hot water heater and the cistern pump.)

"I really wouldn't do that, Mama Bess," I murmured evasively. "Let's not be in a hurry—something is bound to turn up." She was easily dissuaded, of course, and the conversation ended with my giving her a check for sixty dollars, which she took only on condition that I'd tell her if I needed it back. Two months later, the electricity at Rocky Ridge was cut off briefly, until I sold a story to the *Saturday Evening Post* and paid the overdue bill.

Another, more drastic solution, I actually welcomed—at first. Mama Bess came to me with the idea of selling the Rock House and the Newell Forty. Mr. Lynn, who handled farm properties in the area, had told my father that he thought it would sell for seven thousand dollars. The parents could move back to the farmhouse, now that there was electricity and water and an automatic furnace, and they might be able to find someone who could live in the tenant house and do the farm chores and the yard work in trade for the rent. I could go, I could leave. I could escape to New York. I could travel again!

But even as my heart leapt up with a kind of idiotic joy at the thought of getting away, it fell back again under the weight of knowing that the idea would come to nothing. This was an impossible time to list a farm property for sale. Nobody had the money to buy. The banks didn't have the money to lend.

When I pointed this out, my mother replied in a tone of great reasonableness, as if she had also thought about it, that if the house couldn't be sold, it could certainly be rented. She and Papa could come back to the farmhouse and live with me, and we would save money and make money at the same time and be such good company for one another.

I mumbled, again, that we really oughtn't be hasty, that something was bound to turn up, and we should just stay where we were for the time being, in our own two comfortable houses.

Get away—get away! Oh, if only I could! And if only my mother would stay in her own comfortable house, stop dropping in for "just a minute or two" and staying all afternoon, stop telephoning, stop interrupting. She wasn't writing, she announced: that is, she hadn't yet started the book she was calling her "Indian" book. She was at loose ends, with nothing to do and nowhere to go unless Papa drove her to town or a friend came to get her. She was lonely.

I recognized loneliness because I was often lonely, and I felt that she was reaching out, trying to find or create an easier, less tense connection with me. But I was incapable of welcoming that connection, and not just because I resented her interruptions or the unappreciated work I did on her books. In those days, I heard a barb buried in every sentence, an expectation in every offer, a demand in every smiling invitation. She and I were like neighboring states with a long and problematic history, with shared and very porous boundaries, she constantly invading, I continually repelling. I had to fulfill my obligations, but if I were to allow her invasions, I would be overrun, smothered, swallowed up. If I were to be *I,* I had to push her away. When I did, she felt rejected and abandoned and stepped up her demands. These periodic sallies and skirmishes intensified my despair about the situation in which I had been trapped, without hope of release, since I was a child. My sense of guilty obligation was born of those terrible days when I could never do what she asked fast enough or well enough to meet her expectations or her demands, yet I had to try and try again. Here I was at midlife, still trying—and the trying was making me sick.

I was reminded of this on the street in Mansfield one day not long after Roosevelt's inauguration, when Mrs. Watson, who fancied herself something of a seer, looked at my mother's palm and told her that she could always count on getting what she wanted. (Mrs. Watson had known my mother for more than thirty years. I doubted that she had discovered this quite obvious truth in her friend's palm.)

My mother was delighted. "I always have," she replied with her sweetest little smile and looked down at her outstretched palm as if to get what she wanted, all she had to do was hold it out. I heard the complacency in her voice and understood that all my child and adult efforts to please her had come to this: that my mother could get whatever she wanted whenever she wanted it, and she knew it and was pleased. While I, who must pay for everything, would never get anything I truly wanted.

Well. Looking back, I think now that it was this emotional strain that made me physically ill. ("If my subconscious is playing tricks on me I will wring its neck," I wrote in my diary, after one bout of illness). Or it might have been a recurrence of the malaria I contracted in 1922, when Peggy Marquis and I were traveling in the Balkans for the Near East Relief Agency. I spent a week in a private sanitarium in Budapest, and Peggy and I spent another week in the American hospital in Constantinople.

"The malaria of Albania," I wrote to Guy then, "is unmatched for its ferocity." My playful tone didn't match the way I felt. Peggy and I were treated with the usual massive dose of quinine—sixty grains of the stuff twice a week—and spent the days between treatments recovering from the treatments. I've never been sure which was worse: the malaria or the side effects of the quinine. I was so ill that I lost the fear of death.

Now, nine years later, I was sick again, with what might have been a malarial relapse, or a psychosomatic illness, or the flu, or my bad teeth, or a thyroid imbalance (that was the doctor's diagnosis). I knew I needed to use the energy from *Hurricane* to create more magazine opportunities for myself, so between bouts of illness—and operating on sheer will—I managed to drag myself to the typewriter and produce a new story and two rewrites, which I sent to George Bye in April, as well as a third story and another rewrite in May. How I did it, I have no idea. But I had done well: one of the stories sold to *Ladies' Home Journal,* another to *American Magazine,* and the third to the *Saturday Evening Post.* Together, they brought in more than thirteen hundred dollars—a great relief, although it was half of what I'd been getting before everything had gone smash.

The weather, which was simply apocalyptic, made it even harder to work—and might have been responsible for some of my illness. The winter had been warm and dry, except for one mid-April blizzard. Spring was short and hot and dry. Summer was drier and hotter, with a furnace-like wind that exhausted me on the short walk out to the garden, which required constant watering. The newspapers said that the drought in the Midwest and on the Plains, now of two years' standing, had broken a half-century record. Around Mansfield, at the end of June, the summer's hay was cured, uncut, as it stood in the field, while the leaves of the young corn rolled up to protect the plant from moisture loss. Only a couple of hundred miles to the west, dust storms blanketed the land with black, billowing clouds of blown soil; caught on the winds, it fell on us, too.

I lost too many days to illness, but by June I was back at work, despite the awful, mind-numbing heat. George Bye wrote that Erskine Caldwell (the author of *Tobacco Road* and *God's Little Acre*) had contacted him to "nail down" an option for a film adaptation of *Hurricane*. Caldwell was working as a screenwriter for King Vidor at Metro-Goldwyn-Mayer and was responsible for pursuing possible stories. Bye offered a short-term option at seventy-five hundred dollars and authorized the rights to MGM for nine thousand dollars, with the fifteen-hundred-dollar difference to go to Caldwell.

I was hopeful, oh so hopeful. When I imagined *Hurricane* on the screen, I thought of Katharine Hepburn, who was starring that year as Jo in *Little Women*. Hepburn would portray Caroline as a young woman with backbone, endurance, and faith in an unseen future. And the option money would pay my debts and set me free. It bothered me that the fifteen hundred dollars to Caldwell was a bribe, but I was willing to pay it—and more—if it meant that the book would become a movie.

I wrote to George Bye telling him to make the deal if he could. But I might have saved my effort, for the project came to nothing. I learned several years later that Vidor had left the studio at the same time that Caldwell had reached the end of his MGM contract. Out of such small misses and miscues is history made—or unmade. I'm glad I didn't know that then. I wanted the film, oh, yes, and very badly. But would I have wanted Erskine Caldwell's adaptation? I remember *Tobacco Road* and think probably not.

And then I thought of something else I wanted to do—something different, yet related. Years before, in the *San Francisco Bulletin* days, I had written a series of articles called "Soldiers of the Soil," about farming in California's Central Valley. Now that *Hurricane* had established me as a writer on Plains pioneers, I thought of doing an article on the dire situation of wheat farmers on the drought-stricken High Plains. I had been reading about their plight in the newspapers and seeing it in the context of Roosevelt's Agricultural Adjustment Act, which was paying farmers to take their wheat land out of production. I proposed the idea to George Bye and he pitched it to the *Saturday Evening Post*. In mid-July, the *Post* commissioned it.

After Lucille Murphy had returned from our drive to upstate New York the previous autumn, she had decided to give her marriage one more try. "I just don't have the ruthlessness it takes to cut myself loose," she told me ruefully. "At least, not now." I asked her to go with me to do the research for the *Post* article. I broached the subject the week after I heard from the *Post,* one night when she and Eddie had come over for a supper of fried chicken and fresh sweet corn.

"It'll be a two-week driving trip," I said, "across Oklahoma and Kansas. I'm making a list of people I need to interview. We'll see a lot of country," I added, "although it'll be hot. And dusty."

"Sounds nice, Rose," Lucille said, tilting her head. "I'd like to, actually. Just us girls." She glanced at her husband. "I'm sure Eddie can take care of himself while we're gone. He'd rather have chow with the boys at the café than eat my cooking, anyhow."

"Oklahoma and Kansas?" Eddie hooted. "In this heat?" He was a short man, in his thirties and not bad looking but already going to belly. "That's the damn stupidest idea I ever heard, Rose. Don't you know what's goin' on out there, with them dust storms and all? If you gotta go, put it off until the weather ain't so hot."

"I can't," I said, trying to be polite. "The *Post* wants the article for the September issue." I turned to Lucille. "What do you think, Lucille? Are you game?"

"Nothin' doin'," Eddie said flatly, and reached for another piece of fried chicken. "Lucille's got better sense."

That decided the matter. Lucille was in favor of doing anything Eddie didn't want her to do.

"Well, pooh on you, Eddie. You're just an old spoilsport stick-in-the-mud." She puffed out her pretty mouth. "Sure, Rose. I'll go. We'll share the driving. It'll be swell fun."

It wasn't swell fun. It was a grinding trip, a weary, scorching drive across drought-stricken, dust-blighted prairie, with stops in Tulsa, Ponca City, Tonkawa, Enid. North into Kansas, to Wichita and west to Dodge City, then north again to Hays and Salina, then back east to Kansas City and home. During the trip, I interviewed some two dozen people—farmers, ranchers, farm association directors, grain elevator operators, newspaper editors, county agents—and attended several farmers' meetings.

What I saw was deeply dispiriting. From eastern Oklahoma to western Kansas, there was no green to be seen anywhere. What had once been productive wheat land was swept clean by the wind, the soil drifted in brown, wind-sculpted dunes along fences and against buildings. This was not the country of the pioneers I had written about in *Hurricane,* where the wild grasses reached to the horizon in every direction, dancing to the wind that blew out of a clean, bright sky. The grass of fifty years ago was gone, the protective pelt of sod plowed under, the soil, millions of acres of it, sowed to wheat. When the rains stopped, the wheat died. The earth was left bare. What little moisture remained in the subsoil was baked out of it by the relentless sun. The unforgiving wind scraped it up and flung it into the air in boiling clouds two miles high, moving with a blinding force across the land, scouring paint from buildings, blasting the bark from trees, the flesh from animals.

Dust, dirt, wind. "We know where the dust comes from by its colors," one farmer's wife told me, holding her apron across her face. "Red dirt blows in from eastern Oklahoma, yellow-orange comes up from Texas, black comes down from northern

Kansas. Sometimes it's all colors, mixed up together. Sometimes it turns the sun bright orange." She shook her head, marveling at the memory. "I've even seen the sun with a rainbow around it. A rainbow, but no rain."

Lucille and I drove with the windows closed, but the car filled with dust and we had to tie handkerchiefs over our noses and mouths. When we stopped at a roadside café, empty because there was no traffic on the road, there was dust on the table and grit in our sandwiches. In our hotel rooms, the furniture was furred with dust and the floors were gritty underfoot.

The dust wasn't just ugly and unpleasant. It was deadly. In Dodge City, we saw people on the street wearing masks distributed by the Red Cross. In less than an hour, one man told me, a clean white mask would be black with dust. Prairie soil, he said, was rich in silica. It had the same effect on people's lungs as coal dust on the lungs of miners. The *Hays Daily News* reported that in the previous three months, dust pneumonia had killed twenty—half of the victims were children. Cattle and sheep, their lungs filled with dirt, suffocated in the fields where they stood. They didn't fall over: they were held upright by the dust that was blown around and over them.

Businesses were paralyzed. The winter wheat crop was gone, and even when the flour mills could get grain, they often had to send workers home because the blowing dust couldn't be kept out of the flour. Hospitals delayed surgeries because the dust filtered into operating rooms. Foreclosure sales were postponed due to dust storms, and the cattle auctions and feedlots had gone out of business. Dunes drifted across the roads and travelers had to stop and shovel their way through. A locomotive in Kansas was derailed when it ran into a dune newly drifted across the tracks. Roosevelt made a train trip through the Plains states; at one stop, a farmer held up a homemade sign: YOU GAVE US BEER. NOW

GIVE US RAIN. The president shook his head. "Beer was the easy part," he said. He was booed.

I had gone to political rallies before—in Louisiana, where Aunt E. J. was a supporter of the socialist Eugene V. Debs; in New York, to a Communist meeting with Jack Reed—but I had never seen people in such a dark mood. They were angry. They were rebellious. Everything about Roosevelt's New Deal agricultural schemes went against the grain of these yeoman farmers who had never taken a dime—or a dime's worth of advice—from a government agency. Some of them were beginning to understand that their mistakes in land management were as responsible as the weather for the terrible fix they were in, and they could see the need to change their farming methods. They were ready to rotate crops, fallow the land, and abandon their sod-busting ways—whatever it took to make the land productive again.

But the scorching heat, the wind, the drifting dust had already drastically reduced the arable acreage. The farmers felt that Roosevelt's scheme to pay them not to plant was as idiotic as his plan to fix the price of wheat. They feared a famine. They wanted a free market. They didn't believe that the New Deal would help them cope with the dilemma that nature had pressed on them.

Many others swallowed their anger and simply persevered. Like Caroline in *Hurricane,* when the wind blew and the dust came, they lived through moments of blind, blank terror at the vast indifference of nature; moments of courage that made them strong even as they knew the infinite smallness of human life; and moments of pride in their own indomitable efforts. I listened, humbled, as they told me they had read *Hurricane* when it came out in the *Post* and had passed the magazine from hand to hand until the pages felt out. They had seen themselves in Caroline: the waist-deep snows she attacked with her shovel were like the waist-deep dust drifts they had to shovel aside to get to the barn.

The darkness in the heart of her blizzard was the same blackness of their dust storms. They were Caroline. They were metaphors for all Americans, in the bleakness of the Depression, steady in their resolve to stay.

But no, not all. Between Dodge City and Hays, heading west, we picked up a hitchhiker, a dark-haired boy of sixteen or seventeen in a ragged red flannel shirt, the collar frayed, the elbows out, half the buttons missing. He had left his mother's farm outside of Independence, he said, despite her pleas to stay and finish school. His father had died and he was going to California, where he would find work and send money home to his mother and younger sisters.

He grinned when he said that, and added, "Ain't everybody? Going to California, I mean. All the boys I know, they're going to California."

"You don't have to go that far," I said, and something compelled me to add, "We'll be heading back to Missouri in a few days. You might find more work there." I thought of Rocky Ridge and the oats to be cut, the corn to be shelled, the barn to be painted, the weeds in the flower border to be pulled. "I expect you would find work in Missouri," I said, emphatically now. "You'd make enough to be able to send money home to your mother."

"Naw." The boy grinned, showing missing teeth. "It's west for me. Ain't you never heard the old saying, missus? Go west, young man. Go west." He jerked his thumb at his chest. "Me, I'm going west. I'm going west and make my fortune."

Go West, young man, go West and grow up with the country. It was Horace Greeley who wrote that, in 1865, two years before my mother was born, four years before my Ingalls grandparents left their little house in the Big Woods and loaded up their wagon and their two little girls and set out for Missouri and then for Indian Territory, where the native grasses grew tall and the heavy black soil, once broken and sown to wheat, proved richer and more fertile than a man's most optimistic dreams. Where the country had grown up and filled up with farmers and their children and now that fertile black soil filled the air like a boiling black nightmare.

"Yep," the boy mused, staring down the thin thread of road that stretched to the horizon, to somewhere else, to the not-here. "Yep. I ain't gonna be no farmer, not me. Got enough dirt in my lungs to last me a dadgum lifetime. I mean to get me a job in the movies. If I cain't do that, I'll live in one of them Hoover camps and be a picker."

When we got to Hays, the boy left us and headed for the train yard to hop a freight. I gave him three dollars for food, and he gave me a grin, his lips so chapped they were cracking. "Thanks, missus," he said. "Gee, thanks."

And then, as if the boy had opened my eyes, I began to see the other people who were giving up and heading west. I saw old cars and trucks with boxes and bedding piled high and roped on, children and dogs and chicken crates perched dangerously on the lopsided loads. But they weren't all headed west. One farmer told me that his wife had taken their children east to Vermont, to her parents' farm, where they could breathe clean air. If they didn't go, the doctor said, they would be dead before the year was out. The farmer had promised to follow when he could.

The man stared at me for a long moment, his bleak, dark-rimmed eyes sunk deep in a dust-streaked face. And then he said something that struck like a lance to my heart.

"That stuff at the end of your magazine story, about that baby growing up to a big white house and acres of wheat fields—it's a damned lie." His voice was thick and raspy with dust, heavily accusing. "It might make some folks feel good, might even make people back East feel like it's still possible to settle out here and get themselves a farm and make a living off of it. But it just isn't so. If you're going to write any more stories about pioneers, for God's sake, tell people the truth. Don't give them any more of those phony happy endings. Show them this." He gestured, a helpless, hopeless gesture, toward his barn, half-buried under dust dunes, his skeletal cattle, waiting for the federal executioners. "*This* is what it comes to, missus. *This* is your hurricane."

My hurricane. I looked around at the death of the man's dreams, at the end of his hopes. And from that moment on, I could see nothing but blowing dust, starving animals, and people who moved like sleepwalkers and talked in voices so raspy that it was almost impossible to make out what they were trying to say.

Back at Rocky Ridge, I spent four days in early August working on the article, then scrapped what I had done and started over again. It was called "Wheat and the Great American Desert," and it appeared—a dull, bland, badly written piece—in the *Post* in late September. I lacked the courage to include the things I had seen and heard and felt in that desert—and now understood. If I had written the truth, the *Post* would not have printed it. No magazine in the country would have printed it—at least, not then. They were all looking for hope, and I had none.

And then I was sick again—thyroid deficiency, according to Dr. Anderson in Springfield, who sent me home to bed with a half-dozen medicines. Or maybe it was bad teeth, or another malarial relapse. Or maybe it was despair.

"*This* is your hurricane," the farmer had said. My hurricane, and like the dust storms, the black blizzards, it had swept away all hope.

I spent the next few weeks in bed, suffering from aches and weariness and constantly pounding headaches, discovering that the bed was a refuge, the only escape I could manage from the terrible losses the year had brought—the pain, the disappointments, the despair. *All we have to do is remain invincible*: Mary Margaret's glib, facile phrase was now freighted with a cosmic irony. But I no longer thought of being invincible, or even courageous. I was incapable of courage. I knew I had nothing to show of my life but the end of hope, the end of love.

That was why, I thought, that no medicine could stop the pain pounding in my head. And why I so desperately missed little Bunting, the last creature on this earth that had loved me, the last creature that I should ever love.

But I was wrong. There was John.

PART FOUR

12. KING STREET: APRIL 1939

Norma Lee noticed that the rain had started again about the time Russell joined them and they sat down to lunch. She had picked a bowl of lilacs for the center of the table, and they feasted on chicken vegetable soup, cabbage slaw, homemade Sally Lunn buns, farm cheese, and the last of the apple cobbler from the night before, topped with fresh whipped cream.

Mrs. Lane loved to cook, especially when she was cooking for guests, and the food on her table was always abundant and excellent. The cabbage and soup vegetables had come from a local farmer, and the milk, cream, and cheese came from the neighbor who also supplied both eggs and chickens. Norma Lee wasn't sure how she felt about Mrs. Lane's determination to avoid buying government-subsidized foods whenever possible—it meant a great deal of extra work. But she understood the principle and was definitely in favor of fresh farm eggs and cream that could be churned into butter or whipped and sweetened and dolloped onto warm apple cobbler.

It was probably a good idea to buy food from the neighbors, too. With all the scary European news—Mussolini and Hitler joining forces, German children being required to join Hitler Youth, and Stalin demanding a British, French, and Russian anti-Nazi pact—the times were terribly unsettled. Of course, the United States was not going to get involved with whatever happened over there. If it came to war, it was *their* war. Still, lots of people were saying that they aimed to grow as much of their food as they could, just in case. You never could tell what might happen.

Mrs. Lane put down her coffee cup and tilted her head, listening. "Was that the mail carrier's car I heard?"

"I'll get it," Norma Lee said quickly, knowing that Mrs. Lane always liked to see the mail as soon as it came.

"You ladies stay put." Russell pushed his chair back from the table and stood. "It's raining. I'll go out and get it."

"Let me find my umbrella for you," Mrs. Lane said, getting up. "And do watch out when you pull up the lid on the mailbox, Russell. It wants to snap down on your fingers."

"Yes, ma'am," Russell said dutifully and winked at Norma Lee as he followed Mrs. Lane onto the porch.

Norma Lee returned the wink with a smile. Russell called it "Mrs. Lane's mother hen complex"—her habit of looking out for you and everybody else within shouting distance, giving instructions, making sure you had what you needed (or what *she* thought you needed) and then offering more: more advice, more help, more money. She seemed to be motivated by an extraordinary spirit of generosity, giving not just her time and attention but loans and gifts of money, even when she was short of cash—as she always was.

But beneath the surface, Russell had glimpsed something else. "If it moves and breathes," he had told Norma Lee a few days before, "Mrs. Lane will find a way to take care of it. Or mother it, or manage it—comes to the same thing in the end." One eyebrow raised, he regarded Norma Lee. "Including you, wife. You don't get something for nothing, you know."

Norma Lee had to agree. She admired Mrs. Lane enormously and was delighted—thrilled, even—that such an experienced, accomplished writer would be willing to help her improve her writing. She had been surprised, too, when Mrs. Lane had invited her and Russell to come to Danbury and stay for as long as they liked, whenever they liked. At first, she'd been reluctant to impose, but when it became clear that Russell's carpentry skills and her willing help with the housework (Mrs. Lane was *not* a good housekeeper) were a fair trade for their board and room, she felt better about it.

"It's a small price to pay," Norma Lee said. "She's a gifted writer and a wonderful person. And the best teacher I've ever had. Her mothering doesn't bother me in the slightest." She studied her husband. Russell was an easygoing guy, and nothing much ever got under his skin. But even he had his limits. "You don't mind it?" she asked tentatively.

He shrugged. "It's okay with me, hon, if it's okay with you." He paused, raising one dark eyebrow. "Some people can't deal with it, though. They don't like to be told what to do, even if it is entirely well meant. They think they're being manipulated. Pushed around."

Norma Lee knew exactly whom he was talking about. John Turner, whom Mrs. Lane described as her "somewhat-adopted" son, had recently come to Danbury to stay for a few days. While he was there, he and Russell had talked, although Russell actually did the listening while John did the talking. And there was a lot of talk because John had stored up a lot of complicated feelings over the years since Mrs. Lane had taken him in.

"It's tough for the kid," Russell had told Norma Lee at the time. "Her standards for him are always higher than he's able to meet, especially when it comes to academics. He says himself that he's just not disciplined enough for college—that's why he flunked out at Lehigh. Of course, he feels terrible, after all she's done for him. And he can't seem to stop taking whatever she's willing to give him, which only makes him feel worse."

Norma Lee didn't know the details, but she understood that John Turner, now twenty-one, had been Mrs. Lane's project since he was fourteen. She had fed him, clothed him, housed him, and given him a year at a military prep school in New Mexico, as well as a summer's tour of Europe (with a tutor, no less), a year at the Sorbonne, and a semester at Lehigh—until he flunked out.

Then, at loose ends, he declared that he wanted to become a journalist and had gone to New York. Mrs. Lane arranged interviews with magazine and newspaper editors she knew, found him a one-room apartment, and opened a joint checking account in a New York bank for the two of them, where he could draw fifteen dollars a week—enough to live on if he was careful— until he found a job. The interviews were unsuccessful, he had overdrawn the checking account, and he hadn't found a job. It was Russell's impression that he hadn't looked very hard. In fact, John had as much as said, why bother to get work when the checking account was available?

John's guilty resentment had erupted on Sunday morning over a splendid breakfast of pancakes and maple syrup, scrambled eggs, and sausage. Mrs. Lane had asked him to help Russell paint the walls in an upstairs room. He said he was going back to New York. When she insisted (and reminded him of the overdrawn checking account), he had blown up at her, stalked out of the house, and slammed the door so hard that a picture had fallen off the wall with a shatter of breaking glass. Both Norma Lee and Russell had been embarrassed, and Mrs. Lane had turned away to hide the sudden tears that came to her eyes.

But a moment later she turned back, shook her head, and said, quite surprisingly, "I wonder how many times I wanted to walk out on my mother and slam the door, but didn't quite have the courage."

Norma Lee's first thought was that if Mrs. Lane had walked out and slammed the door on her mother just once, her whole life might have been different. But, of course, she didn't say that. Instead, she offered a little story about the time she had told her mother she hated her—and when her mother had burst into tears, she had been so ashamed that they had wept together.

"I think you must have a very understanding mother," Mrs. Lane said quietly, with something like resignation. "I would like to meet her someday." She glanced at Russell's empty plate and got up. "Russell, you're ready for more pancakes. There's plenty of batter left. Shall I fry three, or would you like four?"

Norma Lee thought that armchair psychologizing was cheap and silly. But in one of her college psych courses, the professor had speculated that daughters learned their mothering styles from their own mothers, who had learned from their mothers and so on. Norma Lee found herself wondering whether Mrs. Lane had inherited her "mother hen complex" from her mother, which could account for the fact that Mrs. Lane saw her mother as managing and controlling—even as she felt obliged to manage and mother *her*. That double-faceted irony might have produced the subsidy Mrs. Lane had begun giving her mother in 1920, which struck Norma Lee as something like her own childhood allowance. And there was that expensive little house she had built for her parents, and the books she was ghostwriting for her mother. (She might not like to call it ghostwriting, but if anyone else but Mrs. Wilder's daughter were doing that job—or if Mrs. Lane were doing it for any other author—that's exactly what it would be called.) Generosity, yes. Obligation, yes. But Norma Lee glimpsed something else, although she wasn't quite able to put her finger on it. Something about those books. Something about the daughter creating the mother's warm and happy child-hood, perhaps to make up for her own lonely, poverty-stricken childhood. No, not just that but more: the daughter inventing the mother, giving her the identity she had always wanted, as a famous, prize-winning author. And if that wasn't management and control, Norma Lee didn't know what else it could be.

Yes, cheap armchair psychologizing, and no doubt there was more to it than that. But it was a reasonable explanation for the complex mother-daughter drama in which Mrs. Lane and her mother seemed to be engaged. Norma Lee remembered what Mrs. Lane had said the previous evening, about the battle of wills she had fought with her mother since she was old enough to realize how good it felt to be willful. "She was afraid of what I would come to if she let me go, and I was afraid of what I would come to if she held on," Mrs. Lane had said—which would explain a great deal about the tug of war that seemed to be going on between them. And between Mrs. Lane and John: another battle of wills and a different-but-similar mother-child drama. Russell had said that he wouldn't be at all surprised if John decided to make a complete break, and Norma Lee agreed.

Now, Mrs. Lane came back into the kitchen and sat down at the table. "Do have another piece of apple cobbler," she said, pushing the plate toward Norma Lee. "And there's more whipped cream in the refrigerator."

Norma Lee was trying to think of a way to refuse the second helping when she was rescued by Russell, coming in with the mail. He put two letters and a newspaper on the table beside Mrs. Lane's plate. "Not good news, I'm afraid," he said.

She picked up the newspaper. "Oh, dear," she said under her breath and then read the headline aloud. "FDR Urges 10-Year Peace Pledge in Surprise Note to Mussolini, Hitler." She traced her finger down the column to another story on the same page, reading: "Allies Push Russian Alliance: Three-Power Armed Pact Urged to Bolster Encirclement of Axis." And another: "Poland

Joins with Rumania: Pledges Exchanged for Resistance to Nazi Aggression." She laid the paper down with a frown. "Such a lot of hullabaloo. Newspapers like to make their readers think there's going to be a war—any war, anywhere. They sell more papers that way."

Russell paused at the door, about to go back to work. "You don't think there'll be war?"

"Not if I have anything to say about it." Mrs. Lane gave a short laugh. "Which, of course, I don't."

"Don't be too sure," Norma Lee said. She had read Mrs. Lane's articles on the subject in *Cosmopolitan* and *Country Gentleman* and *Woman's Day*. "You're getting quite a reputation for speaking out on the subject."

"I hope so," Mrs. Lane said, putting the newspaper down. "We all need to speak out wherever we can. Next month, I'm going to Washington to testify before a subcommittee of the Senate Judiciary Committee. They're holding hearings again on the Ludlow Amendment."

"I read that support for the amendment has dropped quite a bit over the past two years," Russell remarked, in an offhand way. The bill proposed a Constitutional amendment requiring a national referendum to confirm a declaration of war, except in case of an attack by a foreign power.

"It's not likely to be brought to a vote again," Mrs. Lane said crisply. "Roosevelt and his allies dug in their heels when the amendment was proposed back in '35. Any president would, since it allows the people to curtail the power of government. But that won't stop me from telling the Senate what I think. A government, any government, always has its reasons for going to war—land, power, political advantage, money. But it's the mothers and sons and husbands and wives who have to pay the real cost. They should be entitled to a direct say in the matter."

She gave Russell a frowning look. "And there's still plenty of popular support for it, Russell. The last Gallup poll said that 61 percent of Americans are in favor. That's almost two-thirds."

What Russell thought of Mrs. Lane's staunch isolationism he kept to himself. It would likely result in an argument he couldn't win. She was too quick for him, too nimble with facts and figures and anecdotes that supported her position. But Norma Lee knew that he felt the amendment was about as smart as calling a town meeting to vote on whether to send the fire department to put out a blaze. People would stand around and argue until the whole town was on fire.

"There are the pacifists who never want to go to war under any circumstances," he'd said to Norma Lee not long ago. "And there are the jingoes who want to go to war even when it's a bad idea. I don't like the idea of turning the say-so over to people who lack the information to make a rational decision."

When Russell put it that way, Norma Lee had to agree, although she wasn't sure what a "rational decision" was when you were talking about war. She was from Missouri, like Mrs. Lane. She understood the isolationist sentiment that was so strong throughout the Midwest, and the thought of war made her feel cold inside. If the United States somehow got involved and began sending troops, would Russell want to enlist? Would he *have* to go?

On the other hand, she was an aspiring journalist and spent as much time as she could studying the newspapers' coverage of current events. She had noticed that while the isolationist movement continued strong—Colonel Lindbergh had just returned from England and was taking up the America First battle against involvement—there were increasingly powerful interventionist forces everywhere. Roosevelt was pushing Congress to revise the 1937 Neutrality Act to permit the sale of arms and equipment to England and France. Headlines like those in today's paper were fuel to the fire.

Russell smiled and nodded. "Thanks for the lunch," he said. "I need to get back to work. I want to finish painting the shelves in your study this afternoon, Mrs. Lane. When they're dry, we can start unpacking your books." He pocketed a Sally Lunn bun, whistling as he left the room.

"Tell you what," Norma Lee said. "I'll do the dishes and frost Russell's coconut cake if you will sit right where you are and go on with the story. We'd gotten as far as your trip through Oklahoma and Kansas with Lucille. The summer of '33, I think." Nineteen thirty-three, the year she had entered college. Only six years ago, but already it seemed like ancient history—or a chapter in a national nightmare.

"Well, then." Mrs. Lane got up from the table. "If you wouldn't mind, when you're done with the dishes, you could peel three or four good-sized potatoes to mash for supper. I thought I'd make a meatloaf."

"I can make the meatloaf," Norma Lee offered eagerly. "It's one of my specialties. I can peel the potatoes, too."

Mrs. Lane looked pleased. "Thank you, Norma Lee." She picked up the letters. "While you get started on the dishes, I'll fetch that box of quilt scraps I've been wanting to sort. I find that stories are easier to tell when my hands are busy." With the letters in her hand, she left the room.

Norma Lee filled the dishpan with hot water from the teakettle and began to wash the glasses and cups. She had seen the return addresses on the envelopes. One was from Garet Garrett, a friend and fellow writer—a regular contributor to the *Saturday Evening Post*—who shared Mrs. Lane's anti-New Deal, isolationist opinions. The two wrote frequently. The other was from John Turner.

When the dishes were done and Mrs. Lane had still not returned, Norma Lee went in search. She found her in her reading chair in the living room. Her eyes were red and her cheeks were streaked with tears.

"Why, Mrs. Lane!" Norma Lee exclaimed, kneeling beside her. "What's wrong? What's happened? Is somebody ill?"

Mrs. Lane held out a crumpled letter. It was from John Turner.

Dear Mrs. Lane,

I should probably be down on my knees thanking you for everything you've done for me in the past six years, the schooling, the travel, the clothes, the spending money. But I can't.

Instead, I hate you for being so generous and I despise myself for being nothing but a freeloader, especially when I know you can't afford it. The only way I'll ever be my own man is to stop taking anything from you, and the only way I can do that is to break it off completely.

I hope you won't take it too hard, or blame yourself. You've done everything for me that my own mother would have wanted to do, if she could. Maybe someday I'll be able to say thank you. But for now, all I can say is goodbye.

John

For a moment, Norma Lee was silent. She was no friend of John, but she couldn't help thinking that the boy had glimpsed what Russell had seen: that generosity as a means of controlling someone is no gift at all. It's a curse. But that could never be said. She put the letter down and took Mrs. Lane's hand.

"I'm so sorry," she said quietly. "I know how hard this must be, after all you've done for him. But perhaps it's for the best. He's hurt you so much. It's not fair for him to take and take and never give anything back, not even respect."

"Hush, Norma Lee," Mrs. Lane said. She pulled her hand back, fished in her apron pocket for a handkerchief, and blew her nose. "You have no idea where the boy started or how far he's come. You can't criticize because you don't know what he did for me. You don't know—"

"What *he* did for *you*?" Norma Lee asked sharply. "Well, if you ask me, he's only made you terribly unhappy. Every time I've seen him, he's been insolent, offensive, and uncouth." She jabbed a finger at the letter. "If he doesn't want your generosity, that's one thing. But to break it off like this—"

Mrs. Lane shook her head emphatically. "He rescued me."

"Rescued you?" Norma Lee frowned, thinking of Rexh Meta, who (as Mrs. Lane told the story) had saved her life in the Albanian mountains some twenty years before. That was a rescue. How could John Turner have—

"I was ill and terribly depressed," Mrs. Lane said. "Then John came along and everything changed. *I* changed. After he came, I had something to live for, someone to take care of, someone to . . . love."

Love? "I don't see how," Norma Lee muttered, feeling the sharp scissor-snip of jealousy. Rose Lane was a highly intelligent, well-traveled, sophisticated woman. How could she love a crude, insolent young man like John?

Mrs. Lane sighed. "I suppose I should tell you about it." After a moment, she pushed herself out of the chair. "But first I'll find those quilt scraps. It's a hard story. I need something in my hands while I tell it."

13. MOTHER AND SONS: 1933–1934

"Simply sunk," I wrote in my August journal after Lucille and I returned to Rocky Ridge from our trip through Oklahoma and Kansas. After I finished the wheat article for the *Post,* I put the journal away in a drawer and went to bed. Writing about how terrible I felt, physically and mentally, exhausted me. It only made me feel worse.

Looking back over the year, I could see nothing but losses. Remaining invincible was a mocking cry, a cruel joke. I had written *Hurricane* as a reply to pessimists and a testimony to the valor of the American spirit—and it was. But after my trip through the Dust Bowl, I also saw the story from the point of view of the people who were facing the worst that nature could inflict, saw how its hopeful optimism could be read as false, a tidy cheeriness that was undone by the fiercely corrosive realities of rainless skies, black blizzards, parched and starving livestock. Living at Rocky Ridge—and oh, how the hard truth of that name struck home to me now!—I was utterly isolated: friends, lovers, all gone, even little Bunting, whom I had never loved enough, never cared for enough. I hadn't heard from Rexh in months—he had finished at Cambridge and I wasn't sure where he was. Only my parents remained, and they were little comfort. My father was as taciturn as always. My mother kept exhorting me to get up and get busy around the house, as if it was sheer lazy obstinacy that was keeping me in bed. It was one of the lowest, darkest months of my life. My hurricane, and I wasn't sure I would survive it.

But by late September, the worst of my physical distress had passed. I was shaky and uncertain on my feet, but I got out of bed one Tuesday morning and forced myself to read the latest issue of the *Saturday Evening Post,* which contained my article, "Wheat and the Great American Desert." A bad piece, maybe my worst, even after it was substantially rewritten by someone in *Post* editorial. If they hadn't commissioned it and paid my expenses, I was sure they wouldn't have published it at all. I thought for a while about going to New York, as I usually did in the fall, and renting a cheap room. The magazine market seemed to be easing somewhat—I had a couple of sales to prove it. Surely I could write enough to pay the bills on both places. Or maybe my parents could move back to the farmhouse and rent the—

But the idea glimmered away into the drifting fog of my malaise. Listlessly, I dressed and went downstairs for lunch—the first time in several weeks. Lucille was coming in for a few hours a day to do the housecleaning and cooking, and she had made a nice meal of scrambled eggs with a bit of ham, with biscuits and hot tea. We ate together, and when she finished, she put on her jacket and a headscarf—the day was gray and drizzly—and went out to the box to get the mail. In a few moments, she was back.

"I need to drive to town for flour and sugar," she said, putting several envelopes on the table in front of me. "And cocoa. I want to bake a chocolate cake."

"A cake? For just the two of us?"

"You're downstairs and that's something to celebrate, isn't it? I could fry up a chicken and make some potato salad and we could invite your parents for supper, if you want. They went to Springfield, but your mother said they'd be back by five. I'm sure she'd be glad not to cook tonight." I nodded without enthusiasm and she took her car keys out of her purse. "Want me to get anything for you while I'm in town?"

"You could get me some Drene shampoo," I said. "I suppose I should wash my hair. And please pick up the latest *Scribner's* if you see it. Oh, and *Country Gentleman*." If New York was ever going to be a possibility for me, I had to earn some money. "I should try to catch up on the latest fiction, to see what the magazines are buying."

At the thought of New York, I felt the fog lift a little. If I couldn't go this fall, I could surely manage next spring.

"Shampoo," she said approvingly. "Hair washing. Magazines. You're on the mend, Rose."

When Lucille left, I poured another cup of tea and opened the *Springfield News & Leader*. The front page was nothing but crime stories. John Dillinger and two of his henchmen had held up an Indianapolis bank and got away with twenty-five thousand dollars. Eight gunmen had taken two cash boxes containing as much as one hundred thousand dollars (nobody knew for sure how much it was) from the Railway Express Company in St. Paul. Over in Hays, Kansas, where I had interviewed a rancher and a grain elevator manager the month before, four masked men armed with machine guns had robbed the Farmers State Bank, taken several hostages, and escaped after stealing a car. Closer to home, in Springfield, someone had broken into a chicken coop and made off with a half-dozen hens. "The crooks must've shoved 'em into a sack," the owner said sadly. "Me and the missus heard nary a squawk." I shook my head, wondering if I should try my hand at crime writing. There seemed to be an appetite for it.

Besides the newspaper, there were three letters and a post-card. Troub wrote that she was working as a private nurse to a wealthy man in Boston. She was thinking of making another stab at authorship—a series of books for older girls about nurses, she said. If I was planning to be in New York this fall, maybe I'd come up to Boston and help her with it. And maybe I could suggest some publishing connections for her.

Mary Margaret wrote from Los Angeles, where she had finally found steady work, writing and ghostwriting pulp biographies of Hollywood movie stars that sold in five-and-ten-cent stores. "Polished off Joan Crawford last week," she wrote. "Next week, Betty Boop and Olive Oyl. I swear." In parentheses she added, "The mighty are fallen and the proud brought low. But I'm broke again. I'll do *anything* to earn money." She signed the letter, "Invincibly yours, MM."

A penny postcard from Catharine Brody in New York said simply, "*Cash Item* out at last, reviews middling good. Thanks for putting up with me. Tell your mother and her friends that I'm back where I belong."

Troub with a new job and a writing scheme in Boston. Mary Margaret, broke but still wry and funny in Los Angeles. Catharine with a new book, belonging in New York. And here I sat, alone, isolated, sick, with nothing upstairs in the typewriter, nothing in my mind. I *had* to find a reason to get started again.

I opened George Bye's letter last. Always the cheerleader (a very good trait in an agent), he wondered plaintively if I had fallen off the face of the earth. "We need another Rose Lane story," he wrote. "Adelaide Neall is begging for more of your homestead fiction." Neall had replaced Thomas Costain as the fiction editor at the *Post*. "She's desperate for a follow-up to 'Hurricane'. Can't you pull another one out of your hat? Please please?"

Homestead fiction. I thought of the farmer with the bleak, dark-rimmed eyes sunk in a dust-streaked face and shivered. "*This is your hurricane,*" he'd said, gesturing to the desolate land. I folded George Bye's letter and put it back in the envelope. What could I say to him? That I was flat out of the happy endings the magazines wanted? That there was nothing in my head or my heart that I could put on paper—nothing that anybody would want to read, that is? He wouldn't like to hear that bad news from one of his writers.

There was a knock at the back door. My mother never knocked, and anyway, she and my father had driven to Springfield and wouldn't be back until suppertime. It might be Jess, but he usually yelled, as well as knocking. Or Angela, his wife, wanting to visit. I made a face. I was feeling better, but I was in no mood for company.

But it wasn't company. The boy who stood at the back door was ragged and dirty, his dark hair long around his ears and uneven, as if someone had chopped at it with a knife. He was in his mid-teens, thin-faced and skinny. He wore a red cap and a frayed blue plaid cotton shirt. His shoulders were hunched against the chilly drizzle. He wasn't wearing a jacket.

"Yes?" I asked, reaching for the screen door hook, latching it. I wasn't afraid of the boy, but with all the crime sprees in the news, it would pay to be cautious. He was just a boy, but he might have a companion, lurking somewhere out of sight. We didn't often see hobos this far out of town, more than a mile from the railroad depot where they got off the freights. But Mrs. Moore, on the other side of the Rock House, had reported that a pair of Mr. Moore's bibbed overalls and one of his flannel shirts had disappeared from the clothesline. She reckoned it was a tramp, needing something to wear against the coming winter cold. "I hate it when somebody steals," she had told my mother, "but it ain't Christian to begrudge a poor fella a clean shirt and a pair of overalls. I figger he must need it worse than Mr. Moore."

The boy's glance followed my reach for the screen door hook. He dropped his eyes, but not before I saw the sudden hurt burn in them.

"Don't mean to trouble you none, ma'am." He shoved his fists into his pockets and added defensively, "I ain't lookin' for no handout. I'll trade a half-day's work for a meal." He glanced over his shoulder toward the barn. "Another half-day for a bed in your loft."

The flare of hurt had gone straight to my heart and I was ashamed. More, there was something about the boy—the quick glance out of those dark eyes, the turn of the head, the stubborn set of the shoulders—that reminded me of Rexh, whom I had met when he was just about that age. Or perhaps it was the red cap, pulled jauntily over one eye.

I unhooked the screen and stepped out, pulling my sweater around me against the chilly damp. "Well, then, if you're willing, you can weed that flower border." I pointed. "Just weeds, now, mind you. Let me know when that's done, and I'll give you something else to do." I thought of Lucille's fried chicken and was glad of the chocolate cake. I'd never met a young boy who didn't love chocolate cake. "We usually eat supper around six."

I went back upstairs, sat down at the typewriter, and answered the letters. The keys were familiar under my fingers, the rhythmic clack-clickety-clack cheered me, and it felt good to see words on paper. When I went out to check on the boy's progress, I was surprised to see that he had done an unusually thorough job in spite of the wet. I gave him an old denim jacket of Papa's that was hanging in the porch and put him to work on the iris bed. Several hours later, when he was through with that, I offered him a hot bath in the basement.

His name was John Turner. Bathed and combed, he was quite good looking, with fine dark hair and dark eyes, straight dark brows, and a firm jaw. He was fourteen, he said, from a farm outside of Tulsa. Both his parents had died of tuberculosis the year before, leaving him on his own. He had hopped a freight to Texas, where he worked until the previous December picking cotton, then attended school in El Paso. He went back to Texas this year, he said, but there was no work because the government was making the farmers plow up half their cotton. He'd had some other clothes and a photo of his mother and father. But they were in his bedroll, which had been stolen by a hobo in the freight yard in Texarkana. All he had was what he was wearing.

My parents came for supper, so there were five of us around the table: Mama Bess and Papa, Lucille and I, and the boy. But before we sat down, my mother pulled me into the kitchen to warn me against taking in tramps.

"People in town are saying that if you feed one and give him a bed, word will spread up and down the railroad line and you'll have a passel of hobos beating a path to your door. And not just your door, Rose, but everybody's. Mine and Mrs. Moore's, too, since we're just up the road." She frowned. "Why, I've heard that they put a secret mark on your mailbox, so the other tramps will know that they can get a handout from you."

Maybe. But it did my heart good to watch the boy tuck into Lucille's crisp fried chicken and rich chocolate cake, as if he hadn't eaten for a week—which was likely the truth. He was polite and considerate, and when we got up from the table, he volunteered to wipe the dishes while I washed. Later that evening, Jess made up a bed in the workshop, which was warmer than the barn, and John slept there that night. He got up with a bad cold the next morning (and no wonder, sleeping outdoors and slogging through the wet with no jacket), so I suggested that he stay on for a day or two. The next time Lucille came out from town, she brought some boys' clothing she borrowed from a friend, so he had something warm to wear. At the end of the week, when his cough was better, he began painting and doing some chores that Jess hadn't gotten around to. He was a willing worker, bright and capable, and he seemed to take directions well.

John wasn't the only young boy on the road, of course. The "boxcar kids," an army of nomadic young people variously estimated from two hundred thousand to one million, drifted from place to place, hitchhiking along the highways or riding the rails—a gang of rabble that some said would turn into lifelong vagrants, bandits, and criminals. Reading of them, I was reminded of the *bezprizorni,* the homeless, hopeless Russian street children who were left orphaned and abandoned after the 1917 Revolution. When I was traveling in Russia, I was warned to keep my eye on my belongings—especially my pocketbook—and to travel always with others. The *bezprizorni* banded together in packs as pickpockets, thieves, and robbers, armed with homemade weapons. They pounced on the unwary like wolves on a stray lamb.

But I could also see these boxcar kids as a generation of young American pioneers, eager to escape from their conventional parents and small towns and venture out into the great unknown. They were nomads eager for adventure, for new lives, pursuing dreams of hope and abundance—like myself, when I was seventeen and escaped from Mansfield by boarding that train bound for Kansas City. Or like the hitchhiking boy in Kansas who had rejected my suggestion that he look for work back East.

"Ain't you never heard the old saying, missus?" he'd asked. "Go west, young man. Go west. Me, I'm going west. I'm going west and make my fortune."

And who could blame him, or any of them? I thought of all the American generations who have believed that growth on our continent lies naturally in a westward direction. Men and women left the East, fenced with stability and permanence and predictability and tradition, to plant farms and build towns and create new lives in the West. They were hungry for movement, for change, for freedom from tradition, and yes, for instability, for risk. They wanted to escape the past. They wanted to belong to the future and to *themselves,* not to somebody else.

That kind of freedom has always been hard won, and during the worst years of the Depression, it was even harder. Too many of the boys, and girls, who set out to look for the pot of gold at the end of their rainbows—east, west, north, south—ended up dirty, cold, sick, hungry, lost. They were reduced to panhandling on street corners and digging crusts of bread and scraps of meat out of garbage pails. And knocking on strange doors, hoping for work that would earn them a hot meal and a bed in a barn. The government proposed to take care of them by herding them together under an agency called the National Youth Administration. FDR was already concocting a dozen ambitious and costly schemes to solve the problem, when what was needed was a little common-sense charity. A little love.

All this was going through my mind as I stood beside the window that first afternoon and watched John Turner, wearing his jaunty red cap and my father's old jacket, his head bent against the drizzle as he weeded the iris bed. But after several weeks, Jess and I ran out of make-work for the boy, and my excuse for keeping him on—work that needed to be done—had worn as thin as that blue plaid shirt. And by that time, I had already developed what I described to myself as a generous and unselfish interest in the boy, whose adolescent energy and claim on the future filled the house that had been empty ever since Troub left.

But even as I professed my altruistic concern, I could see the self-interest implicit in it. I couldn't fool myself that I was doing this for *John.* A month after his arrival, his young, energetic presence had pulled me into a healthier state of mind and body. I wasn't writing yet, but somehow that didn't matter. I had stopped thinking about escaping to New York. I was collecting enough royalties from *Hurricane* to pay the bills and buy the groceries. Troub was gone and so was Bunty. I no longer had someone to care for, someone who *needed* my care. But here was the boy and I was caught up in him—and less wrapped up in myself.

And John was himself, his own person, with his own strength, his own will, his own purposes and intentions and ways and means, quite separate from mine. In a sense, I thought, that made it safe. I had nothing to lose—or so I told myself at the time, not fully understanding just how much a loss might cost me. I had yet to recognize how one-sided my relationships with people had always been, how I had always invested more than I'd received in return, expected more than most people could give, or be, or do. I hadn't quite learned that lesson. John was to teach me. But that was to come.

I told the boy that I hated to turn him out into the coming winter. If he would agree to enroll in high school in Mansfield, keep up his grades, and help with the chores at Rocky Ridge, he could eat with us and sleep in the spare room upstairs, the room that had been Troub's.

He was surprised—and cautious. "I don't understand why you're willing to do this for me, Mrs. Lane. You don't know me, not really. You don't know anything about me."

That wasn't entirely true. By this time, I already knew (I had checked) that his story about going to school in El Paso was a lie, and I suspected that there were other lies, as well. As there were—in fact, his whole story was a fabrication, start to finish. Over the course of the next few months, I learned that his parents were indeed dead, but that they had lived in Springfield, not Tulsa, and that he had an older brother, Al. After their parents' death, the two boys had gone to live with an uncle in the small town of Ava, fourteen miles south of Mansfield. The uncle's wife didn't like either of the brothers, but John had been especially irritating. His habit of slouching around with his hands in his pockets annoyed her, so she sewed his pockets shut. It was the last straw for him, and he ran away. When he knocked at my kitchen door, he had been on the road for six weeks—just long enough to begin to feel desperate, especially as he thought of the winter to come.

When the whole story finally came out, he told me that he had concocted the tale about Tulsa because he was afraid I would call the sheriff and he would be sent back to his uncle in Ava. After that, he had continued to lie because he didn't want me to know that he had deceived me.

"I'm sorry, Mrs. Lane," he said, with what seemed to be genuine contrition. "I know I should have told you the truth. But I wanted to stay here." He gave me an earnest, pleading look. "I want to stay with you."

And with that look, my heart was completely taken, and John moved into the empty places left by Rexh, by Guy, by Troub, and by little Bunting.

I now had to learn to be a mother—never the easiest thing in the world, but even more difficult when the child has already spent fifteen years becoming the person he is. It was a daily struggle for both of us. But as the weeks and months went on and 1933 slipped into 1934, we settled into a more-or-less comfortable family routine. I bought a used 1928 Willys-Knight sedan, and now we had a reliable car for shopping and family errands. Lucille came every morning to do the cooking and cleaning and often stayed overnight; when she did, Eddie sometimes stayed too, and we played chess or did jigsaw puzzles. My mother strongly disapproved of John; she didn't care much for Lucille and even less for Eddie, whom she found "rough." She and Papa came less often in the evenings, and when they came, they didn't stay very long.

But my mother's morning and afternoon drop-ins continued and even increased. *Farmer Boy* had been published in November, and she was writing her third book now, her "Indian story." She had dozens of questions about what to put in and what to leave out. The moment I had settled down to work on something of my own, I could count on her to interrupt.

And with a teenager in the house, there were lots of distracting school doings: homework (I spent one entire evening trying to help John plumb the mysteries of the participle), basketball games, plays, the debate club—as well as card games in front of the fire and automobile drives and evenings at the movies. From the Sears catalogue, I ordered some much-needed new clothes for the boy: shoes, two pairs of brown corduroy pants, two sweaters, and a heavy sheepskin-lined coat.

When John opened the package, he turned pink with surprise and pleasure. "Gee, they're swell, ain't they?" he exulted, and I cringed. His grammar was truly atrocious. If he was going to get anywhere in the world, he would have to learn to speak proper English. Unfortunately, when I tried to help him remember to stop saying things like "ain't" and "he don't," he dug in his heels, mostly to annoy me, I thought. But he wore that sheepskin coat proudly. I loved seeing him wear it and loved knowing that it had been my gift to him.

John played on the Mansfield freshman basketball team, and in February, when Mansfield played Ava, John introduced me to his brother Al and their uncle Jerry, who was the sheriff there. Mansfield High was very small; John's class had only thirteen students. I wanted him to have friends, so I encouraged him to invite the young people to the farmhouse in the evenings. I put out cookies and popcorn and cider and we told stories in front of the fire. The kids especially liked ghost stories and travel tales, and I had plenty of those to tell. It was good to have young people around. I felt energized.

Later that spring, after Catharine came for another visit, John took over the garage, which gave him a place to play his guitar (one that Papa had found for him) and his records. I invited his brother, Al, to visit on weekends and drove down to Ava to get him when his uncle couldn't provide transportation. When the cows freshened, I put John in charge of one of Papa's milk cows: the money from the cream check was his. After he saved five dollars and deposited it into a bank account, I doubled the amount. He was furious, which I didn't understand then but do now. Jess and his family were still living in the tenant house, but on a rental basis because Jess had a job in town. So John earned his allowance by taking over the yard chores: mowing the lawn, trimming the shrubs, and helping me plant the garden.

It was a good time, those months, but there were a few bad patches. John had a curfew; he broke it, then lied about where he had been and with whom. He overspent his allowance and lied about that, too. He refused to speak proper English, neglected his homework, failed algebra. He was often careless around the house, ignored his chores, and talked back.

After one big blow-up, I wrote in my journal that John was a hillbilly and a hoodlum and no amount of effort on my part would ever change him. But just as often, he was touchingly considerate and sweet. Trying to get him to take cod liver oil when he was sick with a cold, I told him that I worried about him because he was precious to me. He shook his head, perplexed, and I said,

"You'll understand the feeling when you have children of your own." And then I read on his face the thought that he wasn't my child and was surprised. In my mind, in my heart, really, he was my son. He occupied a space in my soul that had been empty so long I had ceased to notice the void until he arrived to fill it.

The small, quotidian realities of daily living forced on me by John's presence were surprisingly therapeutic. I found myself coping with the regular imperatives of school lunches, supper on the table, and clean clothes in the drawers, as well as the more challenging domestic tragedies of a burned-down garage and electricity off for days during an ice storm. As my life began to be livened by the unpredictable activities of a teenaged boy, the fog of dull listlessness lifted. I could see more than a day or two ahead. And I was buoyed by the news from Longmans that *Hurricane* had sold more than twelve thousand copies in its first year and was still selling. I was able to go back to work, although the results were mixed.

In March and April, I wrote a serial set in the early 1930s called "The Hope Chest." In the story, Barbara, a spoiled, romantic young woman who cherishes her grandmother's knitting needles and her family's pioneer heritage is engaged to the more practical Harry, a zealous believer in progress who aims to become an electrical engineer. On the eve of the Crash, Barbara's father gives her a hope chest. Looking forward to marriage, she fills it with embroidered towels and good china and silver for the pretty house where she and Harry will entertain in style and—like her parents—lead an easy, affluent life.

But the Depression changes everything. Harry is forced to leave college when the family money disappears. He is unable to find a decent job and refuses, out of pride, to let Barbara take the job she is offered. Their wedding is postponed—like many other weddings in those years.

The circumstances force Barbara to become realistic: "The newspapers were too optimistic," she thinks, "the radio was too cheering. Too many explanations and promises had been made too many times." Searching for a low-rent house that would make it possible for her and Harry to marry, she discovers a rural area where refugees of the Depression, "new pioneers," have moved into abandoned, derelict houses with no electricity, no water, no plumbing, no telephone. They are raising milk cows and chickens and feeding their families from their gardens—reminding Barbara of her grandmother, a courageous young woman who raised three babies on a Kansas homestead claim, doing the plowing and planting herself.

Fired by pioneer idealism, Barbara spots a five-dollar-a-month house that might do for her and Harry, "one of those small houses which, because they are too humble to try to please, are pleasing." Eager and excited, she imagines how she will fix it up—then, daunted, thinks how hard it will be to live in the little house without any modern conveniences. But it doesn't really matter how they live, does it? She and Harry will be together. Together, anything is bearable.

But Harry, firm in his faith in the inevitability of progress (and the need for electricity), rejects the little house, insisting that they keep on fighting for a better life than that of their pioneer forebears. "Damn it all," he explodes, "we've got a right to it! And if we don't keep on fighting for it—we're quitters, that's all." And anyway, "A good bathroom means something."

The mention of a bathroom is persuasive, and Barbara (who has glimpsed the work-scarred hands of one of the "new pioneer" women), gives in. They'll wait to get married, hoping for future prosperity. But at the end of the story, they are stranded beside the road with a flat tire and no spare. In the distance they see the vacant factories and smokeless chimneys of the city—and spears of light, shooting into the darkness, "a beacon for airships."

It was an inconclusive, provocative (I thought), and intentionally ironic ending. But although George Bye was enthusiastic about the story, *McCall's, Saturday Evening Post,* and *Good Housekeeping* turned it down. I was disappointed but not terribly surprised. The magazines were looking for romantic pieces with happy endings and satisfying plot resolutions that reinforced the myth of a disciplined and orderly society. It didn't do to leave the main characters standing beside the road with a flat tire, gazing at an illusory beacon of hope. The day I received the *Good Housekeeping* rejection, a truck loaded with crates of chickens overturned in the ditch outside our house. The absurdity of it was almost funny.

My mother had brought her third manuscript—now titled *High Prairie*—to me in February, but since Harper wasn't expecting it until late summer, I had set it aside in favor of my own work. The Harper editor, Ida Louise Raymond, had written to say that both *Little House in the Big Woods* and *Farmer Boy* were doing well. In January and February (slow months in the book market), *Farmer Boy* had sold 242 copies and *Little House,* 144. She added, "We think this is something to be proud of, and we're looking forward to receiving your next book."

I was at the Rock House for a soup-and-sandwich lunch when Mama Bess showed me the letter. She had multiplied out the two-month sales on a scrap of paper, figuring that if the two books continued to do that well, she might sell more than fifteen hundred copies by year's end. Even with *Farmer Boy's* low royalty rate, the royalties could amount to nearly two hundred dollars. And the addition of *High Prairie* to the list could mean another one hundred dollars or maybe even one hundred and fifty dollars added to next year's royalties.

She ladled chicken soup into our bowls. "That means that I could earn as much as three hundred and fifty dollars in royalties next year."

"Wonderful!" I said enthusiastically. I might have reminded her that she had earned three hundred dollars from the two *Country Gentleman* articles that had appeared in 1925 and that the articles had been easier and faster to write than a whole book. I didn't, though. Articles brought only a one-time payment, while the books could bring her a steady income—perhaps. There was a catch. The backlist—the older books—would continue to sell only as long as new books were added. If there were no new books, the sales would probably decline.

"But *High Prairie* is the third book in the contract," she said worriedly. "The last one. And Miss Raymond hasn't said anything about a fourth book." She sat down, tucking her white hair back under the hair net she wore at home to protect her permanent wave. "Do you think Harper will be interested in another one?" She wasn't looking at me, and I knew she was wondering if I would be willing to do the necessary rewrite. I also knew she wouldn't ask—if she did, she might feel obligated to say please. And thank you.

"Of course, nobody knows what's going to happen these days," I said. "But if the editor likes *High Prairie,* and if the first two continue to sell, yes, it's likely that they'll offer you another contract." I spread some of Mama's homemade mustard on my ham sandwich and added, somewhat more cautiously, "You could probably write a book a year—as long as you feel like writing."

And as long as the books were like *Farmer Boy,* I would have my work cut out for me. I would have to set aside a couple of months for every one of her rewrites, about the same amount of time I had spent ghosting the Lowell Thomas books—for which I had been paid. But I couldn't refuse. The royalty income was important to her and Papa, and the prestige of being an author was increasingly important to her. She couldn't write the books herself. She understood that now, after Harper's rejection of *Farmer Boy*. And much as she might hate to depend on me to do the work, she had no alternative.

"If you wrote a fourth book," I said slowly, "you might expand the Plum Creek section in 'Pioneer Girl.' The grasshoppers eating the wheat, the prairie fire—that would be dramatic."

She picked up her spoon, hesitant. "I've been thinking about that. I suppose I could write about Minnesota and Iowa, but . . ." Her voice trailed off. I knew she was thinking of the death of her little brother, a painful episode in her childhood. "We did a lot of moving around in those days." She dipped her spoon into her soup. "It wasn't a happy time for us, you know. Pa couldn't seem to get settled. He kept running into hard luck of every kind—crop failures, grasshoppers, drought, debts. And there was never any money. I remember what a big decision it was for Mary and me to spend a penny for a slate pencil, which we shared."

"You *shared* a piece of chalk?"

She nodded. "Each of us had gotten a penny for Christmas. We used Mary's penny to buy one slate pencil and agreed that Mary would own half of my penny. We sat on the same bench at school, you see, so sharing was easy. We shared our schoolbooks, too. I was littler, so I read in the front part of the book, where my lessons were, and Mary would read in the back, with pages standing up between." She shook her head. "And now—children nowadays have so much, even in these hard times. Too much, I often think."

I said nothing. I was remembering growing up with my own sense of never having enough of what the other children had. But I didn't have to share my slate chalk.

She looked away, as if she were seeing into the past. "We lived in conditions that people wouldn't tolerate today, no matter how hard up they were. The dugout, for instance. It daunted even Ma, who was so brave about such things. It wasn't much bigger than a fruit cellar, and dug into the creek bank, so close to the water that we had to watch Carrie every single minute to make sure she didn't fall in. And Ma's work . . ." She shook her head and fell silent.

I was distracted by the thought of "The Hope Chest," where Harry refuses to live in what he considers a substandard house, even if it means that he and Barbara can marry. My mother was probably right. Not even the "new pioneers" would live in a dugout—unless it had electricity and plumbing.

I brought myself back to the conversation. "Ma's work?" I prompted.

Mama Bess put down her spoon, her soup untasted. "I'm sure you thought I worked hard while you were growing up at Rocky Ridge. But you have no idea how hard Ma had to work in those years to keep food on the table and her children halfway clean. When it rained, the mud . . . " She shuddered. "And the time the ox ran across the dugout and stuck his leg through the roof and the whole thing caved in and everything we owned was covered with dirt. We couldn't afford lumber—and anyway, there was very little to be had, out there on that prairie. It all had to be hauled in on the railroad. So Pa wove a roof out of willow boughs and covered it with earth and sod. Can you *imagine*?"

I thought of the dirt-stained face of the Kansas farmer whose wife and children had given up in despair and gone back East. The Ingalls had not persevered, either. Grandpa Ingalls gave up at Plum Creek—his last effort at farming—and went to work in Burr Oak, Iowa, where he had helped run the Masters' Hotel.

"And I have the terrible suspicion that we drank creek water without boiling it," she went on. "But I can't put that in the book." She shook her head again. "Today's children get water out of a faucet. Hot water, too. They just wouldn't understand."

"You don't have to tell everything that happened," I said. "As for the drinking water, you could just say that there was a spring." I went back to my sandwich. "This isn't an autobiography, you know. It's a story. A story for children. Make it an adventure. Make it *fun*."

She frowned. "I suppose," she said doubtfully. She picked up her sandwich. "Yes, I think Plum Creek will be the next book, if there is one. But I'll have to leave out an awful lot."

Mama Bess had been pleased with her *High Prairie* manuscript when she brought it to me, saying, quite hopefully, that she felt there wouldn't be much for me to do. If there was, she added, I should go ahead and make the changes, then show her what I had done. "I'm hoping that there won't be very many."

But when I sat down to read the manuscript, I saw that there would have to be quite a lot of rewriting. The narrative wasn't as jumbled as *Farmer Boy,* but the story (which she had based on the opening pages of "Pioneer Girl") needed a proper beginning that would connect it to the previous book. She had included the story of Carrie's birth, but that would be confusing to readers who had read the first book, where Carrie was part of the cast of characters. So I took out the birth story and mentioned Carrie in the first sentence, to make it clear that this book followed *Little House in the Big Woods*:

> A long time ago, when all the grandfathers and grand-
> mothers of today were little boys and little girls or very
> small babies, or perhaps not even born, Pa and Ma and
> Mary and Laura and Baby Carrie left their little house in

the Big Woods of Wisconsin. They drove away and left it lonely and empty in the clearing among the big trees, and they never saw that little house again. They were going to the Indian country.

The plot was simple: The family arrives, they build a house and plant a garden, live there for a time, and then leave. But their coming and going had to be motivated in a way that children could understand. The episodes had to be rearranged for greater coherence and knitted together with clearer time-and-place transitions. And Mama Bess's bare-bones scene sketches had to be filled out with the kind of rich, vital sensory details that keep readers interested. I remembered what George Bye had written about "Pioneer Girl": it lacked the "benefit of perspective or theatre." This book had the same problem. Impatiently, I jotted the Albanian phrase *Shumë keq* in my diary. "Very bad." It was my private writer's judgment on my mother's manuscript. I would never say that in her hearing.

I worked on her book every day for more than a week, early morning to late afternoon—miserable days at the typewriter, because it was late May and the weather had turned very warm. On the thirtieth of May, I noted in my diary that the thermometer at Rocky Ridge had hit 125 degrees in the shade. The day after that, the thermometer broke.

The next week, I gave the rewritten pages to my mother, who had come for tea. She took them home to read and promptly got sick. (Whether there was any connection between the two events, I can't say.) The next day, Papa telephoned me to ask me to come over and take care of her, and I walked the three-quarters of a mile to and from the Rock House four times. Dr. Fuson, who came that afternoon, lectured her about eating too many strawberries.

While I was there, she handed me the material I had given her, with only a few corrections. "I thought I had written a better book," she said regretfully. "But I can see why you needed to make the changes. The story is much improved, Rose. It holds together better, and all your little details make the pictures so much clearer." With a little sigh, she added, "Thank you."

Thank you.

"You're welcome," I murmured and went into the kitchen to make some supper for Papa.

Altogether, I worked on the rewrite of *High Prairie* for thirty-one days, with a break in early June for John's birthday party. The previous autumn, my mother and I had talked about taking what she called a "research trip" to the area some forty miles south of Independence, where she thought Pa had built the little house. But she had been just a toddler when the family lived there and had no idea where the place might be, so we gave up the plan. I didn't know where it was, either, but Lucille and I had driven through that area when I was doing the research for the "Wheat and the Great American Desert" article, and I could fill in the necessary landscape descriptions from memory.

I finished rewriting her book the last week of June and gave it to her, along with a cover letter to George Bye that she could sign and send with the manuscript. George forwarded it to Harper, which accepted it—without revisions—a few months later. It was to be called *Little House on the Prairie,* a title suggested by Ida Louise Raymond, who by this time was head of the children's department. The contract for the fourth book came later in the year, in November, and Mama Bess began to plan the book that would be called *On the Banks of Plum Creek.*

My mother's project had one advantage: it served as a kind of limbering-up exercise that pushed me back toward my own work. When I finished her Indian Territory book, I wrote another

Dakota pioneer story, "Object Matrimony." It had an O. Henry ending—an unexpected twist—that wrapped up the main plot in a few short paragraphs toward the end. Adelaide Neall snapped it up for the *Post*. The story brought enough to clean up the bills and keep us going for another few months.

Looking back, I don't know how I managed to work. The summer was unspeakably horrible, and we suffered through a record string of hundred-degree-days. There was no rain, and the drought was the worst ever for our part of Missouri. When the wind blew out of the west, it carried grit from the plains of Oklahoma and Kansas; everything was covered with a film of dust, even the dishes on the table. I was nearly at the end of my rope when some friends—the writer Talbot Mundy and his wife Dawn— invited me, and John, too, to visit. They lived in Florida, on Casey Key, near Osprey, on the Gulf of Mexico. They encouraged John to bring a friend, and he asked Jackie Mason, whose mother agreed. I didn't have the money for the trip, but Longmans owed me a thousand dollars in royalties for *Hurricane*. George Bye sent a check, enough to fund the trip and handle expenses through the rest of the year.

I stopped work, packed our clothes, and we were on our way. Talbot and I had been corresponding for some time about several historical novellas he had published in the magazine *Adventure,* featuring a fictional Roman adventurer named Tros of Samothrace, who fought with the Britons against Julius Caesar. Talbot's work was good, and I had been encouraging him, by letter, to collect the novellas into book form. Now, they were to be published by Century, which had published *Diverging Roads* and my Hoover book, some fifteen years before. I was glad for the chance to help him.

I was also glad for the sheer, mind-altering relief of three weeks away from the farm. The Mundys' small cottage was tucked into a jungle of palms and pines, with Blackburn Bay at the back door and the Gulf at the front door. John and Jackie were on their best behavior and went off every day, exploring the narrow barrier island. On long tropical evenings, Talbot and Dawn (she was years younger than Talbot, who was nearly fifty-five) taught me to swim in the warm, silver-flecked waves that frothed against the white sand beach. They introduced me to a motley assemblage of local people, all of them enviably tanned and fit and refreshingly cynical and nonconformist—a delightful break from the Mansfielders. We went out on a sailboat and walked down the beach to a local nudist colony for an afternoon game of volleyball. We talked nonstop about politics (the Mundys and their friends were as anti–New Deal as I) and the increasingly troubling European situation.

One week, John, Jackie, and I took a bus across Florida to Miami and then a boat to Havana, where we toured Morro Castle, a sprawling Spanish fortress built in the late 1500s. We indulged in spicy Cuban food (which I regretted afterward) and spent hours in the market, buying little presents to take home. The Cuban parliament had just extended suffrage to women, but General Batista was the acknowledged power behind the presidency and the streets were full of police, a threatening reminder of the military power I had seen in the European states. The boys were both frightened and excited at the sight of the armed and uniformed men, giving me an opportunity to talk about what happens when the state imposes its power over individual citizens—an on-the-spot civics lesson.

In fact, the whole trip was magical for John, and he came to my hotel room that night to tell me how much he appreciated it.

"The island, the swimming, the big boat, and now Cuba— there's no way I could've done this on my own," he said. "I think of where I was just a year ago and I don't know how to thank you, Mrs. Lane. You've changed my life." And then he got up from his chair, came over to me, and put his cheek against mine. "Maybe I don't always act like it, but I know that you're the best thing that's ever happened to me. I would like to call you mother."

My heart was so full I could barely speak. "I would love that," I managed finally, thinking that John was the best thing that could have happened to *me,* and thanking the providence that arranges such things for sending this boy to Rocky Ridge that rainy September day.

At the door, he turned and added, wistfully, "I just wish I could be all you want me to be. I'm afraid I never will."

"Of course you will," I said. It was only later that I thought how that must have sounded.

We had taken the train to Florida but planned to go back to Missouri by bus. John and Jackie were eager to see more of the country, so they left from the Miami bus station at the end of our Havana trip, going back the long way, up the coast to Charleston, then across to Memphis and home. I went back to stay on with the Talbots another few days, then took the bus home alone. The whole glorious, carefree trip had reminded me of how good it was to escape from the isolated, sunk-in-the-muck life I lived at the farm, if only for a little while. If it hadn't been for John, I told Dawn Mundy the night before I left, I might not go back at all.

"John's a swell kid," she said, swinging lazily in one of the twin hammocks that Talbot had slung between two palm trees. "Smart, good-looking, too. I see why you want to do something nice for him." She paused, and the silence was filled with bird song. "But is he worth giving up your freedom, Rose? After all, it's not as if he's your *son.*"

I was startled. Giving up my freedom? I hadn't thought of it that way at all. But from one point of view, it was true. The magazine market was loosening up, and with *Hurricane* so successful, I could count on selling my work. I could leave the farm. I could move back to New York. I could—

But I couldn't. Not yet. I understood why it might seem to Dawn as if I were yielding my freedom to provide a home for John. But I wasn't, not really. I was choosing, *freely*, to commit my time, my work, my attention, my life-energy to the boy. In choosing, I was exercising my freedom. I was not obligated or compelled by any force outside myself to accept responsibility for John. And in some ways, at that moment, remembering that I had freely chosen him made him even more precious to me.

"He *is* my son," I said, thinking of what the boy had said in the hotel room in Havana. "In all the ways that matter."

There was a long pause. "I had a child," Dawn said, so softly that I could scarcely hear her. "A baby girl, last year. She was born when we were in England. She died."

My heart opened to her. "I'm so sorry, Dawn. I lost a child, too. A little boy, at birth. He would have been twenty-four this year." Twenty-four years. Nearly a quarter of a century. A very long time.

Another pause. "Do you . . . do you ever get over it?"

I could hear the hurt. "No, never. But you learn to live with the loss. And even to welcome the flicker of pain, when it comes. You feel it—you know what it is. The pain makes you real, somehow."

She nodded doubtfully. "I suppose that's why the boy. John, I mean."

I thought of a dark-haired youngster with bright eyes and a dirty red fez. "Two boys," I said. "Two sons. My oldest is Albanian. He graduated from Cambridge two years ago and is back home in Tirana. I worry about him, with Mussolini just over his horizon."

"Cambridge," she said in surprise. "Did you do that?"

I smiled. "He's very bright. *He* did it. I only helped."

"Mussolini," Dawn mused. "I can see why you're worried." She smiled pensively. "Two sons. Two adopted sons. Lucky boys."

Talbot came to the door of the cottage with a glass in his hand. "Bar's open," he called. "Either of you ladies want something to drink?"

"Gin and tonic, please, dear," Dawn said, and pushed herself out of the hammock.

Two sons. I didn't know it yet, but by the end of the year, there would be three.

The weather had already changed when I got back to Missouri. It was the end of August and cooler, and that week a long, soaking rain broke the drought. A sad thing: a few days before I got back, Molly (the last of Troub's horses, and the sweetest) had escaped from her pasture and wandered onto the road, where she was hit by a truck and killed. It felt like yet another, even more conclusive ending to all that Troub and I had shared. I sat down and wrote her a sad note.

But Molly's death wasn't the bad omen it might have seemed. In the next day's mail, I got a letter from George Bye, letting me know that George Lorimer, the *Post*'s publisher, had liked "Object Matrimony" so much that he had decided to raise my rates. Bye's letter enclosed a check for an additional two hundred and seventy dollars, bringing the full payment for the story to twelve hundred dollars. I was now among the *Post*'s best-paid writers. I spent the extra money, along with a trade-in of the Willys-Knight, on a secondhand Nash.

School was starting, and the last four months of 1934 were busy, mostly with family. My father bought a flock of goats, which sent my mother into a fit of temper. She came over the next day to complain to me, but I could see his side of it, too (he had always loved goats), and she left, resentful. Lucille and Eddie split up forever, again—I had already lost track of the number of times this had happened—but two weeks later he was coming regularly for supper and on the weekend, he stayed all night.

And then Lucille proposed that she and Eddie—who was still managing the laundry in town—let their apartment go and stay at the farm. In return for their board and room, she could do the cooking and cleaning and Eddie, who was handy with tools, could lend a hand with outdoor work on weekends. That way, they might even be able to save a little money, so that when things got better, they could buy their own place. I didn't much like the idea of having Eddie around all the time. But he *was* good with tools and a paintbrush. I could see advantages on both sides, so I said yes, although as it turned out, Eddie wasn't a very willing worker.

In October, Catharine arrived for another long visit, which meant that my mother (who reminded me once again that Catharine's reputation as "fast" would surely besmirch mine) would not come over nearly so often. To make up for her self-imposed deprivation, I took her on a day-long promised driving trip to see the autumn foliage, which was very pretty that year. The Nash had carburetor trouble near Bradleyville, and I ended up walking into town. But we got it fixed and drove on to Rome and Thornfield and then home. It was a pleasant drive (except for the car trouble), and when she got out of the car, she turned back to say, "Thank you, Rose, for the lovely drive."

John, now a sophomore, had made the Mansfield High basketball squad, so we were scheduling supper around practice and games. He had been with me for a full year now, and we were getting along reasonably well, although he still bridled when I spoke to him about his carelessness with money and clothes and the English language. I had hired Jess to build a new garage to replace the one that had burned—at $60, it was a bargain. John was sleeping out there, and his brother Al was coming up from Ava on weekends. The garage became "the bunkhouse," a place where the boys could make all the noise they liked.

Late in October, we planned a Halloween costume party for John. Al was invited, and Lucille and I contrived ghost costumes for the two boys. The day after the party, Al came into the kitchen, alone, to talk to me. He was a gangly boy, not quite a year older than John but also a sophomore, with brown hair and eyes and a heavy smattering of freckles.

He came straight to the point. "Mrs. Lane, I'd like to come here and live." Then, as a kind of afterthought, he added, "Please."

I was rolling out a crust for a cherry pie. I stared at him in some surprise. "I thought you liked living with your uncle. And you're doing well at Ava High, aren't you?"

He nodded diffidently. "It's just . . . well, I like being with John. And Mansfield is a bigger town—there's more to do here. And my uncle's wife—" He swallowed and dropped his eyes. "Well, that's the big thing, I guess. It's been better since John left, but she's never much liked me, either. She'd be glad to see me gone. And my uncle, too. I'm kind of like a burr under her saddle, and he's the one who gets all the complaints." He raised his brown eyes to mine and I could see the hurt in them. "I feel like . . . well, sort of pushy, asking you this, and I'll understand if you say no. But I'd be really grateful if you could manage to make room for me here."

For the first time, I looked closely at the boy. His hair was badly cut; his bony wrists were sticking out of his too-short sleeves; the knees of his pants were patched; his shoes were worn. It occurred to me that his uncle wasn't making a very substantial investment in his clothes—and, say what you will, clothes are important to youngsters. I ought to know: when I was a child, the other girls judged me (and I judged myself) by their satin-trimmed dresses and patent leather shoes.

"I'll be glad to work for my board and room," he added earnestly. "I can do a lot to help around here, Mrs. Lane— stuff like cutting the grass, doing the milking, working in the garden, scrubbing the floors. I could go over to the Rock House and help your folks out, too." He gave me a lopsided grin. "And what do you want to bet that I could keep John at his chores? All that kid needs most times is a little shove in the right direction. Why, with the two of us, you won't have to pay Jess to do stuff."

My first impulse was to say yes. I liked Al, and I felt he would be a settling influence for John. But I hesitated. It was hard enough to find the money for John. I didn't think I could afford to feed two teenaged boys and keep them in clothes and allowances, no matter how much work they did around the place.

I picked up the rolling pin. "I understand why you're asking, Al, and I'd like to do it if I could." It was best to be honest with him. "But money is a problem. I'll have to think about it." I went back to my piecrust. "I'll discuss it with your uncle. He might not be as willing as you think."

He gave me a hopeful look. "Thanks," he said. "It would be really swell if we could work it out."

Perhaps for his own reasons, John wasn't enthusiastic. "I don't understand why you want to do this," he said darkly. "You don't know anything about Al. You don't know much about me, either."

I thought of the many small secrets that sixteen-year-olds hold in their hearts and nodded. "I'm sure I don't," I said.

My mother was even less enthusiastic. "You've already got your hands full with the one boy, Rose." She frowned. "I don't see why in the world you would want to take on his brother. It's not as if you have any obligation."

Why? Because I thought that Al could use a little help, that's why. But money was still an issue. And then George Bye sent me another royalty check from *Hurricane,* and that decided me. I discussed the details with the boys' uncle Jerry, agreeing to support Al until he finished high school. Then I told the boys that I would be glad to have Al live with us, and early in November, he moved in. My third son.

In one way, Al's coming made things easier, for John liked having his brother with him. With their books and guitars and Victrola records and the radio they were building from a kit, the two boys were good company for one another. Al was even-tempered and easier to get along with than John, did his chores willingly and promptly, and made good grades in school. Lucille and the boys liked one another—she was the understanding "big sister" to whom they could take their troubles—and she was usually available to help. The boys had big appetites, and between the two of us, Lucille and I baked dozens of pies, numerous batches of cookies and gingerbread, and washed thousands of dishes. I was elbow-deep in domesticity.

And at the same time, there were encouraging possibilities for my work. Crane Wilbur, a noted playwright and film director, wrote to me about the dramatic rights to "Hired Girl." The story had been a winning short-short in the 1933 O. Henry Award competition, and he thought it would make a "bang-up" play. It was agreed that the play would be staged by the West Coast Theater Guild—although it wasn't, in the end, because the funding fell through. George Bye was attempting to negotiate a deal with 20th Century Fox for the movie rights to *Hurricane,* but he kept running into snags. The grasshopper plague, for instance, which seemed somehow difficult for the producers to imagine on-screen.

"Oh, come, now," I wrote sarcastically to George. "I can't believe that the Grand Masters of Illusion are incapable of creating a fake cloud of winged insects—or of hiring actors who can register sufficient terror and trepidation to convince an audience that they are being overwhelmed by grasshoppers." If that was beyond their competence, I added, they could film the damn thing as a musical.

And by the end of 1934, I was thinking of another book. A couple of years before, I had suggested to Talbot Mundy that he collect his novellas into a longer novel. His book had just been published—*Tros of Samothrace*—and was dedicated to me. Now I began to plan the same thing. I would gather eight or nine of the published short stories I had written over the past few years and add a preface that would establish a context for the linked stories. The stories I chose had a recurring cast of characters and were set in a typical small town around the turn of the century. I was calling it *Old Home Town.* I didn't give the town itself a name: I meant it to be everyone's hometown. It was certainly mine. It was that Missouri I had thought about a few years before, full of untouched story material that I could use to say whatever I wanted to say about the world.

14. $\mathcal{E}$SCAPE AND OLD HOME TOWN: 1935

The year 1935 was like a jigsaw puzzle. Everything I had put together flew apart, the way a puzzle does when you drop it. When it was reassembled, the picture looked very different.

To put it another way: in 1935, I left the farm and a door opened onto the rest of my life.

The gloomy dark of winter always seems to send my spirits plummeting, and I find myself longing for sunshine and warm breezes. That year, winter dragged on and on, with bitter winds and leaden gray skies roofing a world of frozen mud and brittle trees. There was almost no snow, but we were hit by several ice storms that knocked the power out. Even with the furnace, it was hard to keep the old farmhouse warm, especially upstairs, where I was working. Downstairs, the pipes froze and burst.

The winter was too cold for the boys to sleep in the garage, so they were both sleeping in the upstairs room that had been Troub's. Lucille and Eddie were staying at Rocky Ridge, too, so the house was crowded—and even more crowded when Catharine came. I began to think of building a new bunkhouse for John and Al—a heated place where they could sleep and entertain their friends.

From one point of view, this was not the most practical idea in the world. Even as I was sketching plans (there's nothing I like better in this world than lavishing attention on a house, even a boys' bunkhouse), I was thinking how desperate I was to get away from Rocky Ridge. The boys' high school graduation was two years away, however, and in the meantime, they had to have a place of their own. Obviously, I needed to write—and earn. *Cash cash cash.* My mantra.

But while I had a strong idea for a book—*Old Home Town*—I was having trouble getting enough quiet time to organize the stories, write a new one or two and revise the others, put the collection together, and write an introduction to it. The crowded, noisy house was mostly my own fault, I had to admit, because I had invited all these people to live with me. And each one filled a certain place in my life, so why was I complaining?

Contemplating these contradictory necessities and urgencies, I remembered a scrap of insight I had once jotted into my journal. The problem, I wrote, is my own disorderly mind: I never want things or people or ideas in any logical way but haphazardly, helter-skelter, all at once. And when that commotion of greedy wanting collides with the ordinary commotion of living, the result is a messy confusion. That's what I had now in my life: a chaotic, competitive confusion of the boys, the household, my mother, my work.

Al was solid, dependable, and unfailingly courteous, and I never once regretted inviting him to live at Rocky Ridge. But even though I loved John—he had become my son, in all ways—his behavior was often simply impossible. At school, he was rude to his teachers and his report card was disgraceful. At home, he flared into ugly, combative arguments with me and with Al and Lucille, whom he saw as my allies. Lucille did her best to keep the household running smoothly, but John's ongoing, escalating ruckus—always worse at mealtime and chore time—made it impossible for me to work. And yet I *had* to work in order to pay the rent, buy the groceries, and keep up the bills.

And there was my mother, who seemed to have become more demanding, perhaps because she feared that the boys were pulling me away from her. The telephone calls became more frequent and she came over more often during the day, bringing her notes for *Plum Creek* so that we could discuss them. In early February, she brought the proofs of *Little House on the Prairie* for me to correct. The proofs went back to Harper and also to *St. Nicholas Magazine,* which wanted to publish an excerpt, as they had with *Farmer Boy.*

Mama Bess also asked me to rewrite a chapter from her book that would appear, under her name, in *Child Life.* That was something I thought she might do herself, but she insisted that I do it, and after thinking it over, I agreed. If we were going to maintain the fiction that she was the sole author of the books, all of her published material would have to be stylistically consistent. I could see the dilemma I had created: in helping her build an independent income as an author, I had made her dependent on *me* as her coauthor. If I had it to do over again, I don't think I would have done it. But I hadn't had the luxury of foresight, and what I had begun I had to continue. It was as simple as that.

Mama Bess and I had other topics of conversation besides her books, of course. We both read the newspapers and listened to the radio and had firm opinions about the state of affairs in Washington. Locally, Roosevelt had won by a small margin in the 1932 presidential race, but it hadn't taken long for the Republicans to regroup, and in the 1934 midterm election, Democrat Harry S. Truman was sent to the Senate with only 33 percent of Mansfield's vote. Most people voted a straight ticket, so our district returned Republican Dewey Short to Congress, where he spoke out vehemently against Roosevelt's New Deal programs, echoing the sentiments of the folks back home. *Strong* sentiments. Nobody in Mansfield liked the New Deal.

There was no denying that the programs created jobs, mostly in highway and dam construction. The CCC (the Civilian Conservation Corps) alone employed some four thousand men in building Missouri parks, and the Works Progress Administration was paying women to work in sewing rooms and canning factories around the county. Locally, there was hope for a new grade school building, funded by the government. These jobs meant food on the table and shoes on children's feet, and while people hated to be beholden to the government for work, they did what they had to do to keep their families going. If government work was all there was, people would do it.

But at the same time, resentment stewed. The self-reliant individualists in Wright County and across Missouri hated the idea of the government giving handouts to people who didn't work. Even worse, they hated federal agencies that tried to tell them how to do their business. And the AAA—the Agricultural Adjustment Administration—was the most hated of all.

My father was a good example. There wasn't much arable land at Rocky Ridge, but Papa always planted what he could in oats for his horses and millet for my mother's chickens, as well as a little popcorn for those long winter nights by the fire. He and Buck—his thirty-year-old Morgan—were out one afternoon plowing the bottomland along the creek, when a young AAA agent in a business suit, white shirt, bow tie, and brown fedora parked his coupe beside the road and sauntered into the field. He wanted to warn my father that the new federal regulations prohibited him from planting more than two acres of oats. He cast an eye across the field, took out a notebook, and began writing something.

"Looks to me like you got three, maybe four acres here," he said. "That about right?" Without waiting for an answer, he pointed with his pencil. "I'd say you oughta stop plowing when you get to that maple tree over there. No point in planting unless you just want to burn, come harvest."

My father stared at him with narrowed eyes. "I'd say you oughta get the hell off my land and do it right now," he said in a steely voice. "No point in standing there unless you want to get the seat of them fancy britches speckled with buckshot."

The AAA agent didn't linger to see if my father meant what he said. The boys at the pool hall, where Papa enjoyed his regular Saturday afternoon game, laughed over the story for a long time.

The crowding at the house eased a bit when Catharine got a job as a Hollywood scriptwriter and left for the West Coast. My mother was relieved. She hurried over to tell me the "dreadful gossip" that had apparently been circulating around Mansfield about Catharine and Lucille's husband Eddie. Mrs. Rogers had told her that Mrs. Bates's sister's neighbor over in Mountain Grove had seen the two of them in Eddie's car one afternoon the previous week.

"I told you, Rose," my mother said, with a kind of grim satisfaction. "Catharine Brody is the kind of girl who always gets *talked about*."

"She might have been with him," I objected mildly, "but I'm sure there was nothing to it—at least not the kind of thing that Mrs. Rogers and Mrs. Bates and Mrs. Bates's sister and her neighbor are thinking." Catharine liked to get out of the house, and Eddie had a laundry route that took him to the nearby small towns. She could have gone with him to pick up a few things at the dime store in Mountain Grove, or just gone along for the ride. I had, on several occasions.

"Where there's smoke, there's fire," my mother said darkly. "Mark my words."

I shook my head. I found the whole thing utterly absurd and annoying: Catharine was a sophisticated New Yorker with her pick of men. Eddie, while he might be good looking, was a boorish small-town loudmouth, amusing in his way, but empty. If she had been of a mind to have an affair, she wouldn't have wasted her seductive energies on *him*.

But poor Lucille did not find it absurd. She heard the gossip at the next bridge club meeting and was humiliated and deeply hurt. She came to me, tearfully, one afternoon when I was working.

"Do you suppose it's *true*?" she asked, wiping her eyes. "I've always liked Catharine, even though she's a bit of a flirt. But the idea of her and him . . . " She broke into fresh tears.

"My dear Lucille," I said and put my arms around her. "I am not going to tell you that your husband is above reproach. But I do *not* suppose that he and Catharine were up to anything. Those self-righteous old biddies in town have nothing better to do than wag their tongues." I was sorry to think that my mother might have contributed to the gossip, but I knew she didn't like Catharine or Lucille—and Eddie even less. If she had her way, none of them would be staying at Rocky Ridge.

Lucille blew her nose. "But even if it isn't true," she wailed, "how am I going to face people, knowing what they're saying behind my back?"

"You face people the same way you face any problem," I said staunchly. "You keep your chin up and your shoulders straight. Catharine's gone. In a couple of weeks, they'll have found another victim for their gossip and forgotten all about her."

Lucille's tears subsided after a moment, but I could read the wariness in her relationship with Eddie. It was weeks before she could bring herself to go to a bridge club meeting. And the destructive effects of the town's gossip would linger on. Years later, when I was living in New York, Catharine (wearing a memorable fur coat) stopped in Mansfield on her way back from the West Coast, intending to make a courtesy call on my mother. But when she telephoned from the station, my mother refused to see her.

Small things, tempest-in-a-teapot matters, you might say, but they distracted me from the work I had to do to support our two households. The weather didn't help, either. Everywhere in the midsection of the country, the winter and early spring had been exceptionally dry—so dry, in fact, that my father was hesitant to plant potatoes, wondering if they would make a crop.

To the west of us, where the drought was still deepening, the situation was worse. I read that a quarter of the winter wheat crop in Oklahoma had failed, half the crop in Kansas, and all of it in Nebraska—something like five million acres utterly devastated by drought. By the end of March, the southern Plains had already been hit with two solid weeks of dust storms boiling in huge clouds across the naked land. A few weeks later, I would read in the newspaper about Black Sunday, the nightmare storm that hit the Oklahoma Panhandle and swept like a black avalanche down into Texas. "We thought it was our judgment, we thought it was our doom," Woody Guthrie wrote later, and many people did indeed die. Everyone's nerves were raw in those months, and minor disagreements flared into sullen words that hung like ominous clouds in the air. I decided that if I was going to get any writing done, I would simply have to get away.

And in April, I managed to do it. I couldn't have without Lucille, of course—and I wouldn't have tried, if she hadn't been so willing. "You don't have to worry about a thing," she said reassuringly. "You go and do whatever you have to do, Rose.

Eddie and me will handle the boys. And you'll be close enough in case there's an emergency."

It was true. I wasn't going far, only seventy-some miles, to the small town of Hollister, where I checked into the English Inn. It was a small, inexpensive hotel with decent food, and I had a large room with a table beside the window for my typewriter. It was pleasant, for a change, to look down onto a street where people were coming and going, exchanging hellos, and leaning close together and lowering their voices to exchange the latest Hollister gossip about the latest affair, the latest divorce, the latest unwed mother.

I didn't fool myself that Hollister was any different from Mansfield in that regard, or from any of the myriad other small towns across the country. And, after all, that's what I was writing about in the stories of *Old Home Town*: the life of a small town in all its relentless cruelties, both conscious and unconscious, directed toward those who are condemned to live their lives on the outskirts of the close-knit society.

This was something I remembered vividly from my childhood. Before Mama Bess and Papa and I moved into town, we were country folks, outsiders, strangers—and we were still outsiders for years afterward, in the eyes of the town. I had been able to leave; I could come and go. But my mother had to stay. It had taken her decades to become a full-fledged member of the Mansfield flock, which was why, I supposed, she cared so deeply about the opinions of other members of the flock.

There was some quiet social life in Hollister—I met people at the hotel and was introduced around town and invited to a few dinners and teas. I was lionized, for a great many people had read "Hurricane" in the *Saturday Evening Post* and wanted to tell me how much they liked it, and my other stories, as well. I was also (and inevitably) critiqued and censured, and one of the local

Mrs. Grundys, at a dinner party, made it a special point to inform me that I was also pitied: I had no "Christian faith"—another reminder that I was likely to be an outsider wherever I went.

But most of all, this was a productive time, and exactly the change I needed. I settled in to work and polished off two stories in just over two weeks, one of which—"Nice Old Lady"— would be included in *Old Home Town*. I mailed them to George Bye and he sold both immediately—"Dreadful House" to *Country Gentleman*, "Nice Old Lady" to the *Post*.

The stories I planned to include in the book—already linked by setting and characters—offered the kind of cozy glimpse into sentimental, small-town life that appealed to readers. But I had a larger ambition for the stories as a group than I'd had as I wrote each of them, individually. For the collection, I arranged them in a sequence that I hoped would give them both a cumulative weight and a moral coherence, and I wrote a preface that framed them historically. They were, after all, about small-town life at the turn of the century, thirty years before, not about small-town life today—except that they were both, of course—about *then* and about *now*. Some things, and some people, never change.

The stories were told from the point of view of a young girl, Ernestine. In each story, Ernestine is older and more experienced, growing toward the day when she will leave her hometown. She sees the town's cruelties with a clearer and clearer eye, witnessing the struggles of its hapless victims—widows, spinsters, hired girls, unhappily married women—as they attempt to free themselves from the clutches of the town's oppressive rules and unforgiving rule-makers.

But Ernestine also witnesses occasional escapes, both successful and unsuccessful. In the first story, "Hired Girl," Almantha escapes being "talked about" by killing herself. Mrs. Sims, in "Immoral Woman," escapes to millinery school in St. Louis and eventually to a career as a successful dress designer in New York and Paris. Leila Barbrook climbs into Ab Whitty's buggy and escapes into a freer future.

And in the end, Ernestine also escapes, as I had, by becoming a writer, the creator of the tales in *Old Home Town*. In the last story, "Nice Old Lady," a grown-up, unmarried Ernestine is living in faraway Albania. In a bazaar there, she happens to meet old Mrs. Sherwood, the "nice old lady" who had once loaned her *Quo Vadis* and *The Conquest of Peru,* books that whetted her desire to see the world—and my own, when I was a young Ernestine, borrowing those very books from a neighbor. Mr. Sherwood was a homebody who denied his wife's wish to travel and see the world, refusing even to take her to Niagara Falls on their honeymoon. Mrs. Sherwood—realizing that marriage is the ultimate prison—had told the young girl, with an unforgettable ferocity, "Whatever you do, Ernestine, don't you get married! Don't do it!" Now, encountering the widowed Mrs. Sherwood climbing on a horse in a street in far-off Albania, Ernestine understands that even a "nice old lady," once she has escaped the bonds of marriage, can flee the old hometown, at last a free woman, a world traveler.

When the reviews of *Old Home Town* came out, I found it interesting that while each of them praised the book, not a single one mentioned the central, and deeply ironic, theme of escape. I think no one noticed. Perhaps they read the stories individually and failed to see the linking theme. Or perhaps they weren't looking for irony in stories that were originally published as magazine fiction.

Hollister was less than two hours' drive south of Mansfield. Lucille drove down several times during the three weeks I stayed at the hotel, once with my mother and, for the last weekend, with the boys, who went boating on the nearby Lake Taneycomo.

Then we all drove back to Mansfield. Longmans' contract for *Old Home Town* was waiting for me.

And so was another opportunity, one that would—in the end—take me away from Rocky Ridge and from Mansfield altogether, and for all time. Ernestine had escaped from her old hometown. And so, at last, would I.

"How did you come here?" the Albanians would inquire politely, ritually, of every traveler who reached their mountain village.

"Slowly, slowly," the weary traveler would answer. "Slowly, slowly, and little by little."

"Glory to your lips," the villagers would reply, bowing low. "It is so."

It is so.

It was late April when I returned to the farm, and I settled in to wrap up the manuscript of *Old Home Town,* retype the stories, and ship the thing off to Maxwell Aley at Longmans. (I would correct the proofs in the second week of July and receive my advance copy in late September. The book would be published in October and see a healthy sale.) In May, I made several trips to the dentist, where I left most of my teeth and many of the ongoing problems with my health. As a family, we were all busy with the end-of-school-year activities: the class play (John had a part, Al worked on the set); graduation exercises (Al sang in the boys' quartet); the boys' class picnics (Lucille and I baked multiple jelly rolls); and a party for John's June birthday.

And then another opportunity—unexpected, exciting, and entirely welcome—appeared in the mailbox. George Bye wrote to ask if I would be interested in writing a book on the state of

Missouri for a series about the United States planned by Robert M. McBride. McBride had already published several popular travel books about Czechoslovakia and Germany—popular perhaps because most people couldn't afford to travel, and reading was the next best thing. *Quo vadis,* I thought. Escape, escape. I jumped at the chance.

Years earlier, I had thought that Missouri held a great deal of untouched story material that I understood and could work with. Now, the more I thought about writing a book about "my" state, the more enthusiastic I became. I wanted to do a book that wasn't just a travel book but a story of the state, for I felt that Missouri had its own special character, its own unique personality. I knew the Ozarks and the Ozark people: I had written about them for years. I could learn about other parts of Missouri and reveal it in the way I would show a character in a story, with the actions, the events, the landscapes, and people, all interacting in a multi-threaded plot. It was an ambitious idea, yes, but I saw very clearly how it could be done. All I needed was access to research materials and quiet time to do the writing.

Therein my escape. After a month of flurried activity, I moved to Columbia, just a hundred and twenty miles from the farm, to a comfortable ninth-floor suite in the Tiger Hotel on South Eighth Street. I was able to rent the rooms very cheaply since there wasn't much regular demand for that kind of accommodation in Columbia. The hotel was only a few blocks from the University of Missouri campus and an enjoyable walk to the library and the state historical archives. I expected the research to take several months, and the writing—some of which could be done back at the farm—another few months, perhaps six altogether. The manuscript was due in January, and I planned to have the project finished by that time.

Sadly, the book came to nothing in the end. I turned in the manuscript when it was due, after months of serious work in the library and several weeks of travel around the state. But it quickly became clear that the publisher and I had very different books in mind. I had created a dramatic history of the state, while McBride wanted little more than a tourist guide with anecdotes about contemporary places and people. I took a stab at revising the manuscript, then gave it up and told George Bye that I would return the advance when I had the money. I didn't have to do that, as it turned out, because a few months later, Maxwell Aley, at Longmans, Green, bought the manuscript from McBride for the price of my advance. Despite Aley's best intentions, though, Longmans couldn't find a place for it on their list. The book was never published.

But my move to Columbia produced something better than a book: my escape from the farm, where I was buried under the cascading minutiae of everyday life and subject to my mother's daily attentions. And in my escape, I discovered the seductive pleasures of living alone, truly *alone,* for the first time in my life.

I was actually astonished when I stopped to think about this. I had left home at seventeen, lived with roommates until my marriage to Gillette, then lived with other roommates after the marriage ended. After that, I traveled abroad with various women, lived with Troub, and moved to Rocky Ridge. Always, in all that time, there was at least one other person in my household, often three or four or five. I had lived a crowded life. I had never been genuinely *alone.* Yes, there were days in Columbia when I fell into bleak depression, unfocused days when I couldn't work. But most days, I found myself reveling in the solitude.

I still had my obligation to John and Al, of course, and I took it seriously. I suggested that we rent a small house in Columbia so the boys could join me for the school year. But both of them wanted to spend it with their friends at Mansfield High, and now that the bunkhouse was finished, they had a comfortable living arrangement. Lucille and Eddie volunteered to stay at the farm and supervise them—*in loco parentis,* as it were—so that's how we worked it out.

But my mother wasn't happy that I would be an "absentee landlord," and she didn't like the unconventional situation at Rocky Ridge. "People are *talking,* Rose," she kept saying worriedly. But she could see that I needed to use the libraries, and Columbia was just two hours by car. So the family—the boys, my mother and father, Lucille—drove up frequently and we stayed in touch with letters and telephone calls.

But something else happened that summer—the summer of 1935—that made a significant change in my life. It was another kind of escape, and perhaps the turning point in my life as a writer, and as a thinker and a political person. It was very simple thing, really. I spent two August weeks in a car with a man I barely knew, driving across the Midwest.

And after that, after those two weeks, everything in my life was different. *Everything.*

But not in the way you might think.

15. "CREDO": 1936

I met Garet Garrett in 1923, on board the *Leviathan*, bound from Le Havre to New York. The ship had been built in 1913 as the *SS Vaterland*. But she had the misfortune to be laid up at her dock in Hoboken when Wilson took the country to war against Germany and was seized by the U.S. government for troop transport. In 1923, refurbished and restored to her prewar Edwardian and Louis XVI splendor and sailing to the music of her own ship's orchestra, she was once again in service, the largest passenger liner in the world.

The luxury of the *Leviathan* seemed strange and almost sybaritic to me, and I found myself wandering the decks like a lost soul, unmoored and out of place. I was on my way home after a difficult three years traveling on behalf of the American Red Cross and Near East Relief. I had trekked across the postwar wreckage of Europe, through the Balkans, through Turkey, and into Armenia and Georgia and Azerbaijan. And not in luxury, either: it had been grueling travel in dangerous places where I didn't speak the language, in unreliable vehicles, and with guides I couldn't trust.

During those years, I had been writing what my friend Dorothy Thompson called "sob-sister stuff," magazine and newspaper pieces designed to encourage Americans to open their pocketbooks and support postwar relief. But nothing I wrote in any of those articles—and there were dozens of them—was exaggerated. Every word of it was true, all of the waste and desolation and cruelty and hunger and disease and cold—and the malevolent, willful ignorance that closed its eyes to the helpless. In Etchmiadzin, I was a guest of the archbishop of the Armenian church, where in the company of warm, plump, well-fed monks, I sat down to a magnificent feast. Outside, starving children cried on the cold steps. At the head of the table, the archbishop remarked in an offhand way, "They're always dying out there." He added (thinking that the story I was to write might bring in some foreign money), "Do you have a camera? Be sure and get a photo."

The years traveling abroad changed me in many ways—especially in terms of my political perspective. When I was a child, my parents, along with most of the people I knew, were conservative Democrats of the William Jennings Bryan stripe, believing that the free coinage of silver would help raise farm prices and carry the country back to prosperity.

In high school in Louisiana, I read Edward Bellamy's *Looking Backward* and looked ahead to the perfectly socialist world that would be ours when Eugene V. Debs—whose presidential campaign literature I helped Aunt E. J. distribute—and his Socialist Party of America took the White House. My friends and I continued to bear the socialist torch during my *Bulletin* days in San Francisco, until the Bolshevik Revolution transformed us all into zealous admirers of the great Russian experiment and we decided that we were Communists at heart. This enthusiasm flared gloriously in New York after the war, where several of my idealistic friends—among them Jack Reed, Robert Minor (who had met and interviewed Lenin in Moscow), and Floyd Dell, an editor of *The Masses*—were engaged in forming an American section of the Third International. I might have joined, since in any argument, I have a habit of taking the side of the underdog. But a particularly bad case of influenza kept me in bed and away from meetings for some time. When I recovered my health, I found myself in Europe, attempting to describe the real-world horrors of war's aftermath so vividly that readers in capitalist America would feel the pain and open their purses.

And then, some four years after the Bolsheviks came to power, I traveled to Russian Georgia, where I stayed in the century-old home of a farmer, his wife, and their multitudinous children. The village was a prosperous one: the fields were beautifully maintained, the harvests were abundant, the dairy herds and flocks of chickens were flourishing, and everyone was well fed and warm (relatively speaking—I was wearing all the clothing I possessed and some I had borrowed). The farmers were communists in the truest, most traditional sense of the word, for the village lands and jointly owned resources were allotted to the farming families according to their needs. When needs changed (marriages, births, deaths), the villagers got together and worked out a new allotment. Once a year, the tsar's tax collector rode across the plains at the head of a parade of oxcarts. The villagers loaded their tax payments of grain, chickens and piglets, and woven goods into the carts, and the tax collector rode away again. That, and the occasional conscription of sons for duty in the tsar's army, was the villagers' only contact with a central government.

But things were different now, and my host, a lifelong communist in a communist village, was not happy with Lenin's new Communist (with a capital *C*) regime in Moscow. He complained that the big-city Communists were interfering in village affairs, coming in with rules and regulations for making the land more productive—"reforming" farming practices, it was called. The reforms didn't make sense, he said.

"The government is too big and too far away," he said. "Those men in Moscow, they are city men. They cannot know how we live and work, or how people live and work in the next village or on the other side of the mountains. Why doesn't the government content itself with governing and let us alone? We don't need their 'reforms.'"

That chance conversation with a communist in a communist village changed the way I saw Communism, and I found myself glad that the fates had earlier dealt me such a severe case of influenza that I was thereby restrained from naively pledging allegiance to the Party. It was neither socialism nor communism but good, old-fashioned American individualism I cherished— American freedom of thought and action, American democracy, and the spirit of American enterprise. I was damned sick of the Old World and glad to be going home to the New.

Those were the sorts of thoughts and feelings that were tumbling chaotically through my mind on board the luxurious *Leviathan* on that day in 1923 when I first encountered Garet Garrett. He was a small, jaunty man, powered by a coil-spring of nervous energy and an incisively—and self-confidently—logical mind. He was dressed in tweeds, his bow ties matched the colors of his shirts, and his shoes were handmade and polished to a fare-thee-well. A writer on economic issues, he had been sent to Germany by the *Saturday Evening Post* to cover the German refusal to pay war reparations to the French, and he had a broad and deep understanding of postwar financial realities. We talked for hours about the war and its aftermath, the sights we had seen and the people we had met—about socialism, communism, democracy. About ourselves.

He was, I saw quickly, a passionate man, deeply informed, widely read, a writer and raconteur. His conversation was electric: its jolt left a lingering impression. There was a great deal to learn about him, and I confess to being fascinated—I, who pride myself on not being fascinated with anyone. He was born in rural Illinois and grew up working in the fields of his parents' rented farm near Burlington, Iowa. He went to school only through the third grade and educated himself—as I had—by reading every book he could lay his hands on. He was in Chicago during the depression of 1893 and at eighteen, working in Cleveland as a reporter for the *Cleveland Press*. After that, Washington, D.C., and then New York, where he established his credentials as a financial reporter and served on the editorial council of the *New York Times*. The year before we met, he had become the *Saturday Evening Post*'s lead writer on economic issues. He was to go on to become one of the New Deal's sharpest critics.

I got Garet's letter the week before I moved to Columbia. He had been assigned by the *Post* to write a series of articles about the effects of the New Deal agriculture programs on farmers. He had read my article on wheat farming in the Great Plains and wondered if I would be free to go with him on the two-week research trip he planned to take through Nebraska, Kansas, Missouri, Iowa, and Illinois.

"Yes," I said and wired him that he could find me at the Tiger Hotel in Columbia.

"*No!*" my mother cried, appalled. "Two weeks with a man in a car, going God knows where! Rose, you can't! What will people think? What will they *say*?"

"Don't tell them," I said. "It's none of their damned business."

Garet and I left Columbia on a bright, hot morning and drove east into Illinois, then west across Missouri to the Great Plains, interviewing farmers about their responses to the New Deal. What we heard was similar to what I heard on my trip two years before. But this time, there was a deeper anger and a broader disillusionment, for people had had two more years of experience with the dictatorial Agricultural Adjustment Administration, which had authority to manage soil erosion, reforestation, and flood control projects and to loan money to farm tenants, croppers, and laborers to buy their own farmland. The AAA was paying farmers to take thirty million acres out of production in order to keep farm commodity prices high. But at the same time, it was bringing millions more acres into production through drainage and irrigation and pushing new farmers into accepting loans for land and equipment that they couldn't afford.

"Don't make no sense a-tall," we heard from one glum farmer after another. "Just don't make no damn sense, what them Washington folks are doing with the land and the crops."

After my wheat farming research trip two summers before, I was familiar with these problems. But although Garet had understood the situation in a theoretical way and from a distance, he was now confronted, as he put it, "with the facts and the faces." As we traveled, we heard a great many stories that reinforced my fears about the farm crisis and gave to his fears a new and appalling reality. He became more pessimistic with every mile.

We were both dismayed by the freedoms the farmers were required to give up in return for the cash the government gave them. If you wanted to grow potatoes on your farm, for example, the Roosevelt administration would tell you how many bushels of potatoes you could grow and sell, tax free. Your tax-free potatoes, when they went to market, would go in a federal package, bearing a federal stamp, by permission of a federal bureau. If you wanted to grow and sell more potatoes than the law allowed, you had to pay a tax of forty-five cents a bushel. If you got caught bootlegging potatoes, you and your customer would be fined a thousand dollars. Get caught again and you went to jail—and your customer as well.

It didn't matter how many potatoes you could grow on your property, or how many hungry neighbors might want to buy your potatoes, or what price they might be willing and able to pay. "The Law of Potatoes," Garet called it, was immutable. And what was true of potatoes, he wrote in one of his *Post* articles after he got back from our trip, was true of wheat, cotton, and corn. This might still be a "free country"—for some people. But it wasn't free for farmers, who even on good ground and with good weather and for a decent local market were no longer at liberty to choose the crops they would grow on their own land.

But what struck both of us most forcefully was the plight of farmers who were living on marginal land the government wanted to redevelop as grasslands or forests. In southern Illinois, for instance, in Pope County, the administration had decided to create the Shawnee National Forest, from a quarter of a million acres of land that (the government said) was over-cropped and eroded. It was true that some of the land badly needed reclamation—but not all. Yet *all* of the people who lived on those acres were being enticed to sell their farms and homes in return for cash and government loans so they could relocate to "better" areas or to villages being built by the Resettlement Administration. If the owner was unwilling to sell, the land would be condemned and the owner would be forced to leave with little or nothing to show for his or her time and work and cash investments. We met one Pope County woman of seventy who lived with her ailing husband in a neat frame house on thirty acres of good, well-managed soil, with no erosion. The pair, by themselves, had cleared that land of timber and it had supported them for a half-century. They didn't want to sell out, but what choice did they have? They couldn't continue farming. They had no children. Where could they go? How could they support themselves?

But at the same time, I saw many more people, who as individuals, *free* individuals, were finding their own way to survive the impositions of the bureaucracy, using the American wealth of resources and their own wealth of creativity. I saw farmers who refused to accept checks drawn on the public funds. I saw men and women quietly paying their debts and going about cheerfully in the daytime, finding God only knows what strength during the dark nights. I saw Americans still paying the price of individual liberty, which—like it or not—is individual responsibility *and* insecurity. I saw courage and endurance and strength.

After the first day or two, our trip wasn't just business, and our relationship was not just an intellectual one. We were an unlikely pair of lovers, I suppose. I was nearing fifty, feeling—and looking, I feared—very much my age. Garet was seven years older, short, stout, and balding, missing several fingers and with a voice that was husky from a bullet he'd taken in the throat during a shooting in a restaurant five years before. He was irascible, a pessimist by nature, a thinker of cynical thoughts, and he rarely saw the funny side of anything. I was . . . I was my own greedy, disorderly self, wanting haphazardly and helter-skelter, wanting everything and all at once. And when I was with him, countering his pessimisms, I began to find my own optimism. In an odd sort of way, his darkness lightened mine.

Yes, unlikely lovers. But lovers we were, compelled by an undeniable physical need, attracted by an intellectual magnetism that was all-powerful, wholly irresistible. Lovers who lay awake, talking into the warm, sweet night, with the heavy richness of someone's cigar drifting into the room on the breeze that stirred the curtains at the open window. Lovers who woke each other, not with a kiss, but with a "Did you ever read—?" or a "What do you think about—?" Lovers who buried themselves in their newspapers at the breakfast table and in their books until bed-time. Lovers from that first night until the last morning when we said good-bye.

And then he drove away, and I was utterly miserable for weeks, for months. I was suspended in a kind of unbelief, as lovers are, waiting for the blue envelopes that brought his letters, for the strong, almost illegible scrawl of his handwriting, for the cigarette smoke that scented the paper.

"Rose, dear," he wrote, "it is all more than I can comprehend. You shake me in the fixed principle of my life. I am angry and happy. I once wrote that a man would give everything he has in the world to find her—that woman, that one woman, that other part of himself. I thought to find her only in fragments, a glimpse here, a thought there, and never enough in any one place to be satisfied with. And now, we two! We ought to be in a rowboat somewhere in the middle of the Pacific. We ought to be on a distant island. I want to see you and yet I dread it."

I said earlier that after those two weeks with Garet, every-thing in my life was different. *Everything.* But not in the way that might be expected when two people are so suddenly and fiercely attracted as we were to each other. He might be shaken in the fixed principle of his life, but my own determination still held firm. A rowboat for two in the Pacific, yes. A distant island, visits when we could manage them, letters, and always a terrible longing, oh yes. But not marriage. Not marriage. Oh no, not marriage.

And when I knew *that*—that I could not marry even such a man as Garet Garrett—I knew everything about myself and was resigned to my new freedom.

But our time together gave me more than longing and more than resignation. It gave me my voice. And that is what I mean when I say that after our trip together, everything was different. Everything.

One night in a Wichita hotel, a red neon light blinking like an erratic pulse in the dark street below, I told Garet about the great divide, the chasm I had not been able to bridge in the twenty years of my writing life. I could easily and skillfully produce the most insignificant, entertaining, *popular* nonsense for money, but when it came to saying something worthwhile, writing something that *I* thought and felt and believed, I was mute. I had no words. I had no voice.

"Bullshit," he rasped, and threw a companionable arm across me. "You've got a voice, Rose, a damn strong one, a passionate one. I've been hearing it ever since we left Columbia, haven't I? Every time we turn a corner, see a new sight, you're telling me what you think, how you feel, what you believe." There was a rueful smile in his voice. "What the hell do you mean, you have no words? You've got more words than any woman *I* ever knew—and I've known plenty in my time."

"But that's politics," I protested. "We've been talking politics. And history and government and the national spirit. And individual freedom, what makes us free and what it costs. I'm a fiction writer. I can't sell—"

"Then give it away." He sat up and reached for a cigarette, the match flaring into the dark. "Hell's bells, Rose. You are a damn fine *writer*, and you've got to stop disparaging the work you do. So what if your fiction isn't that high-culture crap? So what if it's low-brow, middle-brow, commercial? You get paid for it, don't you? So write what sells and sell it for enough money to live on, and go off somewhere and write your passion—politics, history, government, freedom, all that optimistic stuff you've been preaching to me. Fiction, nonfiction, what the hell does it matter? Write it and give it away, if you have to, although you probably won't. Write your passion and somebody will pay you for it." He stuck his cigarette in the corner of his mouth, pulled me against him, and softly, fondly rapped my skull. "Dolt. Idiot. If we were in the kitchen, I'd throw a plate at your head."

I lay against him, breathing him in, loving the strength of him, the wisdom. Simple. So simple. I thought of the chaos that was my life—the boys, the farm, my mother, my work—and sighed. Sell my fiction, give my passion away. Was it really just that simple?

I went back to Columbia, to my research in the archives and the library. Garet went back to the East Coast, to his small farm in Tuckahoe, New Jersey, and immediately wrote three articles about what he learned on our trip. They were published in the *Saturday Evening Post* in October and November. Reading and rereading, I devoured every word, hearing his raspy voice speaking to me as if he were in the same room, loving the sense of it, the rhythms, the density of the sentences, the clear, strong logic of each paragraph, each section, the whole. I didn't agree with him on all points and as the years went on, our disagreements would widen and deepen. But they never diminished my admiration for his intellect, his logic. Ah, that mind. *That* was what I loved of him then, and still love, and will love, wherever he is, wherever I am.

And yes. It really was that simple. Garet had been gone just four days when I began writing. Earlier in the year, the *Post* had asked their lead writers for a thousand words for a "Who's Who" profile. About myself, I had written: "I am now a fundamentalist American. Give me time and I will tell you why individualism, laissez-faire, and the slightly restrained anarchy of capitalism offer the best possibilities for the development of the human spirit."

"We'd like to see more along these same lines," *Post* editor Adelaide Neall had written to me, just before I left with Garet. "Send us something else."

So I sat down at my typewriter and began to write, my understanding sharpened by two weeks of day-long, night-long talks with Garet. I called it "Credo." I wrote that every American is governed only by the principle of personal responsibility and that his or her most important freedom is the absolute freedom to flourish or fail. The question each person must answer is whether that freedom is worth the terrible effort, the never-lifted burden, the price of individual self-reliance and insecurity. Yes, insecurity. Because if we are aiming to be genuinely self-reliant, we must learn to embrace uncertainty and anxiety. If we fail, there will be nothing to break our fall—nothing but whatever cushion we have managed to create for ourselves.

Credo. I believe. And as I wrote, I realized that it was the first time in my life that I was writing exactly *as I believed,* without compromising my truth for an editor or for a reader or for *cash cash cash.* Two weeks and twelve thousand words later, I finished the piece and sent it to Adelaide Neall for her opinion. She sent it back. Too long, she said, too political, too polemical, too passionate. The *Post* had opposed the New Deal since Roosevelt's election, but this was too outspoken even for them.

I wasn't surprised. I wasn't dejected, either. I hadn't written it for Adelaide or for the *Post,* or for anybody. I had written it as my essential claim to my own deepest, truest freedoms, and that was enough. I sent it to Garet, of course, who wrote that it sounded like my voice—the voice he'd been hearing for the two weeks we were on the road—and that eventually Adelaide Neall and the *Post* would come around. If they didn't, well, damn their bloody eyes. I should publish it myself.

But they did come around. I sent the piece to George Bye, a long-time liberal Democrat, a Roosevelt supporter, and Eleanor Roosevelt's agent. But none of that deterred him. He said the essay should have been read by the nonfiction editor and resubmitted it to the *Post*. It was accepted immediately and published in early March 1936, to an enthusiastic reception. Herbert Hoover wrote to me, praising the piece and promising to see it widely distributed. *Reader's Digest* reprinted it as an article, and Maxwell Aley at Longmans, Green reprinted it as a booklet, under the title *Give Me Liberty*. It was ironic, I thought, that the one thing I hadn't written for money was bringing me money—but not much, for I insisted that the reprints be priced as affordably as possible.

Cash cash cash would have to continue being my mantra, because I still had debts to pay and a family to support. But Garet had been right: I could write what sells *and* write what matters—what mattered to me, what I cared about most deeply. It was true. I had found my voice.

Slowly, slowly, and little by little.

Glory to your lips.

It is so.

16. ON THE BANKS OF PLUM CREEK: 1936–1937

I was still in Columbia when "Credo" appeared in the *Post* in March 1936. Lucille and Eddie Murphy were living at the farm, running the household for me. The boys were still there too, completing the year at Mansfield High, and there were regular weekend visits back and forth. I had finished the Missouri book and turned it in: publication with McBride was out, but it looked like Longmans would publish it.

"Well, good," my mother said with satisfaction, when I told her that the Missouri project was concluded. "I hope this means you'll be coming back to Rocky Ridge." She gave me a long look. "I don't think it's good for you to stay away, Rose. Your father and I don't trust the Murphys to take care of the place. And Jess says that Eddie is stealing water from the well. He fills up big cans and takes them into town for his laundry."

I turned away. Jess didn't like either of the Murphys and was always complaining about them to my parents. But "stealing water"? It was a trivial thing, and I was sick of trivial complaints.

I could no longer claim to be staying away because I was doing research work at the library. But now that I had escaped, I couldn't bring myself to move back to the isolation of the farm, to the long, dull days filled with my mother's phone calls and visits and my own temptations to domesticity. In Columbia, I wasn't inclined to bake cookies or make soup or clean the living room or reupholster the sofa. I was there to write and that was what I did. And because it was a university town, there was enough going on—lectures, concerts, films, and the like—to fill any empty hours: important to me because it helped keep depression at bay. The people I had met were nice, too, educated, informed, interesting, and tolerant—no Mrs. Grundys. I had once planned to keep the farmhouse as a writing retreat, a place to live between visits to New York and elsewhere. Now, I no longer wanted that. My mother was able to take care of herself and my father, and she had royalty money coming in. All I wanted was to bring the Rocky Ridge chapter of my life to a close.

And I could do it, for the boys would be gone. They planned to spend the summer with me, studying with a tutor from the university in preparation for the coming school year. John had applied to a military school in New Mexico and Al had decided to do his senior year at the University High School in Columbia. After that, I had promised them a summer of travel in Europe and then college. When they had embarked on their lives in the world, I would be free to live where I chose. And George Bye had been encouraging me to come back East, where I could be in closer touch with the magazines that purchased my work.

My mother kept after me to stay. "Tell the Murphys to move out," she instructed me. "You won't need them after the boys are away at school. But you don't have to come back and live in the farmhouse, you know. Your father and I think we should just trade houses."

"Actually, I don't—"

But she was going on, with an enormous enthusiasm. "It would be just perfect, Rose. We know you love the Rock House—you put so much time and effort and money into building it and it's such a *pretty* little place. It will be just the right size for you when John and Al are gone and you're free of that burden."

"They're not a burden," I said defensively. "Let's just leave things as they are for a little longer," I added, not wanting to have this confrontation just now.

"And it will be so good to have you with us again," she went on, as though I hadn't spoken. "Whenever I need a little help with my writing, you'll be handy. And you know, dear, your papa and I are lonely out there, all by ourselves."

Of course I would be "handy." If I were at the Rock House, she could drop in or telephone any time she wanted. But I heard the wistfulness in her voice and remembered what she had once said to me, when Guy Moyston left Rocky Ridge and the house felt dismally empty: "Now can you imagine what it is like when you go, and there is nobody? *Nobody.*" I heard both her plea and her demand, and I felt sorry for her. But it was time to take a stand.

"I understand," I said. "But I've already decided. Once the boys are gone, I'm going back to New York to live."

"New York!" My mother's eyes widened and she flinched as if I had struck her. "Oh, no! Oh, please, let's not hear anything about that!" She put her hand to her heart as if she were holding herself against a sudden pain. "Really, Rose—the Rock House would be just perfect for you."

I turned away with another vaguely evasive answer, but she was not deterred. Over the next couple of months, she interspersed her pleas with a litany of complaints about the Murphys. (I called them "yowls" in my diary, but I was angry when I wrote that.) I was paying rent, which gave me the right to use the place as I pleased, and I knew Lucille well enough to be confident that she was taking care of the house and yard.

But at last I got fed up with the complaints. By that time, the boys were with me in Columbia, so I wrote to Lucille that she should close up the house and take the furnishings to her place in Mansfield. I told my mother that she could do whatever she wanted with the place. I wasn't coming back to Rocky Ridge.

And once I made my decision clear, my mother accepted it and the tensions in our relationship subsided. That spring, she came to Columbia with her manuscript of *On the Banks of Plum Creek,* the fourth of her books. *Little House on the Prairie* had come out the previous November to a strong review in the *New York Times.* Harper was publishing the books every two years now to build a broader readership base. I would have plenty of time to work on this one.

"Here it is, Rose, dear." She put the now-familiar stack of orange-covered tablets on my desk. "I've done the best job I could, but it was harder than I thought." She paused, thoughtfully. "I left out Pa's moving us to Walnut Grove, as you suggested, so the action would be less confusing. It all happens at Plum Creek. We didn't have Jack, the bulldog, then, but I put him in anyway, because I think the children like him. Oh, and I left out the baby. Freddy."

We had talked about that several times. The baby's birth and death had been included in "Pioneer Girl," but she had written that version of her life for what we thought would be an adult audience. These books were for children. And since Freddy had died before his first birthday, she decided that he shouldn't be mentioned at all. I had agreed, regretfully. Between us, there were three dead boys: her brother, her own nameless son, and mine. Three little boys, never forgotten, but never spoken of. Perhaps my three living sons were a kind of memorial. I hoped so.

But one other thing was obvious. She had stopped insisting that her story was the literal truth. Confronted with the need to craft a *story,* she was beginning to think of her work as fiction, rather than autobiography.

I picked up the first tablet and began leafing through it. "Any special instructions?"

"Well, of course, I'm hoping that the way I've written it is good enough to stand as it is," she said, taking off her gloves and her hat. She was staying to tea at the hotel, and then we were going shopping. "I've done such a lot of writing and rewriting, you know—you should see my pile of little scraps and scribblings! Naturally, I'm happy with the way I've done it. I hope you won't have to spend a lot of time on it." Her tone became conciliatory. "But your judgment is always better than mine where these things are concerned. Whatever you decide to do will be fine with me." She smiled. "You'll have the last word."

Later, I noted in my diary that *Plum Creek* had me "stopped flat," so I set it aside for a few weeks while I worked on several things of my own. When I went back to it, I found—as I had with the drafts of the earlier books—that the manuscript left open a great many questions that would have to be answered in the book. The central question was the theme, the idea that should hold the story together from beginning to end and motivate the actions of Pa and Ma. In my mother's draft, that wasn't clear, but when I asked her, she wrote to me with a ready answer.

"It's the wheat," she said. "The fields of wheat spread out on both sides of Plum Creek. All that growing wheat gave everybody a false sense of security. They had no idea it could be destroyed. They thought it was going to make them rich." When she made that clear, it gave the novel its structure: the wheat that the inexperienced settlers were so proud of was vulnerable to catastrophes that they couldn't predict.

That was decidedly helpful, and I kept it in mind as I did the rewrite. At the beginning of the book, Pa promises Ma that she would have to live in the dugout only until the first wheat crop. Then she would have a fine house, and he would have horses and a buggy. At the end of the book, Pa is still counting on the good wheat crop to come—although I knew from "Pioneer Girl" that the Plum Creek episode had ended in disaster. The grasshoppers came again, and Pa had had enough of farming. He was ready to move on again, even if that meant leaving everything behind.

I also needed more concrete details to flesh out the thin narrative, so I wrote Mama Bess a two-page letter with specific questions. She had the girls going to school during hay-cutting time. Did they have school in July? What schoolbooks did Laura and Mary have and where did they get them? What did Pa wear when he dressed up? What were Laura's school dresses like?

She sent me the answers I needed. Their school dresses were sprigged calico made with tight waists, buttoned down the back. For Sundays, Pa had a black silk tie, a coat and vest, and Ma's handmade calico shirts. School started in spring, so it probably wouldn't be still going on during haying time, so I should just leave that part out. She had no idea where they got the schoolbooks; Pa probably found them in town. (I thought they should be Ma's books, since she had been a schoolteacher herself, so that's what I wrote.) She gave me a full description of the schoolhouse and desks, which I was able to use.

Concerned about length, I sent her some pages and she returned them with a few cuts that worked. She proposed other cuts, though, that were far too drastic—the ox going through the roof, for instance, which was wonderfully dramatic—and I kept the material in. "Sorry it is such a mess," she wrote at one point. "You must be awfully tired of this story."

Once I got started, I kept at it steadily. I reconstructed the action so that the narrative covered just a little more than a year; cut the episode of Ma's illness since there were already so many wretched hardships; and cleared up the point of view problems. All told, I put in two months' work on *Plum Creek* during that long, hot summer—so hot that I worked as I had one long-ago summer in Athens, wearing as little as possible and showering several times a day.

I finished the revision and sent the full typescript to my mother in late September, with a draft of a cover letter she should send to George Bye, asking him to negotiate better terms for this book than he had for the last. There was a compelling justification for the request: she had just received an eight-hundred-dollar royalty check for the first six months of 1936. The books were selling well and Harper could afford a better royalty. Miss Raymond accepted *Plum Creek*, with no requests for revisions. It was to be published in October 1937.

The boys were settled for their school year and I was working, but my general spirits that fall and the following spring were gloomy. Garet and I had comforted ourselves with the thought that the country had not yet had the opportunity to vote on the New Deal. We had heard so many angry denunciations of the Roosevelt administration on our trip through the Farm Belt that we were both hoping that Alf Landon, the governor of Kansas and the Republican presidential candidate, might defeat Roosevelt in the November 1936 election.

But Roosevelt won in the biggest landslide in history. He captured all but eight electoral votes, in Vermont and Maine. It was a hard blow, and Garet and I had the bleak sense that American public opinion was hostile to what we believed so strongly: the freedom of the independent, self-reliant individual who had the strength to withstand the power of the state. The Supreme Court had struck down eight of FDR's New Deal programs, and immediately after his January inauguration, Roosevelt himself submitted a plan for "judicial reform" that would pack the nine-member court with seven new appointments. The plan failed. But the court caved in and began upholding several parts of the New Deal, including the minimum wage and the National Labor Relations Act.

Garet, always pessimistic, was even gloomier now. "People want manna and milk out of the rock," he wrote. "I wanted people to stay hard and fit and self-sufficient, so that they could go on under their own power. Now, they'll get their manna and milk, and it will render them powerless."

Still, 1936 wasn't a bad year, as far as my income was concerned. I earned nine thousand dollars—my best year since 1926. My short fiction was bringing in as much as twenty-five hundred dollars now, and the magazine markets were improving. I sold all the short pieces I wrote, and I was making a start on the project that—eventually—would make me financially independent.

And by the following fall, the fall of 1937, my family life was entirely changed. John and Al had graduated high school—John in New Mexico, Al in Columbia—and were spending the year in Europe, studying, traveling, learning about the great, wide world beyond the Ozark Mountains. Rexh wrote to say that he was to be married to the childhood sweetheart whom he had courted in the traditional Moslem way, by arranging their marriage through her father. I sent them my love and congratulations and two hundred dollars for a honeymoon trip to Budapest. And while I had rejected George Bye's suggestion that I write an article about my sons, I found it in my heart to write a short story about my Rexh, his courage and perseverance in his love for his bride. It was called "The Song Without Words." It was published in *Ladies' Home Journal.*

And my parents? They had moved back to the old farmhouse—modernized now with electricity, plumbing, hot water, and a furnace so it was easier for them to manage. Mama Bess abandoned her efforts to persuade me to live in the Rock House and rented it out. With the rents from the Rock House and the tenant house and the royalties from the *Little House* books increasing by nearly a thousand dollars every year, my parents would have enough reliable income to support them, I hoped, for the rest of their lives.

Ironically, then, things had worked out the way I planned, more or less. The Crash had radically altered the plans and dreams and hopes of everyone in the country, and I was no exception. But if the Crash hadn't happened, would my mother have gotten serious about writing "Pioneer Girl," from which we drew all the other books? If the Crash hadn't seriously reduced the magazine markets, leaving me stranded at Rocky Ridge, would I have had the time to rewrite her drafts enough to make them publishable? I doubt it. I seriously doubt it.

Sweet are the uses of adversity. Yes—and I felt good when I thought about my parents' situation.

And about my own. Among the magazines, I was once again in demand. Jess Gould, the editor of *Ladies' Home Journal*, wrote to ask me about the possibility of a collection of my letters, which I quickly declined. George Bye wrote to let me know that 20th Century Fox was interested in seeing the manuscript of my Missouri book, and he offered an idea for an around-the-globe travel series called "Before I Die." The *Post* liked it, but preferred me to write about little-known spots in the United States. The *Country Gentleman* offered eight thousand dollars for a three-part serial, yet to be written. Mrs. Roosevelt read *Hurricane* and wrote about it in her "My Day" column. In all this hurly-burly, I sold four more stories: two to the *Post*, two to the *Journal*.

And then I was back in New York—and free.

17. KING STREET: APRIL 1939

"New York. That's where Russell and I tracked you down," Norma Lee said. Finished shaping the meatloaf, she went to the sink and washed her hands. "We had just married, and you were living at the Grosvenor and tearing your hair out over *Free Land*." She laughed. "And then the *Post* bought it for twenty-five thousand dollars and it went on to become a best-selling book and earn you pots more money."

Norma Lee was too easily enthusiastic, Rose thought, but then, she was young. She would learn that while money was important, it wasn't the only measure of the worth of a piece of writing. Rose laid out another piece of green-print cotton fabric and began to chalk an outline around a diamond-shaped cardboard template.

"I'm always in despair when I'm partway through a long project," she said. "I remember telling Adelaide Neall that I was heartsick about the damn thing. I didn't dare look at it critically because then I would know it was no good at all and I'd have to abandon it."

It was true. From the day she'd begun professional writing—almost thirty years now—she had always felt that way. Whatever she was writing—it just wasn't good enough. It didn't meet her expectation of what it should have, could have been. And she always felt, once she'd finished a piece of writing, that it was the last one she'd be able to write, that there would never be another. That had never been true, though, until this time. This time, maybe she was right. Maybe *Free Land* really was the last. The effort to produce it—the eighteen-hour days, the seven-day weeks, month after month—had exhausted her.

And there was worry, too, for *Free Land* was very good. Editors would expect that level of work from her, whether the piece was long or short. But she had no ideas, no energy for beginning something new. *What has become of my ability to write a story when I had to?* she asked herself plaintively and heard no answer.

But perhaps the truth lay in the competitive demands of real life, which—now that she owned her own little house, at last—were simply too interesting, too compelling. Fiction, and especially the kind of happy-ending fiction demanded by the magazine markets, didn't seem worth her time.

And, of course, there was the other writing, the political writing, what Garet called "writing your passion." She was doing plenty of that, articles arguing against any U.S. entry into the European conflict and pieces on the importance of personal self-reliance. There would be a dozen out this year. It was true that they were mostly in women's and small-circulation magazines—*Woman's Day, Good Housekeeping, Cosmopolitan, Liberty*—but while they didn't bring in much money, she didn't need much. She no longer had to support her mother. Al and Rexh were self-sufficient, and John had cut himself off. And she was trying to avoid earning an income on which she would have to pay income tax or the new Social Security tax.

Norma Lee got two cups out of the cupboard and began making tea. "Of course, I had never known any serious writers before I met you. But when I saw you at the Grosvenor, I remember being frightfully impressed with your working schedule. You were working even harder than you did in Columbia. You were spending all day and half the night at the typewriter."

"I needed the money," Rose said ruefully. "I was nearly broke when I got to New York. I had seven dollars in my pocket after I paid a week's rent for a furnished flat. I unpacked my typewriter, settled down to work, and wrote 'Home Over Saturday.' It was a Dakota pioneer story based on an episode in my mother's 'Pioneer Girl.' When I asked her if I could use it, she told me to go ahead since the story was so frightening she couldn't put it into a book for children." She shook her head. "The story *was* horrible. It involved a woman with a butcher knife who seemed bent on slashing her husband to death. I gave it one of those O. Henry plot-twist endings that the *Post* likes so much. They snapped it up and I had money again."

"And then you moved to the Grosvenor Hotel?" Norma Lee brought two cups of tea and her cigarettes to the table. She sat down, frowning. "I seem to remember that somebody else lived there once—another writer, I mean. Who was it?"

"Willa Cather and her friend Edith," Rose said. "For five years." She rotated the template on the fabric and marked again. "You know, it's funny. Back in Columbia, I had a ninth-floor suite with the morning sun and a thirty-mile view of the Missouri hills. At the Grosvenor, I had a swank address—the corner of Fifth Avenue and West Tenth—and a three-dollar-a-night, handkerchief-sized room that looked out on an airshaft. For a dollar-fifty more, I could have had one with a window on Fifth Avenue. But I needed to write, and the airshaft provided fewer distractions."

She picked up her scissors and began to cut diamonds out of the fabric. "Except, of course, for the pigeons that perched on the windowsill, so tame they would eat out of my hand. I've always loved pigeons. And the young woman on the floor above, who was also on the airshaft. She was a tap dancer. She would shove the furniture back and tap for hours. She had a Victrola but just one record. 'Let's Call the Whole Thing Off.'"

"Oh, that's from *Shall We Dance*," Norma Lee put in eagerly. "Fred Astaire and Ginger Rogers. They danced on roller skates."

Rose nodded. "I think she danced on roller skates, too. On my ceiling, hour after hour. I thought of complaining to the hotel manager, but she was a nice girl. The poor thing had to practice somewhere." She put down her scissors and reached for her cigarettes. "Anyway, she didn't last long. She ran out of money and moved into a flat with two girls she'd met in a coffee shop." She lit a match to her cigarette. "I was glad she was gone. I was afraid that the lyrics of 'Let's Call the Whole Thing Off' were going to turn up somewhere in *Free Land*. David Beaton might start humming it." David was the protagonist, a Dakota homesteader.

"But he didn't," Norma Lee said comfortably. "He's like that dancer. She kept tapping. He just puts his head down and keeps on plugging. Blizzards, droughts, storms, bad luck, Indians, horse thieves—he doesn't give up, no matter what."

"That's the point I wanted to make," Rose said, pulling on her cigarette. "Anybody who really wants to do something can do it, if they put enough effort into it. David isn't a hero or a superman. He's an ordinary person with an ordinary person's weaknesses and frailties. He married the wrong woman. He makes bad business decisions. But he loves the land. And he endures." She smiled crookedly. "He doesn't succeed, he doesn't triumph—unless success and triumph are measured in simple endurance, as they should be. He just remains . . . invincible." She thought of Mary Margaret McBride, who had outlasted the Depression and now had her own hugely popular radio show.

Norma Lee put down her teacup. "Invincible," she repeated thoughtfully. "Yes, I think that describes him, in the end."

Rose frowned. "The *New York Times* reviewer complained about that ending. He said it was false. 'It leads one to believe that David conquered. Some did and do conquer. But the odds!' That's what the reviewer said."

"I didn't think the ending was false," Norma Lee ventured slowly. "But perhaps just a . . . bit optimistic?"

"It's not optimistic," Rose replied, remembering the gaunt Kansan wheat farmer who had sent his wife and children back East in search of clean air. "There's no guarantee for David, and he knows it. He understands that he's free to leave, to go someplace safer, but he chooses to stay. He knows the odds. He could lose his crops and his health—my father did. He could lose his wife—many women died in childbirth. He could lose a child: my grandmother did, my mother did, I did. David knows all this, and as Thomas Paine said, it has never been discovered how to make a man unknow his knowledge. Knowing and choosing—that's what makes him invincible."

She turned to look out the window, at the forsythia beginning to bloom in bright yellow-gold arcs against the pale greens and browns of the woods. She thought back over the years, her writing, her travels, her effort to build a home in Albania, her retreat to Rocky Ridge, the Crash and the terrible Depression, the emptiness left in her by all her losses.

Had she succeeded in any of it, in anything she had ever wanted to do?

No, not in what she had planned or in the way she had planned. But there was the forsythia, as golden as the sun, outside her own window, and over her head, the roof of her own little house.

Slowly, slowly, and little by little.

Glory to your lips: it is so.

It is so.

EPILOGUE

The Rest of the Story: "Our Wild Rose at Her Wildest"

Rose's career as a fiction writer was not over, although *Free Land* is the last novel that bears her name. After she finished rewriting *By the Shores of Silver Lake,* she coauthored three more books with her mother: *The Long Winter, Little Town on the Prairie,* and *These Happy Golden Years.* In the last three books, Rose seems to be working more independently than ever, and there are no surviving letters attempting to solicit information or coach her coauthor to improve her writing. According to her biographer, William Holtz, Rose rewrote her mother's tablet pages, "expanding, condensing, and shifting material, sharpening drama and dialogue, and composing new episodes out of whole cloth." The *Little House* series was at last complete. (The name has since been trademarked by the publisher and merits the trademark distinction: ®)

At some point, probably in the last few years of the collaboration, Laura produced the manuscript of *The First Four Years*, the story of her early marriage to Almanzo. In late 1937, she had suggested the project to Rose. "I could write the rough work. You could polish it and put your name to it if that would be better than mine." But Rose (who was hard at work on *Free Land* at the time) didn't offer to help, and Mama Bess didn't pursue it. When the book was finally published, after both Laura and Rose's deaths, readers were more puzzled than enthusiastic. The stumbling prose and the clumsily developed story were not what they had come to expect from Laura Ingalls Wilder. For some, the book made them consider the possibility that Rose had been more involved with the writing of the series than anyone knew.

From time to time, Rose privately lamented her inability to write more fiction: "I have no ideas whatever, no spark, I see no more stories," she wrote in her journal. "What has become of my ability to write a story when I had to?"

But that didn't mean that Rose's writing life was over. The rest of her days were dedicated to her passion: the active practice and advocacy—through publications, letters, and teaching—of the libertarian philosophy that she had begun to pursue in the early days of the New Deal. Her next project was *The Discovery of Freedom: Man's Struggle Against Authority,* published in early 1943. In that book, she saw America as an exceptional nation, a "totally new world," unaffected by Old World races, classes, or creeds and separated from the European past by a radical new conception of individual autonomy. At its best, she argued, America offers the utopian potential for human growth and human liberty, both of which thrive under laissez-faire and are stifled by governmental and economic controls. "An eccentric and spirited statement of a certain strain of the modern libertarian character . . . historically visionary," one critic has called the book.

The Discovery of Freedom was written "at white heat," Rose said, and published during wartime. It ends on a fervent wartime declaration that for many would echo long after the war was over:

> Win this war? Of course Americans will win this war. This is only a war; there is more than that. Five generations of Americans have led the Revolution, and the time is coming when Americans will set this whole world free.

Although Herbert Hoover praised the book, reviewers largely ignored it, and because it was wartime, people's energies and attention were elsewhere. *Discovery* went out of print at Rose's wish: true to form, she saw it as topical and flawed and planned to revise it. She never did.

Instead, beginning in 1943, she worked as a newspaper columnist, writing regular "Rose Lane Says" columns for the *Pittsburgh Courier,* an African-American weekly newspaper that, at its peak, had a national circulation of about two hundred thousand. Always written with passion and great energy, her columns ranged from political history to laissez-faire economics, from radical individualism to civil rights. In 1945, she moved from the *Courier* to the National Economic Council's *Review of Books,* where she wrote monthly book reviews through 1951. One of her reviews, a detailed and hostile reading of a 1947 Keynesian college economics textbook by Lorie Tarshis of Stanford University, earned her considerable attention in the academic world.

Rose had always paid taxes on her income, but as her distrust of the government deepened, she found ways to reduce her taxable income. In 1943, she planned to create a trust into which her royalties and writing income would be paid; she would receive just enough to live on (frugally) and the rest would be donated to charity. (The scheme never came to fruition.) She was deeply opposed to the Social Security program and refused to get a Social Security number: "I will have nothing to do with that Ponzi fraud," she wrote with characteristic fervor, and she never did. Her passionate crusade against government programs did not always sit well with her friends and editors. As the war ground on, the *Saturday Evening Post* became (in Rose's view) far too liberal. One of her intemperate letters prompted fiction editor Adelaide Neall to write across the page: "Our wild Rose at her wildest."

The war, which Rose had resisted in print until Pearl Harbor, moved her to invest more time and energy in her garden. She refused to get a ration card, for she believed that rationing "causes more shortages than it relieves" and requires people to submit to "bureaucratic regimentation." She enlarged her garden and went shares with her neighbors on chickens, pigs, and a cow. "I raised a pig," she was quoted as saying in a New York newspaper article, "butchered it last fall, 600 pounds of beautiful pork. I get around the butter and sugar rationing by making my own butter and using honey as a substitute for sugar." By war's end, she had become known for her cellar full of meats, fruits, and vegetables. "Aladdin's cave," she wrote, "glittering with jewels—all those colors in glass, with the gold-colored metal rings on the tops of the jars." She was known, too, for her frugality: she was living, she said, on just fifty dollars a month, six hundred dollars a year. Her independence, self-reliance, and frugality were political statements.

A lifelong letter writer, Rose continued to explore her political philosophies through correspondence. From 1946–1968, she carried on a correspondence with Jasper Crane, a DuPont vice president. The first of Rose's letters (January 26, 1946) is typical: "You'll find that I don't 'pitch into' anyone; I am much more appalling than that; I actually say what I honestly think.

It seems to me that the time is a little too late for anything else." Twenty years and hundreds of letters later, she was still at it: "It isn't money that moves the world," she wrote to Crane in 1966. "It is faith, conviction, ardor, fanaticism in *action*." Wild Rose.

She continued to say what she honestly thought as a teacher at Robert LeFevre's Freedom School, created to educate people about the nature and meaning of freedom and free market economic policy. When she arrived in late 1958, she found that the school was about to close: it owed fifteen hundred dollars on its mortgage and was out of money. As it happened, she had sixteen hundred dollars in her checking account. She wrote the check, and Freedom School survived and thrived. It, and the people she met there, would become her community of friends and correspondents through the rest of her life.

Over the years, Rose's family changed. The break with John Turner was complete; he did not see Rose again. He became a lieutenant commander in the Coast Guard, completed three engineering degrees, and went on to a successful career. Al Turner also became an engineer and went to work for McDonnell Douglas. Rexh Meta was imprisoned during the war but was released at war's end and went on living quietly in Albania, keeping in touch with Rose when he could. His daughter, Borë-Rose, and her children would later immigrate to the United States, with the help of another of Rose's protégés, Roger MacBride. Mr. Bunting's place was filled (although not the hole he had left in her heart) by two Maltese terriers named Jonathan Edwards and Henry David Thoreau, and when they were gone, other Maltese carried on.

Norma Lee Browning and her husband Russell Ogg would continue in Rose's orbit for the rest of her life, traveling with her and keeping up a regular correspondence. A talented and persistent writer, Norma Lee became a much-published investigative journalist for the *Chicago Tribune*. In her thirty-year career, she wrote award-winning stories on murders, medical quackery, presidential elections, and Hollywood life. She also did her share of ghostwriting, even though Rose advised against it: "It's all to the good to LEARN to keep out of these ghosting and collaborating jobs. You are much too good EVER to have got into anything of that kind." Russell became a well-known freelance photographer and collaborated with his wife on several book projects.

Rose's decade-long friendship with Helen (Troub) Boylston seems not to have been renewed after Troub left Rocky Ridge. Troub continued to be employed as a nurse, but, left to her own devices (and needing money), she put her writing skills to work. In 1936, she published the first book in a series called Sue Barton, Nurse. The seven books in that series have sold millions of copies and have stayed continuously in print. Troub also wrote a series featuring a young actress, Carol Page, and a young adult biography of Civil War nurse and founder of the American Red Cross, Clara Barton.

The most important addition to Rose's family was her "adopted grandson," Roger MacBride, the son of a *Reader's Digest* editor. They met in 1943, when Roger was fourteen, and became deeply attached. MacBride went to Princeton and Harvard Law and was awarded a Fulbright in the early 1950s. He would go on to serve as Rose's attorney, agent, trustee, and close personal friend. He also carried on her political agenda, becoming the Libertarian Party's presidential candidate in 1976. He was on the ballot in 32 states, but won no electoral votes.

Rose's parents lived comfortably on the ever-increasing royalties from the books and the income from the sale of the Rock House and other pieces of Rocky Ridge Farm. As the years went on, Laura may have begun to feel somewhat conscience-stricken about those royalties. In July 1949, a few months before

Almanzo's death at the age of ninety-two, she wrote to George Bye, assigning a 10 percent share to Rose "for helping me, at first, in selling my books and for the publicity she gave them"—a stunning understatement, apparently designed to continue the literary deception by deflecting Bye's suspicion that Rose was more deeply involved in the books' authorship.

In Mansfield, others were puzzled by Laura's apparent literary prowess emerging unexpectedly so late in life. Stephen W. Hines, who collected her *Ruralist* articles, also interviewed a number of the Wilders' fellow townspeople. Here is his summary (his phrase "under the name" introduces what is perhaps an intentional ambiguity):

> Mrs. Wilder's fame has always bewildered her adopted town of Mansfield. She lived as a farmer's wife and an active rural neighbor to the town for almost forty years before writing a published book under the name Laura Ingalls Wilder.
>
> By the time she did this radical thing—writing a book— her daughter, Rose, was the town's famous cosmopolitan citizen, a world traveler who had eschewed further voyages to return to her native village—population approximately eight hundred—to write. The town recognized Mrs. Wilder as a former correspondent for the *Missouri Ruralist*. But by her late fifties she had given up even that modest task, and the Wilders were supposedly in retirement. Thus, it took Mansfield many years to become reconciled to Mrs. Wilder's latter-day fame as a famous storyteller.

Almanzo's life appears not to have been touched by his wife's local celebrity. He was generally thought "aloof" by his neighbors (as was Laura), was remembered as a hard worker who was at his best with cows and horses, liked a good cigar, and enjoyed a game of pool. He worked in his tool shop, read the newspaper and an occasional book, shared his wife's and daughter's strong political views, and told Rose that his life had been mostly "disappointments." He died at the age of ninety-two in 1949.

After Almanzo's death, Laura lived on at Rocky Ridge, which the Wilders had sold on a lifetime lease. Rose visited for a week or two at a time, usually in the winter, when her mother needed more help. In late 1956, she arrived to find her mother delirious. Laura was diagnosed as diabetic. She was hospitalized, then returned home, with Rose and several local women as her nurse.

"I am indeed frantically busy," Rose wrote to Jasper Crane on January 20, 1957. "No help of any kind is available here, and I am houseworking, nursing, cooking and figuring out diabetic diet at high speed all day long . . . . She is holding her own and perhaps gaining a little strength. I wish she would stay with me in Danbury but of course I understand her attachment to her home."

And it was in her home that Mama Bess died, with her daughter beside her, on February 10, 1957, just three days past her ninetieth birthday. She was buried beside Almanzo in the Mansfield cemetery. Several friends formed a nonprofit organization to repurchase the house and grounds and create a permanent museum. After objecting that the books should be her mother's memorial, Rose endorsed the project and contributed the money to acquire the land, build a curator's house, and fund the maintenance.

Rose lived for eleven years past her mother's death. She wrote an introduction and conclusion to the journal Laura kept of the trip from De Smet to Mansfield in 1894. The book was published as *On the Way Home* in 1962. She continued to be active, engaged, and energetic in her expression of her political beliefs, and she was interested in many things.

Needlework had always been a major interest in her life, and in the 1960s, she wrote a series of articles about American needlework for *Woman's Day,* based on pieces she had written in 1941–1942. The articles were collected in a book, *Woman's Day Book of American Needlework*, published in 1963. *Woman's Day* also sent her as a correspondent to Viet Nam in July 1965, when she was 78 years old. Her article, "August in Viet Nam," was published in that magazine in December 1965. She had just celebrated her seventy-ninth birthday.

In the last few years of her life, Rose traveled with friends around the United States. She found someone to live in her Danbury home and bought a house on Woodland Drive in Harlingen, Texas, in the Rio Grande Valley. She sent her books (reportedly ten thousand volumes) to Roger MacBride in Vermont, who had added a wing to his house for her. Her health was relatively good, although she was concerned about diabetes, since her mother and two of her mother's sisters suffered from the disease. She began to think of traveling abroad and planned a trip to Europe and beyond. Intending to sail from New York on November 9, 1968, she went back to Danbury to prepare for the trip. She baked several loaves of bread, went upstairs to bed, and died in the night. She was eighty-two.

But death did not end the what-belongs-to-whom controversy. Rose had been the beneficiary of her mother's estate—at eighty-eight thousand dollars a sizeable one—including annual royalty payments on the books. But Mama Bess had assigned her copyrights and the income they produced to her daughter only for her lifetime. At her death, they were to go to the Mansfield Public Library. Rose, however, had renewed the six expiring copyrights in Roger MacBride's name. She left her entire estate to him, and as additional copyrights expired, he renewed them for himself. After MacBride's death, the library sued for the copyrights to the two books still in Laura's name. The claim was reportedly settled for $875,000.

The nature of the mother-daughter collaboration has been the subject of scholarly debate since the 1970s, when Rosa Ann Moore and William Anderson published articles examining the discrepancies between the manuscripts and the early books and speculating that Rose had a significant hand in their production. William Holtz's biography, *The Ghost in the Little House: A Life of Rose Wilder Lane,* published in 1993, argued that Rose was essentially the ghostwriter-behind-the-scenes. It was met with a great deal of vocal opposition by fans of the series and the later TV shows, who resisted the idea that their heroine might be involved with a literary deception.

I don't think it began that way, though. I think Laura simply believed Rose's assurances that the books were *hers* and that her daughter was doing nothing more than any good editor would have done. Laura may have been uneasy with this explanation, but she was isolated from the literary community and had no experience of authorship against which to test what her daughter told her. From this point of view, there was only a naive and simplistic understanding of the full dimensions and responsibilities of authorship and an eager acceptance of the unexpected prestige (Laura's word for what she wanted) that came with being an "author." I admit, however, that this explanation doesn't fully account for Laura's participation in the elaborate concealment of the collaboration from her agent and editors. At some point, I think, she must have recognized that this was an unusual arrangement, to say the least.

It's easier to understand the situation from Rose's point of view, especially with a careful reading of her journal. She undertook to "fix" and market the material that became *Little House in the Big Woods* in order to gain some writing income for her mother. She did whatever it took to get the book published without considering the possibility of future books. Once it became clear that there could be additional books, she might have requested a jacket acknowledgment of her contributions, but that would mean backtracking on claims she had made to agents Carl Brandt and George Bye and editor Marion Fiery. If she had known that she was obligating herself to eight books, and that those eight books would go on to make literary history—and a great deal of money—it might have been a different story. We might remember, though, that the largest sums of money didn't arrive until after Roger MacBride helped to produce the long-running television adaptation of *Little House on the Prairie*.

It's difficult and perhaps even painful to dismantle a long-standing myth, especially one in which the myth's heroine is as lively and authentic-seeming as the young Laura and as sweetly ladylike as the older Laura. But whatever we have learned in the past few decades about the real circumstances of authorship, the books themselves remain exactly what they were when you and I read them for the first time and fell in love with Laura and her resourceful family. Rose and Laura's stories are a continuing testament to the strength, resilience, and courage of American pioneers and to our enduring belief in what it means to be an American.

$\mathscr{A}$UTHOR'S THANKS

I owe a very special debt of gratitude to William Holtz, whose masterful biography of Rose, *The Ghost in the Little House: A Life of Rose Wilder Lane,* established the factual basis on which my fiction is built. I am grateful, as well, for the published work of many other scholars, notably that of John E. Miller, William Anderson, Anita Fellman, Ann Romines, Janet Spaeth, Stephen W. Hines, and Nancy Cleaveland (whose "Pioneer Girl" website has inspired many readers to further research). Additionally, William Anderson made careful notes on the manuscript and generously shared both advice and his knowledge of Wilder/Lane history.

Thanks, to, to the patient and helpful archivists at the Herbert Hoover Presidential Library and at the State Historical Society of Missouri, who helped me assemble copies of the documents on which I relied, and to Kerry Sparks at the Levine/Greenberg Agency for her enthusiastic support and her help in putting this book in the hands of readers.

And of course to Bill Albert, again and always.

$\mathscr{H}$ISTORICAL PEOPLE*

Rose Wilder Lane (1886–1968, RWL), only surviving child of Laura and Almanzo Wilder. Author of *Let the Hurricane Roar* (1932), *Free Land* (1938), *The Discovery of Freedom* (1943), and other fiction and nonfiction; unacknowledged co-author (with her mother, Laura Ingalls Wilder) of the Little House® series.

Laura Elizabeth Ingalls Wilder (1867–1957, LIW), daughter of Charles and Caroline Ingalls. Author of articles for the *Missouri Ruralist* and other farm publications; co-author (with her daughter, Rose Wilder Lane) of the Little House® children's books. Called "Bessie" by her husband, "Mama Bess" by Rose.

Almanzo Wilder (1857–1949), married (1885) to LIW. Known for his farming skills and horsemanship. Called "Manly" by LIW.

Eliza Jane (Aunt E. J.) Wilder Thayer, Almanzo's sister. Invited RWL to live with her in Crowley, Louisiana, and attend high school.

Ethel Burney, Rose's Mansfield friend from youth until her death; married Paul Cooley.

Rexh Meta, the Albanian boy whom RWL met in 1921 and adopted informally. She sponsored his education in Tirana and at Cambridge University and helped to support his family through the rest of her life.

John Turner, Rose's second informally adopted son. She cared for and supported him from 1933–1939.

Al Turner, John's brother. Rose's third informally adopted son.

Helen (Troub) Boylston (1895–1984), RWL's friend, travel companion, roommate, and confidante. Author of the young adult series, Sue Barton, Nurse (1936–1952) and Carol Page, Actress (1941–1946).

Norma Lee Browning (1915–2001), close friend and confidante of RWL from 1936 until Rose's death. Born in Missouri and educated at the University of Missouri and Radcliffe. Award-winning *Chicago Tribune* feature writer and columnist for thirty years, author of more than a dozen books. Married (1937) to Russell Ogg, who became a well-known newspaper photographer.

Carl Brandt, RWL's literary agent, 1920–1930.

George Bye, literary agent for RWL and LIW after 1930. His client list also included Eleanor Roosevelt, Charles Lindbergh, and Frank Buck.

George Q. Palmer, New York stockbroker for RWL, LIW, Helen Boylston.

Genevieve Parkhurst, friend and occasional guest of RWL at Rocky Ridge. *Pictorial Review* editor.

Catharine Brody, friend and frequent guest of RWL, author of several best-selling novels in the 1930s, including *Nobody Starves, Cash Item,* and *West of Fifth.*

Mary Margaret McBride, friend of RWL, later a famous radio talk show host. Rose stayed often in New York City with McBride and Stella Karn.

Berta Hader, friend of RWL, children's book illustrator. Berta introduced Marion Fiery to Rose to promote "When Grandma Was a Little Girl."

Marion Fiery, editor and head of the children's book department at Knopf, who first (1930) agreed to publish "When Grandma Was a Little Girl" (the material that became *Little House in the Big Woods*).

Virginia Kirkus, director, Harper Books for Boys and Girls, who agreed (1931) to publish "When Grandma Was a Little Girl" after Fiery left Knopf.

Ida Louise Raymond, Harper Books for Boys and Girls, who oversaw the production of the Little House® series.

Adelaide Neall, *Saturday Evening Post* fiction editor, with whom Rose worked on her stories in that magazine.

Garet Garrett, anti–New Deal critic, *Saturday Evening Post* leading political writer, close friend of RWL after 1935.

*The names of most of the Wilders' neighbors and friends have been altered to protect their privacy.

$\mathcal{F}$OR FURTHER READING

For more of the story behind the story, check out the Reader's Companion, available from www.AWilderRoseTheNovel.com.

The Little House® Books

Little House in the Big Woods, 1932. New York: Harper & Row.
Farmer Boy, 1933. New York: Harper & Row.
Little House on the Prairie, 1935. New York: Harper & Row.
On the Banks of Plum Creek, 1937. New York: Harper & Row.
By the Shores of Silver Lake, 1939. New York: Harper & Row.
The Long Winter, 1940. New York: Harper & Row.
Little Town on the Prairie, 1941. New York: Harper & Row.
These Happy Golden Years, 1943. New York: Harper & Row.

Works by Laura Ingalls Wilder

West From Home: Letters of Laura Ingalls Wilder to Almanzo Wilder, 1915. Ed. Roger MacBride, 1974. New York: Harper & Row.

The First Four Years. Ed. Roger MacBride, 1971. New York: Harper & Row.

Laura Ingalls Wilder, Farm Journalist: Writings from the Ozarks. Ed. Stephen W. Hines, 2007. Columbia & London: University of Missouri Press.

Works by Rose Wilder Lane

Henry Ford's Own Story, 1917. New York: Ellis O. Jones.

Diverging Roads, 1919. New York: Century Company.

The Making of Herbert Hoover, 1920. New York: Century Company.

The Peaks of Shala, 1923. New York: Harper & Brothers.

He Was a Man, 1925. New York: Harper & Brothers.

Hill-Billy, 1926. New York: Harper & Brothers.

Let the Hurricane Roar, 1933. New York: Longmans, Green & Company.

Old Home Town, 1935. New York: Longmans, Green & Company.

Give Me Liberty, 1936. New York & London: Longmans, Green & Company.

Free Land, 1938. New York: Longmans, Green & Company.

The Discovery of Freedom, 1943. New York: John Day Company.

Woman's Day Book of American Needlework, 1963. New York: Simon & Schuster.

Travels with Zenobia: Paris to Albania by Model T Ford, A Journal by Rose Wilder Lane and Helen Dore Boylston. Ed. William Holtz, 1983. Columbia & London: University of Missouri Press.

Dorothy Thompson & Rose Wilder Lane: Forty Years of Friendship. Letters, 1921–1960. Ed. William Holtz, 1991. Columbia & London: University of Missouri Press.

The Rediscovered Writings of Rose Wilder Lane: Literary Journalist. Ed. Amy Matson Lauters, 2007. Columbia: University of Missouri Press.

Works by Rose Wilder Lane and Laura Ingalls Wilder

On the Way Home: The Diary of a Trip from South Dakota to Mansfield, Missouri, in 1894. With a Setting by Rose Wilder Lane, 1962. New York: Harper & Row.
A Little House Sampler: Laura Ingalls Wilder and Rose Wilder Lane. Ed. William Anderson, 1988. Lincoln: University of Nebraska Press.

Manuscript Sources

Lane, Rose Wilder. Papers. Herbert Hoover Presidential Library, West Branch, Iowa.
Wilder, Laura Ingalls. Her letters are part of the Lane Papers, labeled "Laura Ingalls Wilder Series."
----------. Papers, 1894–1943. Joint Collection, University of Missouri, Western Historical Manuscript Collection, State Historical Society of Missouri, microfilm.

Selected Sources

Anderson, William. *Laura Ingalls Wilder: A Biography.* New York: HarperCollins, 1992.
----------. "Laura Ingalls Wilder and Rose Wilder Lane: The Continuing Collaboration." *South Dakota History* 16, No. 2 (1986): 89–143.
----------. "The Literary Apprenticeship of Laura Ingalls Wilder." *South Dakota History* 13, No. 4 (1983): 285–331.

Campbell, Donna M. "'Written with a Hard and Ruthless Purpose':
Rose Wilder Lane, Edna Ferber, and Middlebrow Regional
Fiction." In *Middlebrow Moderns: Popular American Women
Writers of the 1920s.* Ed. Lisa Botshon and Meredith Goldsmith,
25–44. Boston: Northeastern University Press, 2003.

Ehrhardt, Julia C. *Writers of Conviction: The Personal Politics of
Zona Gale, Dorothy Canfield Fisher, Rose Wilder Lane, and
Josephine Herbst.* Columbia: University of Missouri Press, 2004.

Fellman, Anita Clair. "Laura Ingalls Wilder and Rose Wilder
Lane: The Politics of a Mother-Daughter Relationship."
Signs: Journal of Women in Culture and Society 15, No. 3
(1990): 535–561.

----------. *Little House, Long Shadow: Laura Ingalls Wilder's Impact
on American Culture.* Columbia & London: University of
Missouri Press, 2008.

Hill, Pamela Smith. *Laura Ingalls Wilder: A Writer's Life.* Pierre:
South Dakota State Historical Society Press, 2007.

Hines, Stephen W. *I Remember Laura.* Nashville: Thomas Nelson,
1994.

Holtz, William. "Closing the Circle: The American Optimism
of Laura Ingalls Wilder." *Great Plains Quarterly* 4 (1984):
79–90.

----------. "Ghost and Host in the *Little House* Books." *Studies
in the Literary Imagination* 29 (1996): 41–51.

----------. *The Ghost in the Little House: A Life of Rose Wilder Lane.*
Columbia: University of Missouri Press, 1993.

----------. "Rose Wilder Lane's *Free Land:* The Political
Background." *South Dakota Review* 30 (Spring 1992):
56–67.

Miller, John E. *Becoming Laura Ingalls Wilder: The Woman
Behind the Legend.* Columbia: University of Missouri Press,
1998.

----------. *Laura Ingalls Wilder and Rose Wilder Lane: Authorship, Place, Time, and Culture.* Columbia & London: University of Missouri Press, 2008.

Moore, Rosa Ann. "Laura Ingalls Wilder and Rose Wilder Lane: The Chemistry of Collaboration." *Children's Literature in Education* 11, No. 3 (1980): 101–109.

----------. "Laura Ingalls Wilder's Orange Notebooks and the Art of the Little House Books." *Children's Literature*, No. 4 (1975): 105–119.

---------. "The Little House Books: Rose-Colored Classics." *Children's Literature*, No. 7 (1978): 7–16.

Romines, Ann. *Constructing the Little House: Gender, Culture, and Laura Ingalls Wilder.* Amherst: University of Massachusetts Press, 1997.

Spaeth, Janet. *Laura Ingalls Wilder.* Boston: Twayne Publishers, 1987.

Zochert, Donald. *Laura: The Life of Laura Ingalls Wilder.* New York: Avon, 1976.

Books by Susan Wittig Albert

An Extraordinary Year of Ordinary Days
Together, Alone: A Memoir of Marriage and Place
The China Bayles Mysteries
The Darling Dahlias Mysteries
The Cottage Tales of Beatrix Potter
Writing From Life: Telling the Soul's Story
Work of Her Own

With Bill Albert
The Robin Paige Victorian-Edwardian Mysteries

Edited Anthologies
What Wildness is This: Women Write about the Southwest
With Courage and Common Sense: Memoirs
from the Older Women's Legacy Circle

CPSIA information can be obtained at www.ICGtesting.com
Printed in the USA
LVOW10*0743301113

363322LV00004B/9/P

9 780989 203517

DEC – – 2013